THE LONG WAY HOME

Visit us at www.boldstrokesbooks.com

Praise for Rachel Spangler's Fiction

Trails Merge

"The meeting of these two women produces sparks that could melt the snow on the mountain. They are drawn to each other, even as their pasts warn of future pain. The characters are beautifully drawn. Spangler has done her homework and she does a great job describing the day to day workings of a small ski resort. She tells her story with wonderful humor, and gives an accurate voice to each of her characters. Parker Riley's best friend Alexis is as true to the sophisticated "City" girl as Campbell's father is to the country. Trails Merge is a great read that may have you driving to the nearest mountain resort."—*Just About Write*

"Sparks fly and denial runs deep in this excellent second novel by Spangler. The authors' love of the subject shines through as skiing, family values and romance fill the pages of this heartwarming story. The setting is stunning; making this reviewer nostalgic for her childhood days spent skiing the bunny hills of Wisconsin."
—*Curve Magazine*

Learning Curve

"Spangler's title, *Learning Curve,* refers to the growth both of these women make, as they deal with attraction and avoidance. They share a mutual lust, but can lust alone surpass their differences? The answer to that question is told with humor, adventure, and heat."
—*Just About Write*

"[Spangler's] potential shines through, particularly her ability to tap into the angst that accompanies any attempt to alter the perceptions of others…Your homework assignment, read on."—*Curve Magazine*

By the Author

Learning Curve

Trails Merge

THE LONG WAY HOME

by

Rachel Spangler

2010

THE LONG WAY HOME

ISBN 10: 1-60282-178-X
ISBN 13: 978-1-60282-178-1

This Trade Paperback Original Is Published By
Bold Strokes Books, Inc.
P.O. Box 249
Valley Falls, NY 12185

First Edition: September 2010

CREDITS

EDITORS: SHELLEY THRASHER AND STACIA SEAMAN
PRODUCTION DESIGN: STACIA SEAMAN
COVER DESIGN BY SHERI (GRAPHICARTIST2020@HOTMAIL.COM)

Acknowledgments

There's a common narrative in gay and lesbian fiction in which a young person grapples with her sexuality within the confines of her small town, surrounded by small-minded people and overbearing family members. The protagonist somehow finds some reserve of courage hidden deep inside herself to come out and make her getaway, leaving all the small-town narrow-mindedness behind as she bravely chases her dreams to the big city. Those are common themes in our books because for a long time those were common themes in our lives. For many of us, the need to get away in order to find ourselves is still part of our coming-out stories, but this is not one of those stories.

This is a book about going back and having the courage to stay. Mostly, this is a novel about being wise enough to look past stereotypes and caricatures and learning to see our friends, neighbors, families, and even ourselves as complex, dynamic human beings with the capability to change and grow.

I've done a lot of changing and growing over my last few years at Bold Strokes Books. Radclyffe has surrounded me with an amazing support staff (Connie, Lori, Kim, Cindy, etc.) and provided me with the best cover artist in the business in Sheri, who somehow manages to outdo herself every time, even with authors like me meddling with her vision. Shelley Thrasher is more than an editor. She's a professor who has taught me more than even I can put into my very wordy sentences, but any improvement you see in my writing should be credited to her. Stacia Seaman, copy editor extraordinaire, does a job I could never do, and she does so with a ceaseless efficiency. Thank you also to the bigger Bold Strokes Books crew of authors who never fail to offer support and advice, or even a playful distraction, all while continuing to raise the bar for me as an author.

I have amazing friends who've challenged and supported me both as a writer and as a person through the creation of this book. Toni Whitaker and Barb Dallinger served as beta readers, and God bless them, they are the sweetest, kindest, gentlest souls who understand that they have been entrusted with my baby. Neither one of them made a sharp or hurtful comment throughout the process and yet still somehow managed to guide several characters into much stronger, more refined positions. This story is fuller because of their input. Outside of official beta readers, I've also gotten boat loads of attabois and confidence boosters from Will Banks, Georgia Beers, Lori Ostergaard, Jamie Glass, Lynda Sandoval, Jove Belle, Kim Baldwin, Smitty, Lee Lynch, Elaine Mulligan, Cate Culpepper, Heather Lohnes, Gill McKnight, Rev Cynthia Wickwire, JLee Meyer, Cheryl Craig, Carsen Taite, VK Powell, Gill McKnight, and the FSU Rock Band/Theological Poker Night Crew.

And to the people who keep me coming back for more, thank you to every reader who's ever bought and read one of my books, and even more gratitude to those of you who took the time to write, ask questions in the VLR, e-mail, or comment on my Facebook wall, and say what you liked (or didn't) about it. Y'all have taken a hobby of mine and transformed it into a passion.

Finally, to my family, the people who've shaped who I am, I cannot thank you enough for the love and support you continue to give me. I've pushed you all out of your comfort zone a time or two, but you've never failed to rise to the challenge. I know there've been times when you've been a lot more patient with me than I was with you, and I appreciate that. To Susie, who continues to be the single biggest influence in my life and writing, I don't know why an amazing woman like you would ever take a chance on a boi like me, but I'm so glad you did. You are the reason I want to keep getting better, come what may. And to Jackson, you're teaching me more about life than I'm teaching you. Thanks, Jackie boy.

Most importantly, thank you to my Creator, Redeemer, and Sanctifier, for giving me such a long list of people to thank.

Dedication

To all who have the courage to live the life
they want to live regardless of what the world tells them
life is supposed to look like and to every person in a small
town who refuses to be typecast as small minded.

And to Susie—whether you believe it or not,
this one is your fault, too.

CHAPTER ONE

August 1

Ali was sexy as hell, but she was awfully high maintenance for a sometimes lover. Now she wanted to go downtown to the theater.

Raine said, "For the fifth time, I'm broke and out of energy. And I told you I don't want to go anywhere right now. I'm staying in and trying to find a way not to get evicted."

Ali rolled her eyes. "You won't get evicted. No one in Boystown would evict their Little Orphan Annie. You've spent ten years playing the disowned teenager. Why stop now?"

"I'm not seventeen anymore. Eventually I'll have to—"

The phone rang, mercifully saving Raine from having to come up with an end to that sentence. How could she get her life back on track? Change her act? Find a new career? She didn't like to think about either of those options. She glanced at the caller ID and saw the number of her agent, Edmond Carpenter. "I have to take this."

"We're already late," Ali whined.

"We're done, Ali." Raine turned her back to the living room and answered the phone. "Edmond, please say you've found me a job."

"Who loves you, baby?" Edmond asked a second before Raine's front door slammed shut. Ali had recognized her cue to exit.

Raine chuckled. "I hope you do, because I'm pretty sure Ali doesn't."

"Another one bites the dust. Good riddance to bad trash, there're other bitches in the sea, and all those standard breakup clichés that are supposed to offer comfort."

"I don't need comfort. I need a job."

"How about a job, room and board, and a chance to get published again?"

Raine flopped onto her couch, dizzy with relief. "Oh my goddess, you're shitting me."

"Ugh, you can't be that vulgar if you accept an academic position at a liberal arts college, especially since they've offered to put you up on campus as their guest lecturer for the year."

"A lecturer position?" Raine felt giddy. "That's exactly what we wanted. Could it be more perfect?"

"Now before you get all excited, it's not totally perfect. It's four hours away from Chicago." Edmond's voice pitched a little higher, a sure sign he was tense.

"That's not necessarily a bad thing. This place is starting to wear on me."

"It's at a small college. You'd be their first guest lecturer."

"I'm a trendsetter."

"You'd have to start in two weeks."

"Edmond, I'm out of options and my rent was due yesterday. I'll take anything."

"I hoped that's what you'd say." Edmond didn't sound relieved. "The job's in Darlington."

"That's not funny." Raine struggled not to let the mention of her hometown dampen her mood. "Seriously, where is it?"

"I'm serious. It's at Bramble College in Darlington, Illinois."

"Are you out of your fucking mind? I've spent my entire life getting away from that place. I'm Raine St. James, the one who survived." Raine needed to remind herself that she'd made it out alive.

"Exactly. You made it, you beat the odds, you made something of yourself, and now you're a local celebrity ready to return triumphantly. Think about the articles you could write. Hell, maybe even a book. You'd be a hero."

"No, I wouldn't. In Darlington I'm just Rory, a dyke who disgraced her parents and snuck out one night, forever. Those people have no idea who I've become. They don't read *The Advocate*. They've never seen any of my articles or heard any of my public speeches."

"Well, somebody at Bramble knows who you are, because the dean's office contacted me. They want you there. They're offering you a prime job with a place to live, two classes of your choice. . ."

Raine didn't hear any of it. Her chest ached and her head throbbed as memories of her youth rushed back. The angst, the fear, the self-loathing—she could summon it all so easily even after a decade. No way could she take that job. She wasn't that desperate, was she?

❖

August 14

Raine didn't need the GPS in her Toyota Prius to tell her which exit to take off I-55. She'd learned how to drive on these roads. The four-lane highway had been her way out, her path to freedom, though she'd been heading in the other direction back then. The only time she'd driven toward her hometown in the past ten years had been in her dreams.

Her memories had faded to black and white over time, but they never disappeared. If not for the vivid colors around her now, she could convince herself that what she was seeing was nothing more than a memory. The cornfields still rose in every direction as if attempting to swallow her whole. The August heat was every bit as oppressive as it'd always been. The only sign of life was the occasional truck, tractor, or freight train, all of them old, run-down, and covered in rust, like the people who drove them.

The shrill ring of Raine's cell phone interrupted her thoughts. She glanced down at the caller ID display and hesitated. If she hadn't been alone in the car for four hours, she wouldn't be speaking to her agent, but Raine was an extrovert by nature. She gave in and answered.

"I hate you, Edmond Carpenter."

"Oh, good, you're speaking to me again." Edmond had been her agent for almost as long as she'd been in Chicago, and though Raine currently wanted to hate him, she had to admit he was her closest friend. "Are you there yet?"

"I can still turn around if you've found me another job."

"We've been through this, Raine." They'd reviewed her options every day for the past two weeks, and Raine had wrestled with the decision until she received her eviction notice. She didn't have a choice.

"I don't have to like it, or you." Raine pouted.

"Don't kid yourself, honey. You love me more than pussy."

"Fuck off."

"Seriously, Raine, you have to learn to control your mouth. You're about to become a college teacher. You have to play your cards right. This job could revive your career."

"I know how to behave." Raine sighed as she drove into town. "I went to college, you know?"

"I know, cupcake. I got you the scholarship."

"Yeah, and you would've skimmed ten percent off the top of that, if you could've figured out a way to." Raine knew she was acting like a petulant child, but she couldn't help it. She felt like a child again. Returning to Darlington made her revert to her teenage mentality. "I'm sorry. I'm in town now, and I don't have the energy for witty banter."

"I understand." Edmond's voice softened. "If you need someone to talk to tonight, you know my number."

"Thanks." Raine flipped her phone shut and focused on the road ahead. The cornfields gave way to homes that became increasingly closer together as she approached a large green sign proclaiming Darlington City Limits, Population 5,000. *City, my ass. I've lived in apartment complexes that housed more than five thousand people.*

She slowed to thirty-five miles per hour and scanned her surroundings. The gas station had a new neon sign, but it still didn't stay open twenty-four hours a day. The high school looked exactly like it had the day she graduated. All of the little houses still had their perfectly manicured lawns and patriotic bunting strewn on porches. The grocery store still used the same weather-worn banners to advertise double-coupon day. The town square was ringed with American flags and yellow ribbons probably left up since the first Gulf War. In fact, the only significant change was that the Walmart had been super-sized. To anyone else this ride would've been a nostalgic peek into small-town America, but Raine fought to swallow the bile that rose in her throat.

Perfect. That's what they want, perfection. White picket fences and brightly colored flowers lined each walkway. The women she saw through store-front windows wore dresses, and the men wore ties. Everyone was clean-cut, clean-shaven, and clearly gendered. That's why she'd never belonged. She wasn't the perfect all-American girl to fit in the perfect all-American town. She was an outsider and an outlaw. *Homo*, *dyke*, *faggot*—she knew all the names people here called people like her, but she also knew the worst one. *Queer.* It didn't just mean *gay*. It meant *different, strange*. It meant *not like us*. It was the antithesis of Darlington, where team play and conformity were valued above all else.

How could this be happening? She'd vowed that she'd never come back, and she had no idea what she'd do now that she'd returned. Just a few years earlier she'd been the toast of Boystown, a hero in her own small circle, a disowned gay teenager who'd shown the world what she was made of. She'd spoken at colleges and community centers across the country. Everyone had wanted to hear her story, a young woman who had beaten the odds. Her audiences had been so impressed when she was seventeen. Few people had met a more resilient twenty-year-old. Even when she was twenty-five, most college students saw her as one of them, part of a new generation of out-and-proud lesbians.

When had that changed? At first she'd had only a few less speaking engagements each year, but then her articles began to be rejected. Editors had asked her if she had anything new, as if being disowned once wasn't enough. At twenty-seven she was still gay, and she still had the same message. Why was a story about running away from home less interesting when someone nearing thirty told it? Yes, the events that had shaped her might have happened a decade ago, but they still felt real. The memories flooded Raine's mind so thoroughly that she worried she wouldn't be able to drive.

Mercifully, Raine saw the sign for the college entrance and turned onto campus. She had no memories here. Local girls weren't encouraged to go anywhere near Bramble's campus, and the college students and faculty rarely ventured farther than the string of taverns directly across from its well-tended grounds. While Darlington was a town with a college, it wasn't a college town. The only area where the two interacted was sports, and even then the interactions were more competitive than conversational.

The college was small, with large trees shading the winding lane that bisected the campus. All the buildings were brick, most with long strands of ivy wandering up their outer walls. Raine passed several small dorms, the library, and the gym before she stopped in front of a building different from the others only because it had a large sign labeling it the Department of Academic Affairs.

Once inside, Raine had expected to have to ask around to find the dean's office, but a young man behind a large mahogany desk immediately jumped up. "You must be Raine."

"Yeah, Raine St. James. I'm the new guest lecturer."

"I know who you are." The man gave her a little wink that caused her to inspect him more closely, from his Kenneth Cole loafers to his immaculately pressed suit and his perfectly coiffed blond hair. Raine finally recognized the welcome. *He's as gay as a field full of daises.*

"I'm Miles Braden, Director of Financial Aid." He extended a well-manicured hand.

"Nice to meet you, Miles." Raine returned the handshake with a genuine smile. A gay man with an administrative position in Darlington. Maybe some things had changed. "Could you point me toward the dean's office?"

"She's in a meeting, but I'll let her know you're here." Miles stretched over the desk and pressed a few buttons on his phone. "She'll want to see you."

"Flores, Raine St. James is here."

Not thirty seconds later a door off the entryway opened and a striking Latino woman in a brown pantsuit smiled broadly at Raine. She had short black hair and wore no makeup.

"Raine, I can't tell you how happy we are to see you. I'm Flores Molina, the dean of academic affairs and a big fan of your writing."

"Really?" The warm welcome surprised Raine and made her wonder if she was getting the same kind of vibes from Flores that she had from Miles, but when she discreetly raised an eyebrow in his direction she received an equally discreet shake of his head. Raine didn't let her disappointment show. *A gay man and a lesbian would be too much to hope for.*

"I'd love to show you around, but I'm in the middle of a meeting, and I'm sure you'd like to settle in."

Raine forced a nod but couldn't bring herself to make peace with the idea of getting settled in Darlington. "Why don't I walk you to the library and introduce you to Beth Devoroux. She's made your housing arrangements."

"That would be great," Raine said, but Flores was already headed out the door. Raine barely had time to wave good-bye to Miles before she jogged to catch up with the dean. Between her angst caused by her drive through town, her surprise at meeting a gay man in Darlington, and her race to keep up with Flores, Raine didn't have time to process the notion that the name Beth Devoroux sounded awfully familiar.

Beth read a list of the Bramble College journal subscriptions, trying to decide which of them needed to be renewed in print and which should be bundled together through online services. She'd already spent too much time on the detail-laden task. Though she was good at the minutiae that were part of a librarian's job, today she kept thinking about all the things she'd rather do.

The students would be back on campus this weekend, and classes would start Monday. She'd give tours of the library to all incoming freshmen as part of their introduction to composition classes. Then general use of the library would increase sharply over the next two weeks as due dates for assignments and papers invariably snuck up on students who were rusty from their summer vacations. Beth enjoyed interacting with her students and connecting them to information that would help them grow, change, and see the world in new and exciting ways. However, in order to focus on the things she loved about her job when the students arrived, she needed to finish her administrative work now.

The buzzer on the library's front door interrupted her. She fell prey to a convenient distraction again and went to see who was at the door. When she turned the corner from her office to the small lobby and nearly bumped into Rory St. James, her stomach flip-flopped.

It was clearly Rory. She hadn't changed much since the last time Beth saw her. Her chestnut brown hair was shorter, and she'd filled out into her medium build, but her essence was the same. She stood confidently, one hand shoved casually into the pocket of her cargo khakis, her eyes hidden behind a pair of square-lens sunglasses. When she saw Beth, a rakish grin of recognition broke across her face and caused her disarming dimples to appear at either corner of her mouth. For a moment Beth couldn't think of a thing to say. Thankfully, Flores never had that problem.

"Raine, this is our librarian and the head of our personnel committee—"

"Little Beth Devoroux?" Rory removed her sunglasses, revealing her emerald green eyes. "I hardly recognized you. Wow, time has been good to you."

Beth's face flushed at both Rory's characterization of her as "little Beth" and her compliment. Even though the last decade had certainly not all been good, she was glad the strain wasn't evident. Rory's appreciative gaze made her feel like she was in high school again.

"Hi, Rory." The words left her mouth before Beth could catch them.

Raine winced, and her smile twisted into a grimace. "No one's called me Rory in ten years."

"I'm sorry. I don't know why I said that. I realize you go by Raine now." Beth mentally kicked herself for botching the reintroduction. This really was like high school.

"You two know each other?" Flores asked, then answered her own question. "Of course you do. You both grew up here. I always forget that you're a townie, Beth. Why don't I leave you to get reacquainted, then you can show Raine to her apartment?"

Beth didn't have time to explain that they hadn't known each other all that well or that Raine really wasn't a townie, the term people at the college used for life-long Darlington residents. Before Beth could say anything, Flores was out the door, leaving an awkward silence.

"She's a bit of a whirlwind," Rory finally said.

Beth smiled both in humor and relief. "Yeah, she's always on the go."

"I know the type."

Was Rory alluding to a friend, a colleague, a lover? It was best not to pursue that line of thought, so Beth said, "I bet you're exhausted from your drive. Why don't I show you where you'll be living?"

Beth led the way out of the library and onto the quad. "We've had one of the dorms converted into apartments for students with families and our around-the-clock security staff. It's not fancy, but it's quiet and convenient when the weather turns bad."

"And it's free," Rory deadpanned.

"Yes, there's always that," Beth responded carefully. While part of her had hoped Rory was here out of some desire to reconnect with her roots, deep down she knew she was being naïve. Still, she was a little disappointed that Rory had come home only out of necessity.

They walked across the small quad toward Weaver Hall, another brick building, several stories tall. "So, little Beth never left home." It sounded more like a statement than a question.

"I went away to college for a while before I transferred to Bramble and finished here." Beth didn't go into any more details since Rory didn't seem interested. They entered the apartment complex, and Beth waved to several of the employees.

"You always were such a good girl," Rory teased, but Beth could sense condescension. "I bet your daddy's so proud of you he can hardly contain himself."

A sharp pain pierced Beth's chest and she stopped. She hadn't felt that once-familiar sensation in a long time. It rarely crept up on her anymore.

"What is it?" Rory's cocky demeanor faltered as she obviously read the hurt on Beth's face.

"My parents died in a car accident eight years go," Beth stated as evenly as she could. She hadn't had to tell anyone that for ages. Everyone she was around knew her family and their history.

"Beth, I'm so sorry," Rory whispered, and placed a hand on her shoulder.

The touch comforted and warmed Beth, and the concern in Rory's emerald eyes made her stomach tighten. The pain once again faded. "Thank you. Your room is here on the right." She fished the key from her pocket and handed it to Rory, who opened the door.

"It's not big but—"

"It's free," Rory stated again. She made no move to invite Beth in.

"There's a parking pass in your mailbox in the lobby and a laundry room in the basement. If you need anything, dial zero for the campus directory and ask for me."

"I'm sure I'll figure it out." Rory had clearly dismissed her. "I've been on my own for a long time now."

"All right, I'll leave you to it." Beth turned to go. Was Rory watching her walk away? Probably not. She seemed too absorbed in her own demons to pay attention to anyone else right now.

"Hey, Beth," Rory called after her.

"Yes?" She turned around to get one last look at the striking woman in the doorway. She was strong and proud and every bit as stunning as she'd been ten years ago. Seeing her like that, Beth could almost convince herself that no time had passed at all.

"I really am sorry about your folks," she said sincerely.

"Thank you," Beth said, then pivoted before her tears fell, the illusion of timelessness broken. It wasn't ten years ago. She wasn't carefree and innocent anymore, and neither was the woman behind her. The ache in her heart reminded her of all they'd both been through. Having the past surface so unexpectedly jarred and disconcerted her. Beth rarely had to confront the loss of her family anymore. Her students didn't usually ask personal questions, and outside of them, Beth seldom met anyone new.

Then again, Rory wasn't new. Beth had known Rory for eighteen years. She'd known her number on the softball team, twelve; her favorite drink, Coke cold but no ice; and her favorite music, John Cougar Mellencamp. But the woman she'd just seen wasn't Rory. Rory was easy-going, warm, gracious. Rory would've hugged her hello. Rory would've invited her in to get reacquainted. Rory would've known her parents were dead. Rory didn't exist anymore. The woman who'd come to Darlington, Illinois was Raine, and Raine was a new story entirely.

CHAPTER TWO

August 15

Raine stayed in her tiny apartment alone for almost twenty-four hours. She paced around her small living room and smaller kitchen. Then she lay awake for hours, staring at the wall of her single bedroom. Finally, after dawn crept pink across campus, she went to the bathroom and got acquainted with her new shower.

She unpacked the three boxes of personal belongings she had moved from Chicago, mostly clothes and CDs. She ate the entire box of cereal she'd brought with her, and she didn't own a TV. She would lose her mind if she didn't get out of here soon, but where could she go?

If she was in Chicago, she would've strolled down Halsted Street, where she knew all the shop and bar owners. But no way could she ramble around Darlington. She was bound to run into someone she knew here too, and that prospect wasn't nearly as pleasant as it was in Boystown. Sooner or later she'd have to venture into town, but she was still hoping for later.

She pulled on a pair of blue jeans that she had bought already faded, then searched for a shirt. She wasn't sure what style to go for since she didn't know where she was going. After holding up several T-shirts, she settled on a cream-colored polo and popped the collar as was the trend in Chicago. With a pair of Birkenstock sandals she was decidedly casual. She even tousled her short hair to make it seem windblown. She'd spent a lot of time learning to look good without letting anyone know she cared about her appearance.

Outside the apartment building she simply wandered. If she let herself dwell on where she was she'd chicken out and hide in her apartment again. As long as she stayed on campus she should be fine. There were no memories to haunt her there. She strolled across the open, grassy quad and under the shade of the big oak trees that lined the main lane.

Passing several dorms as students and parents unloaded trucks and SUVs piled high with clothes, food, and mementos of home, Raine watched curiously. These would be her students on Monday. They were all so young and full of life. Why would they spend the final years of their youth going to college in a place like Darlington? How would she have felt about this place if she weren't gay? Wouldn't she still have found it oppressive, limiting, or dull? Sure, some people were stuck here in town due to a lack of skill or education, or because they didn't understand their options, but the young people who attended Bramble College didn't fit into those categories. Why would anyone actually choose this life?

Raine shrugged and moved on. Perhaps some people were built differently. Maybe there was a small-town gene. Surely not everyone in Darlington was miserable. She'd gone to school with plenty of kids who fit the mold. Perhaps some people were born for small-town life. As if on cue, Beth Devoroux rounded the corner.

Raine watched Beth approach. *Damn, she's grown up nicely.* Back in high school she was a skinny little kid who was always hanging around, but now she was a beautiful woman. She'd developed curves in all the right places. Her dark hair was still curly, but no longer unruly. Instead it cascaded lightly across her shoulders. When she saw Raine, Beth broke into a huge smile, one sweet enough to remind Raine of the girl she'd once been, but not so innocent as to blind her to the woman Beth had become.

"Good morning." Beth's greeting was warm.

"Morning." Raine returned her smile. It was hard to remain sullen when Beth grinned at her like that. "What are you doing at work on a Saturday morning?"

"I can't stay away on move-in day. I need to stop in at the library to make sure all my flyers and information pamphlets are out where the new students can find them. Then at noon I'll help the orientation committee serve lunch on the quad." Raine was only half listening because Beth was wearing a short-sleeved, light blue shirt thin enough for Raine to see the outline of a sexy little tank top underneath.

Geez, I'm staring at her chest. Raine lifted her line of sight to Beth's baby blues. The chest was great, but it was attached to Beth Devoroux, in Darlington, and that meant trouble. The last thing she wanted was for sweet little Beth to think she was some kind of leering, predatory dyke. What a way to start a new job.

"Sounds like you're pretty busy," Raine finally managed to say. "I'll let you go."

"I'm always busy." Beth chuckled. "I can't ever say no."

Beth had always been a joiner, even in high school, unlike Raine, which was another thing that set her apart from the Darlington crowd. She'd always been independent, while people like Beth were so eager to be part of a team that they exhausted themselves trying to please everyone. "Admitting it is the first step to recovery."

Beth regarded her quizzically. "I wouldn't have it any other way."

During the moment of awkward silence between them, Raine felt the impact of their disconnect. Beth was sweet and welcoming in a place where she'd expected only hostility, so she'd started to relax. But Beth was also a townie, a small-town farm girl, and a straight woman.

Raine was about to excuse herself and leave when Beth waved to someone across the quad, then clasped Raine's arm. "Come on. There's someone I want you to meet."

A young blonde in cargo khakis, shorts, and a red tank top approached them. "Patty, this is Raine St. James," Beth said. "Raine, meet Patty Spezio."

Raine and Patty scanned each other up and down as they shook hands. This woman was smoking hot with toned legs and arms that made it obvious she took great care with her figure, and a tan that suggested time spent outdoors. She wore no ring, but a small silver lambda hung on a chain around her neck.

Patty, for her part, seemed equally pleased with what she saw in Raine. Her smile turned suggestive, and her grip lingered longer than necessary. "Raine, I'm so excited to meet you. I've read all your writing."

"Thanks, it's nice to meet you too," Raine said as she processed this new bit of information. *She cute, she's a lesbian, and she knows who I am. She's a fan.* Raine was back in familiar territory, and after her disconcerting lapse with Beth, she welcomed the chance to be in control again. She'd grown accustomed to this type of interaction over the past ten years, and while she was a little surprised to find one in Darlington, the setting generally didn't change the outcome.

Beth continued her introduction. "Patty works in the athletic department, and she's one of the advisors for the gay-and-lesbian student group on campus."

Raine was genuinely surprised. "I didn't know Bramble had a GLBT group."

"It's not a big one," Patty said. "We usually have about ten students per meeting. They're a good group, though, very active on campus." She added, more suggestively, "You should come with me sometime."

Raine felt her grin widen at the double entendre. "I'd really enjoy that."

"Well, Patty, I didn't mean to interrupt you," Beth said.

"No, I'm glad you did." Patty stared at Raine even though she was answering Beth.

"I'm sure you're busy today."

"I'm working move-in at Preston Hall. You know what a madhouse that'll be."

"Yup, better let you get to it."

Beth was clearly dismissing Patty, but if Patty knew it, she ignored the message. Maybe Beth was eager to get to work or, more likely, was uncomfortable with the lesbian mating ritual playing out in front of her. Although Beth was stunning standing there in the summer sunlight, Raine forced her attention back to Patty. Beth was dangerously off-limits, but Patty gave every indication she was available, and right now Raine needed to feel in control again.

"Sounds like a big job. Why don't I come along and offer a hand?" Raine asked.

Beth cut Patty off before she could respond. "Raine, you don't have to do that. You just got to campus."

Raine shrugged off Beth, who was obviously being gracious. "I don't mind. It'll be a good way for me to get out of the apartment and meet some people."

Beth glanced back and forth between Raine and Patty as if she wanted to say something more, but instead she sighed. "Have fun."

"You too," Raine said as she and Patty turned to leave.

"See you and Kel Sunday," Patty called over her shoulder, and they were off.

What was that about? Who worked on Sunday, and more importantly, who the hell was Kel? Beth's husband? No, she didn't wear a ring, and she still had her maiden name. A boyfriend? Raine tried to recall if she'd gone to school with any Kels, or Kellens, but couldn't come up with anyone. But she'd been gone a long time. Beth could've met any number of good ole boys. In fact, it would be odd for a woman as beautiful as her not to be dating. Girls married young here in farm country, had a litter of kids, and turned into their mothers. That fact of life depressed Raine, but she couldn't avoid it. Besides, who Beth spent time with wasn't any of her business.

But why was she obsessing over Beth? She'd just found a real, live lesbian in Darlington, Illinois, one that appeared eager to take her mind off her old demons and her new surroundings. Patty brushed against her as they walked. Her body was fit and firm, and Raine was going to spend the afternoon watching her lift heavy furniture. She had a brief image of flexing muscle and sweat glistening on skin, only neither of those things happened in a dorm lobby. Beth Devoroux and Kel whatever-his-last-name-was be damned. Raine needed to focus on getting better acquainted with Patty.

❖

Beth slammed the stack of flyers on the front desk a little harder than necessary. Thankfully no one else was in the library to hear the satisfying snap of paper against Formica. She was still fuming about the way Patty had practically jumped Raine in the middle of the quad. That woman was shameless, flaunting her lesbianism and making blatant sexual overtures. Raine asked genuine questions about the campus climate, and Patty turned them into a come-on.

"You should come with me sometime." Beth mimicked Patty. How tacky could she be? And dragging Raine to work move-in when she should be settling in herself was poor manners. Beth wanted to pull Raine aside and let her know that Patty was young and impulsive, flighty, even, but Patty didn't give her a chance, and then they ran off before Beth could warn Raine. Beth shouldn't have introduced them. She was trying to put Raine in touch with professional connections. How was she supposed to know Patty would throw herself at her? The way Patty prattled on was embarrassing, but Beth couldn't resist the urge to imitate her one more time. "I've read all your writing."

"Beth?"

She jumped and yelped before she turned to see Kelly enter the room. "You scared me."

"Sorry." Kelly peeked around the desk suspiciously. "I came in the back door. I didn't know where you were, but I could hear you talking to someone."

Beth blushed at her own silliness. "No, I was talking to myself."

"There's no one else here?"

"No, everyone is working move-in today."

Kelly checked over her shoulder one more time before seeming to accept that they were really alone, then kissed Beth, a light peck on the lips. "I missed you, so I thought I'd stop by and help in the library."

"That's sweet, but I don't have much to do around here. I was about to go help in the dorms."

Kelly frowned. "I don't know if I should show up with you. It might raise suspicions."

Beth nodded. She'd long ago given up trying to convince Kelly that simply being seen together didn't mean they were publicly declaring their relationship. It wasn't much of an issue with them anymore. Kelly was a private person, and Beth respected that fact even if she did find it inconvenient.

"There's really nothing for us to do in here?"

Beth tried to think of something to kill time on, but she was ready to get out and interact with some of the students. "Yes. I should've been over there already, but I ran into Patty, and when I introduced her to Raine she got all goofy."

Kelly stiffened immediately. "What were you doing with *her*?"

"Nothing." Beth steeled herself for Kelly's moral indignation. "I wasn't really with her. I bumped into her on the quad right before Patty came by, so I introduced them and Patty pretty much took it from there."

Kelly snorted. "I bet she did."

"She was all over Raine, telling her how much she loved her writing."

"Raine? God, Beth, you don't actually call her that, do you?"

Beth tried to shrug the comment off, even though she found the name change disconcerting too. "She's very sensitive about being called Rory. She's been Raine for ten years, so I guess it's weird to go back."

"It's weird to change in the first place. Weird and pretentious. Who does that? And 'Raine' of all things. It's not like she went from her nickname back to her full name, Loraine. At least that would've made sense." Beth watched her pace. Kelly could be quite imposing, especially when she was agitated. Her eyes and hair were such a dark shade of brown that they were almost black, and they offset her pale skin. Her high cheekbones and the sharp line of her jaw only accentuated the stark contrast in her coloring, though her cheeks became increasingly pink as she continued her rant. "Raine isn't even a real name. She made it up to get attention."

"Well, Patty gave her plenty of attention." Beth's frustration built again. "She practically swooned for her."

"I bet Rory loved that. She'll do anything to get noticed."

"Not everyone wants to be closeted all the time." Beth immediately regretted the statement.

"Closeted? You mean discreet, respectable, or tasteful? She's a disgrace to herself and this whole town. Whoever invited her back here should be fired."

Beth winced. She hoped Kelly was too absorbed in her tirade to notice how tense the comment had made her. She didn't know why Kelly always made her feel defensive, but instead of defending the decision to hire Raine or explaining her own involvement in the hiring process, she tried to defuse Kelly's anger with a diplomatic answer. "The college wanted someone edgy but with local ties to help the school seem less conservative."

"Fine, let them turn the guest-lecturer position into a freak show, but Rory better stay away from me," Kelly said resolutely, then added, "At least Rory and Patty will keep each other busy for a while. They deserve each other."

At that comment Beth's mind began to race with images of Raine and Patty together, and her face flamed with anger. She wanted to run over to Preston Hall, but why? What would she say? So Patty came on to Raine, why should she care? Raine didn't seem to mind. Patty hadn't dragged her away. Raine had gone willingly. Beth wasn't Raine's mother, or girlfriend, or even her friend. She was only some girl Rory had barely known was alive in high school. Her stomach turned at the thought.

"Hey, you okay?" Kelly asked.

"Yeah, I'm fine. I need to get going."

"Sure. I understand."

"Can you come over tonight?" Beth made the request without stopping to consider it fully.

Kelly was plainly surprised. "I've got church tomorrow morning, and we'll see each other at Miles's in the afternoon."

"I know that, but…I don't know. It would be nice to spend some time together."

Kelly brightened and snuck another quick kiss before she headed for the door. "I could stop by for an hour or two."

Beth watched her go, wondering what had just happened. Kelly probably thought that by "spend some time together," Beth meant "have sex." Maybe she had. She wasn't sure what she'd meant.

But she needed to get her mind off Raine, and Kelly was the most pleasant distraction she had.

❖

The steady stream of students that had filled the dorm lobby all day dwindled as the afternoon faded into early evening. With little left to do, Raine propped herself against a soda machine outside Preston Hall and watched Patty lift a mini-fridge out of one of the last pickup trucks. *God, she's ripped*, Raine thought, not for the first time that day. Patty's body was more than toned. She had firm muscles and a chiseled torso. She moved effortlessly even when carrying heavy or bulky items, and the display of power was a big turn-on. Raine would never have thought of herself as a size queen. In fact, most of the women she'd dated recently were absurdly thin, but watching Patty's biceps flex and contract while she worked, Raine could certainly see the appeal in sporty dykes.

Patty turned around and caught Raine watching, but Raine held her stare, and Patty rewarded her boldness with a smile. "You didn't have to stay all day."

"I don't have anywhere else to be," Raine said honestly. "Nowhere with such a pleasant view anyway."

Patty's blush was clearly visible in the dim light of dusk. "Well, we're done here now, but we could go somewhere else if you want, maybe pick up some dinner."

Raine had a momentary flash of panic. She didn't want to go out in Darlington. She'd done a great job of forgetting where she was all day, but if they left campus, she wouldn't be able to escape the fact that she was back in her hellhole of a hometown. "I'm pretty sweaty and not really dressed for that."

Patty seemed disappointed.

"We could do something less formal, though," Raine said. While she wouldn't go out in Darlington, she'd love to do some other things with Patty in a more private setting.

Patty brightened but seemed nervous. "I've got a frozen pizza and a case of beer at home."

"Lead the way."

Raine followed Patty to her little Ford Tempo and prayed she didn't live too far from campus. She knew she was being a little silly and that sooner or later she'd have to go into town, but she didn't look forward to it.

"What's it like to live in Chicago?" Patty asked as she pulled out of the college's main entrance.

"It's a great city. Nightlife, sports, theater, shopping, any kind of food you'd ever want." Raine wasn't interested in small talk. She was too busy scanning her surroundings. They were a few blocks into an older area of Darlington now. Raine's grandparents had lived in this part of town, though they had passed away when she was in high school.

Patty cut into Raine's memories. "Is it bigger than St. Louis?"

"What's that?" Raine tried to refocus her attention. "St. Louis? That's a great city too. Very different feel from Chicago, though, being right on the Mississippi."

"I go to St. Louis sometimes on the weekends to get away from this place. There're some good gay bars…"

Raine drifted off as she remembered what it used to be like to run for the nearest city. As soon as she was old enough to drive, she'd started sneaking down to St. Louis. Though it was an hour away, it was the closest thing she'd had to freedom at the time. The memories were still so fresh—confusion at being different, fear of being found out, anger at having to hide who she was. The houses they passed started to close in on her. This was the place she'd run from all those years ago.

They pulled into the driveway of a small cottage-style house, and Raine breathed deeply to steady herself. Patty, thankfully, seemed oblivious to her discomfort and kept chattering about her trips to St. Louis all the way up her front steps and into the house.

"Do you mind if I take a shower before I start dinner?" Patty asked once they settled in.

"Not at all."

"Great. Help yourself to a beer. They're in the fridge."

Raine watched her go, trying to refocus on her body and away from the world outside. Patty paused, turned around once more, and gave her a good look up and down.

"What?" Raine asked.

"I can't believe Raine St. James is in my living room," she said, then continued into what Raine assumed was a bedroom.

The comment jolted Raine out of her maudlin mood, and she chuckled as she went to the kitchen and grabbed a beer. She heard the shower turn on as she stood staring out the front window. Some children were playing Wiffle ball in the yard across the street while a few adults sat on the porch watching them. A few minutes earlier this familiar scene from her childhood might have panicked her, but now she felt calm.

Yes, she was in Darlington. No, she didn't fit in, but she wasn't seventeen anymore. She wasn't even the girl who had grown up here. She was Raine St. James, famous for being a survivor. She'd created a new identify for herself, had a new role in life, and she'd learned to play it well. Raine was confident and defiant. Women admired her, wanted to be like her, wanted to be *with* her.

Raine drew a long swig of her beer, her confidence increasing. Rory might've been scared into inaction when faced with a return to Darlington. Rory had bad memories. However, Raine had never even been here before, and Raine was here now. Rory had learned to be Raine in order to survive the fear and doubt that had consumed her. Patty wanted Raine, so she would get her.

She strode purposefully down the hall and into the room Patty had entered. Raine noted the large bed to her right, an antique dresser and nightstand, and then a half-open door through which she could make barely make out the shower because of all the steam in the room.

"Care for some company?" she called.

"Um, sure."

The mix of nervousness and anticipation in Patty's voice was obvious. Despite her early bravado and innuendo, she probably didn't do this much, and Raine had to admit she was being a little forward even by her standards. She usually got to know women before she slept with them. She always provided drinks, dinner, and some nice conversation so she could get a feel for her date's personality. She hadn't had a lot of serious relationships, but she hadn't had many one-night stands either. Tonight, though, she was eager for the main event. Sex was familiar. She was good at it and craved the control it provided.

She quickly shed her clothes and opened the shower door. Patty's firm body was everything Raine imagined it would be, but she hadn't expected the uncertainty in Patty's eyes and the shyness of her grin.

"I've never done this before," Patty said softly.

"Never?" Raine stopped abruptly.

Patty laughed. "No, no, that's not what I meant. I mean I've never done it so soon after meeting someone."

Raine relaxed. "We can take all the time you need." She kissed Patty, lightly at first before she ran her fingers up Patty's arms to gently massage the tense muscles. As the kiss deepened, Patty's mouth opened to accept Raine's tongue, and she relaxed more fully to her touch. Raine cupped Patty's small, pert breasts in each hand, and Patty's confidence seemed to grow steadily as she put her hands on Raine's hips and pulled her closer. Their slick skin slid together under the water, causing it to pool between them before it spilled over.

When they finally broke their kiss long enough to catch a breath, Patty practically panted as she said, "Okay, I'm ready now."

Kelly rolled off Beth, and they lay still and silent. They didn't need to talk. They knew each other's bodies well after nearly eight years together. While the spark of the early days was gone, so was most of the awkwardness. They had a routine, a comfortable rhythm of lovemaking. The thrill of the unexpected had vanished, but the excitement of being together remained. When Kelly made love to her, Beth felt cared for.

Kelly propped herself up on one elbow. "What's on your mind, babe?"

"I was thinking how good it is with you," Beth said as she rolled on her side to face her lover.

"It's good with you too." Kelly kissed her, a slow tender kiss. "I wish I didn't have to go."

"Already?" Beth was surprised that the time had passed so quickly, but not that Kelly was leaving. They rarely spent the entire night together in order to avoid arousing the suspicion of their neighbors.

"Yeah, I'm serving communion at church tomorrow." Kelly sat up and reached for her pants.

Beth watched her dress in the pale moonlight. She was attractive in any setting, but Beth found her most alluring without the sharp attire and power persona she wore in public. Beth liked to see Kelly's dark, shoulder-length hair in disarray and the pale shades of her skin left uncovered. This Kelly was gentler, less guarded, more human than the image she projected to the rest of the world. This was the side of Kelly she wished she could have in her life full-time instead of only a few times a week.

"Okay. I'll see you out." Beth began to get up.

"No, stay." Kelly kissed her once more. "I'll see you at Miles's tomorrow afternoon. Until then I want to hold on to this image of you."

"I love you," Beth said. It was the only thing to say when Kelly talked like that.

Kelly stopped in the bedroom doorway and smiled. "Love you too."

Then she was gone. Beth stared at the ceiling, listening for the door to close and the car to pull out of her driveway. She didn't know when she'd begun the habit, but it was part of her wind-down routine now. Once the sounds of Kelly's departure faded, she relaxed fully into her bed.

She had asked Kelly over impulsively but was glad she had. After her odd reaction to Rory and Patty, she needed to get her bearings. She was still confused about why the thought of the two of them together had upset her. She wasn't the jealous type, and even if she were, what did she have to be jealous about? Patty and

Rory were adults, free to do what they wanted. Rory didn't need her protection, and Beth didn't need to be concerned about her. Besides, Beth had Kelly, and tonight they had reaffirmed how good they were together. They had shared a lovely dinner, caught up on the events of their week, and made love, sweetly and gently.

Kelly had been everything Beth needed to get her mind off the earlier events of the day. In fact, Beth hadn't thought of Rory all night.

Until now.

CHAPTER THREE

August 16

"We're going to a super-secret-society meeting of queer Darlington?" Raine asked Patty on Sunday afternoon.

"Something like that." Patty laughed easily. The awkwardness of their earlier interactions had faded after the many hours of sex last night and again this morning.

"If it's such a secret, then why are you taking me? We barely know each other. I might be a spy," Raine teased. Patty was good for her ego. Now instead of the total panic that had accompanied her drive through Darlington, she was only mildly queasy.

"After the things you did to me last night, I can vouch for your lesbianism." Patty pulled into the driveway of a brick ranch home near campus. "I'm not closeted, but some of the other members are, so we can't advertise. We find each other by word of mouth."

"It's so very 1950s." Raine didn't know whether to be impressed or horrified that an underground group of gay and lesbians met in Darlington.

"Welcome to small-town America."

Patty barely knocked before she let herself in, and Raine followed. The entryway opened into a living room where several people lounged on large black leather couches around a glass table covered with decadent snacks. A gay man had to be their hostess. But Raine was more curious about the people who would attend an event like this than the decor.

The young man she'd met in the dean's office, Miles, jumped up to greet them. He barely acknowledged Patty before he turned his attention to Raine. "Look what the cat dragged in. It didn't take you long to find us."

Miles was even gayer here than he was in the office. "I work quickly."

"So I've heard. Every one of your references said you were absolutely explosive, so we're all eager to see you in action here in Darlington. Looks like Patty already got a sneak peek."

As much as Raine liked for people to be aware of her sexual prowess, she wasn't big on having them turn her night with Patty into a tawdry joke. Instead of responding to Miles's comment, she moved past him to a middle-aged Asian man who stood to greet her.

"I'm Raine St. James." She extended her hand.

"I'm Wilson Taguchi. You're a celebrity here."

"Maybe at the college," Raine conceded, "but I doubt the rest of town would agree with you. I'm more infamous than famous."

"That's not true," someone said from behind her.

Raine spun around. She'd heard the words clearly, and now she saw who had spoken them, but she still couldn't connect those two things.

Beth Devoroux stood in the doorway to the kitchen, looking every bit as startled as Raine. They froze there a few silent seconds and stared.

"I don't suppose you stopped by to borrow a cup of sugar." Raine's attempt at humor fell flat.

"No," Beth said, as if weighing her words. "I'm a member of this group."

"A member of the group, Beth? Like it's the Rotary Club?" Raine didn't know why she was reacting this way, but the words poured out. "I think you meant to say you're a lesbian. Isn't that what you meant, Beth?"

Beth opened her mouth, but her words faded quickly when a dark-haired woman entered the house.

Raine scanned her features as tendrils of recognition tugged at her memory. The woman turned first to Beth, her smile fading before she faced Raine. The images flooded back. Her hair had been longer, her appearance more refined, but her expression was the same—disgust.

Ten years earlier they'd stood staring each other down in much the same fashion. Raine had been hungover at school the morning after a big party at the lake and was doing a terrible job of hiding her condition. She had finally had to make a break for the bathroom, barely entering the stall before she vomited. When she pulled herself together enough to stand up, she was face-to-face with the judgmental, condescending eyes of the class tattletale, Kelly Rolen.

"Why are you here?" Kelly practically spat, bringing Raine back to the present.

"I'm here for a super-secret gay-and-lesbian meeting," Raine said, smiling slyly. Even after all these years, it was still fun to piss off this holier-than-thou bitch. "You see, Kelly, I'm a lesbian, a big one, so I've got a good reason to be here. The bigger question is why are you?"

Kelly's face burned red as her forehead wrinkled and she clenched her fists at her side. "You lazy, selfish, good-for-nothing piece of trash. When the hell will you grow up?"

Raine feigned boredom as the other people in the room shrank from the conflict. Raine thought for a minute that Kelly might actually hit her, but she was pretty sure she didn't have it in her, so she stood her ground. "I don't know what you're talking about."

"You think you can just waltz in here after everything you wrote about this town and all of us who live here? You think you're welcome or that any of us want you around? You're a joke, a flaming dyke mascot." Kelly radiated anger, and Raine felt satisfied that she could still get such a rise out of her, so she let her continue to rant. "We all live nice, quiet lives. We don't need you and your cavalier attitude making us out to be some kind of a freak show."

"You're the one who's bent out of shape. I'm having a lovely time getting to know everyone." Raine chuckled. "Why, Beth and

I were having an unbelievably enlightening conversation when you interrupted."

"Beth?" Kelly turned her attention back to Beth, whose face plainly displayed turmoil and fear.

"Raine," Beth pleaded. "I know you're surprised, but you've been gone a long time. We've all changed. We've chosen different lives. I respect the choices you've made."

"I don't," Kelly mumbled, but seemed to regret her words when Beth looked at her with a gentle reprimand.

"I'm asking you to respect our right to live our lives in the way we see fit," Beth said.

Raine shrugged, the fun of her attack on Kelly diminished. "Whatever. If you want to camp out in the closet, that's none of my business, but I won't lie about who I am."

"We aren't asking you to lie. We're asking you not to out us."

"Not me," Patty interjected.

"Shut up, Patty," Kelly shot back. "You've got the decorum of a toddler."

"God, Kelly, you haven't changed a bit. You're still as self-righteous as you were in middle school." Raine laughed.

"And you're still as reckless."

Raine smiled. That was mostly true. She'd always had a rebellious streak, even when she was Rory. It had kept her from going insane worrying what other people thought of her. The few times that façade had cracked were none of Kelly's business, so she was more than happy to let her think of her as carefree. "Patty's got a good point, though. If I'm going to respect your wishes, I should at least know what they are, right? Who's out, and who's a closet case?"

Kelly flinched at the derogatory term, but Beth cut her off. "That's fair enough. I'm out only to a few people, so it's best not to mention my sexual orientation around campus."

"I'm gay as the day is long," Miles interjected. "I couldn't hide it if I tried."

Raine was glad he recognized that fact because she would never have been able to keep up that charade. "What about you, Wilson?"

"I prefer to focus on my career and not my personal life," he said timidly. The earlier confrontation had probably shaken him up.

"Got it," Raine said with a wink that elicited a small grin from him. "And I think I know where Patty stands, so how about you, Kelly?"

"You know how I feel," Kelly said through gritted teeth.

"I don't want to assume anything." Raine liked to watch Kelly Rolen squirm.

"My private life is private. You don't have the right to say anything about me to anyone, ever. Is that clear?"

"Crystal." Raine saluted and then flopped into a large armchair. "Now that's out of the way, let's get this party started."

Raine saw a cryptic look between Beth and Kelly, but Miles soon distracted her. He wanted to know about every musical she'd ever seen in Chicago. The group settled into a casual truce, and conversation flowed much easier.

Two more hours passed before everyone began to head home. Wilson was the first to leave, saying he wanted to get a good night's sleep before classes started in the morning. Then Beth began to pack her things, and Patty joined her.

"I guess tomorrow's a big day for all of us," Raine said, thinking about her first day of teaching. She probably should have been thinking about it a lot more this weekend. "I don't feel ready at all."

"I never do," Patty said.

"I haven't found my classrooms, met my department chair, or picked up my class list," Raine said. "I haven't even been to the store. I'd better do that, or I'll starve."

"What did you do for Sunday dinner?" Beth asked sincerely. "Did you go to your mama's?"

"Hell, no." The fierceness of her reaction surprised Raine, and she toned it down immediately. "I mean, I haven't seen my parents for ten years."

"You haven't seen your mother since you got home?" Beth stared at her like she'd grown a set of horns and a forked tail.

"No. I thought you said you read my writing. They didn't want a gay kid, so I got lost," Raine said flatly. She'd told the story so many times she'd learned to speak without revealing the pain that still ran beneath her cool exterior.

"Do they know you're here?"

"I have no idea. Someone may have told them. You know how word gets around."

"Yes, I do, and that's why you need to go over there," Beth snapped. For as smoothly as she'd handled the earlier conflict, her vehemence on this issue seemed disproportionate. "What if they heard it from someone else? Or what if they saw you at the store? For God sakes, Rory, think about what that'd be like for them."

Raine winced at the sound of her old name, but she didn't back down. "Think about them? That's rich. Why don't you think about what it'd be like for me?"

"I know you're upset with them, but they're your parents. The least you can do is let them know you're less than a mile away." Beth's forcefulness was out of character for her and caught Raine off guard, but it couldn't override the natural defenses she'd built up over the years.

"I haven't been hiding. If they were concerned about me they could've said something, but they didn't. I never got so much as a 'how're you doing?' from them. They don't want me."

"Rory, you're being stubborn and childish. Your mama and daddy are right across town. They at least deserve to know you're here." Raine tried to turn away, but Beth stepped into her way, refusing to let her disengage. "Don't make them hear that from someone else. You need to be up front with them. You're a grown woman. When do you plan to act like one?"

"What do you expect? She's got no respect for anyone," Kelly quipped.

"Not now, Kel," Beth said sharply.

"Kel?" A connection snapped into place and Raine recalled Patty's earlier reference to someone named Kel. Why hadn't she remembered that sooner? Kel wasn't a Kellen. It was Kelly. "You two are sleeping together?"

They turned and stared at her open-mouthed. "Wow, Beth Devoroux and Kelly Rolen. That's a couple. Two of Darlington's finest. Now I get the whole closet-case routine. Wouldn't want to tarnish those perfect images of yours, right?"

"Rory, please..." Beth didn't seem to know what else to say.

"Talk about being up front with people. You hypocrites. You're lecturing me about taking responsibility for my relationship with my family?"

"Our relationship is private," Kelly said firmly, but Raine could clearly read the fear of exposure in her body language.

"Then so is my relationship with my parents," Raine said resolutely before she stormed out the front door.

CHAPTER FOUR

Beth stared at the door Rory had slammed behind her. What had just happened? She thought they'd made peace after the earlier fight. Why couldn't she leave well enough alone when Rory said she didn't want to see her parents?

"Whew, I don't think we're in Kansas anymore," Miles finally said.

"I told you she'd be trouble," Kelly added. "Why do you even try to pacify her?"

Beth held up her hands. "Not now. I've had enough of this for today."

"You're right," Kelly said, but Beth knew she was the one being pacified now. If it were up to Kelly, she'd go on about Rory all night.

"Thank you for hosting, Miles. I'll see you tomorrow." Beth kissed Kelly briefly, more out of habit than desire. "And I'll see you Tuesday."

Beth arrived home still as confused and frustrated as she'd been when she left Miles's. She began to dust, as if cleaning her home could also clean her mind, and right now she desperately needed a clear head.

Dust rag in hand, she wiped her way around the living room of the old farm house, picking up photographs and knickknacks. After she inherited the house and farm from her parents, she'd had to sell all the land her father had grown corn and soybeans on. She'd also cleared out their things from the bedroom and donated their clothes to charity, but she couldn't part with the house or the mementos that tied her to the past.

She missed her parents. She had no siblings, and her grandparents had died before she was born. Her own family tragedy was responsible for a lot of her outrage at Raine's cavalier attitude toward her own family. Though the St. Jameses weren't perfect and had obviously made a horrible mistake in how they'd treated Rory, they were still her parents. Didn't they at least deserve a visit or a phone call? Rory had a second chance with them, a second chance to show the whole town who she really was. Why was she so content to squander it?

Beth set down a ceramic angel she'd been dusting and gazed at a picture of her and Kelly. It was the only one she displayed in a public area of the house, and nothing in it suggested they were anything more than friends. It had been shot in St. Louis at a Cardinals baseball game. They stood smiling in the sun, both dressed in red and white, with the expanse of the old Busch Stadium behind them. A casual observer would assume they were two young friends at a ball game, but Beth saw the first morning they woke up together. They'd stayed at a hotel in the city, away from the watchful eyes of neighbors and closed off from Kelly's fears of being outed. Beth was twenty-one years old, and for the first time since her parents died she felt truly safe.

She loved Kelly, and Kelly loved her, but Rory did have a point about their hypocrisy. She'd asked Rory to respect them but hadn't told her the truth about what she wanted respect for. She'd yelled at Rory to be up front with her parents, when Beth had refused to be up front with her. Then again, she had every right to keep her private life private. Rory had broadcast her history with her parents in every gay and lesbian publication for years. She and Kelly, on the other hand, had worked to protect what they had together. Telling Rory about their relationship would not only endanger Beth, it could hurt Kelly too. Was she really supposed to feel guilty about protecting Kelly from a virtual stranger?

A stranger? Was that what Rory was? Her head knew that was true, but her heart wouldn't give in. She hadn't seen her in a very long time, and even before that they'd never been close. So why did she feel connected to Rory? Why had she worked so hard to get her the job at Bramble? She'd chaired the committee that hired her, made all her living arrangements, and contacted her agent personally. Why was she so invested in Rory's well-being?

Did she have a lingering high-school crush? Surely she wasn't that pathetic, and if Rory's behavior so far was any indication, they had nothing in common. Rory was angry, insolent, and promiscuous. She'd arrived with Patty in the clothes she'd worn the day before. Beth's stomach tightened. Did it upset her that Rory and Patty had slept together?

"This is ridiculous," she said aloud, and tossed the dust rag down the laundry chute. *I don't have time to obsess over other people.* Classes started tomorrow, and she needed to get some sleep. If Rory didn't care about what she was throwing away, Beth shouldn't have any problem with it either.

Raine couldn't get out of her car yet. After Patty had dropped her off at the college she was too agitated to stay in her apartment. She'd spent an hour wandering around campus trying to burn off her energy, but when that didn't work she found herself in her car. She drove automatically, the echoes of her fight with Beth overwhelming her consciousness.

Beth was a hypocrite, but that shouldn't surprise her. Darlington was full of hypocrites. Why had she let Beth get to her like that? Who cared if she and Kelly were together? They were perfect for each other. Prim and proper small-town girls who probably spent more time worried about getting caught than thinking about each other. A pair of closet cases that still believed lesbians had to hide in the shadows. It amazed her that they'd found each other. How did they even have time to date with all that fear and self-hatred they were so invested in? Beth and Kelly reinforced everything Raine ever wrote about Darlington.

If that's how they wanted to spend their relationship, more power to them, but where did Beth get off lecturing Raine about being up front and responsible? Who was she to talk about Raine's relationships when she couldn't even admit to having one of her own? Why all the concern for Raine's parents if she was too scared to come out herself? Raine was the one who'd been rejected, disowned, betrayed. Why should she care what her parents, or Beth, or Kelly, or anyone else thought she should or shouldn't do? Raine was right. She was sure of it.

Yet here she was, parked in her parents' driveway.

Fuck it, I'm going in. She wanted to pretend she wasn't scared or that she was proving to herself that her parents held no power over her, but the weakness in her knees and the rapid beat of her heart suggested otherwise. She honestly couldn't say why she was here.

She paused for another second before she rang the doorbell. It was strange, even after all her years of feeling so disconnected from this place, not to walk right in. She'd grown up in this little blue and yellow farm house on the edge of town, the place she'd called home for seventeen years, but it was also the place she'd run from when she'd had to choose between safety and freedom.

She had so many memories of coming and going through this very doorway. The last time had been in the dead of night. She'd told her parents she was gay in one of those impetuous moments typical of her age and was immediately made to regret it. They yelled, cried, and threatened, and then fell silent. She felt her parents' disappointment, disapproval, and disgust. Unable to live with their demands, she took the only other option available and left the only place she'd ever called home. Now she stood on the front porch ringing the bell like a visitor, a stranger.

The door swung open and Raine's breath left her. In front of her was her mother, who appeared equally shocked. Her hair now more gray than brown, she seemed smaller too, certainly shorter than Raine. But, amazingly, Raine could see relief on her face as she glanced heavenward before she motioned for Raine to enter.

"Well, don't stand there on the porch."

Raine still couldn't speak. During the early years she'd often imagined seeing her parents and wondered what it would be like. In her mind she always said something witty, something elegant and persuasive. Her parents would feel terrible for all their awful words, and she'd be vindicated. Now she stood in the entryway, obsessively wiping her sandals on the rug and worrying about tracking dirt across her mother's clean floors.

"Have you eaten?" her mother asked, wringing her hands.

Raine knew how she felt. Her own insides were roiling with emotion. "No, ma'am. Not since lunch."

"It doesn't look like you've eaten in a month." She headed toward the kitchen. "Supper will be ready in ten minutes."

Raine was dumbfounded. *That's it? Supper's in ten minutes? She hasn't seen me a decade and that's all she has to say?* The whole thing felt surreal.

"Your father and your brother are out back. Why don't you go say hello?" her mother called from the other room.

Might as well get it out of the way. Raine wasn't eager to see her father. She could still hear him shout in his booming voice, *"You're not gay. Don't you ever say that again."* While she had said it again, thousands of times in fact, none of those times had been in front of him. She liked to think she'd be able to do so now without fear, but she doubted it.

Raine opened the back door, squared her shoulders, and set her jaw. She silently vowed that no matter what her father said, she wouldn't cower the way she had as a teenager. As she stepped into the backyard, poised for a confrontation, the sight of her younger brother, David, knocked the fight out of her.

"Davey" was all she managed to say when he noticed her. He wasn't the gangly adolescent she'd last seen. He'd grown several inches and a goatee. He was a man now, but he'd always be a little boy to her.

"Rory." He jumped to his feet.

Somehow hearing her old name spoken with such love didn't bother her. She actually liked it. This was her baby brother. The one regret she harbored about leaving was not getting to explain things to Davey, but it wouldn't have been fair to him. He was only fourteen at the time and didn't need his sister's burdens. She'd sent him birthday cards and a graduation gift, but she knew that wasn't enough. Tears gathered in her eyes.

"What are you yelling about, David?" Her father strolled out of the garage, immediately halting their reunion. Raine faced him and watched as recognition spread across his features, and then they hardened.

"Hello, Daddy," Raine said, then lowered her head. *Damnit, so much for steady*. She didn't manage to look up during the heavy moment during which she waited for him to speak. She feared his reaction, feared what she might see in his eyes, but most of all she feared her own response to the disapproval she knew was there.

"You cut your hair," he finally said, his voice gravelly but gentle.

"Yes, sir." She forced herself to meet his eyes, the absurdity of the exchange compounded by the fact that she immediately recognized that she had his chin. His nose, too.

"It makes you seem older, like David's beard does."

Raine glanced at her brother quickly. He did appear older, but she hadn't credited his facial hair so much as the long years that had passed.

"She looks like you," David said flatly.

Oh my God, are we seriously having this conversation or am I dreaming? It wasn't a dream, though. She was sure of it. In her dreams her family yelled.

"Supper's on," her mother called from the kitchen window, and both men headed inside, leaving Raine with nothing to do but follow.

Raine sat in her seat at the table, where she'd sat as a child, across from David with her parents at either end. She bowed her head. "Bless us, oh Lord, for these thy gifts…" she prayed. She hadn't prayed over a meal in years, and she couldn't believe she was doing so now, but she couldn't stop herself.

With grace finished, they passed the food and her mom sliced the meat loaf. The sights and sounds of her childhood engulfed Raine, but she felt like she was watching from afar. The conversation picked up around her. Her mother remarked on the recent heat. Davey and her father spoke of the corn crop. Raine said nothing. She didn't have anything to say until dinner was over and her mother began to clear the dishes. On one of her trips between the kitchen and table her mother paused and said, "I could change the sheets in your room if you want."

Raine had a hard time comprehending the words. *My room? Sheets?*

"No, thank you." She slowly pieced together that her mother was asking if she'd be staying the night. "I've got an apartment here in town, on campus."

"Oh." Her mother gathered another handful of dishes and headed back to the kitchen.

"Are you going to school?" Davey asked.

"I'm teaching at the college this year."

"Davey's girlfriend is a teacher," her father said.

"Oh?" *What the fuck?* Raine wanted to scream. She told them she had moved back to Darlington after all these years and all he said was that Davey's girlfriend was a teacher. She seemed to have stepped into some alternate universe, some alternate family, where instead of fighting they avoided discussing anything relevant.

"Niki Belliard, she was two years behind you in school," Davey said, as if that would help. "She teaches kindergarten."

"That's great," Raine said, not because she remembered Niki or cared what she taught, but because it seemed an appropriate response for the conversation they'd had all night.

Davey and her father both nodded, and something inside Raine snapped. She couldn't do this anymore. She couldn't pretend like everything was okay, like nothing had happened and they were one big boring, happy family. She'd spent ten years anticipating this moment and had thought she was ready for anything. She was prepared to be thrown out or to face another rejection. She was ready for a fight. Part of her, though she'd never admit to hoping for it, had even considered the possibility of a warm welcome accompanied by apologies and requests for forgiveness, but this scenario, this nothingness, had never entered her mind. It was maddening, and she wanted to scream at them, but she couldn't even do that because they were all so damn polite.

She pushed back from the table abruptly. "I've got to go."

Her mother appeared in the doorway of the kitchen. "Will you be back next Sunday?"

Raine fought down a bitter laugh. "Yes, ma'am."

She meant to go home. She needed to sleep, to get ready for class, to gain control of her raging emotions, but she didn't do any of those things.

Instead, she fell into Patty's arms the second she opened the door.

"I'm glad you came," Patty said as they stumbled down the hallway, groping and tearing at each other's clothes.

"I haven't come yet," Raine panted, "but I will soon." And so would Patty. She'd remind them both that she wasn't Rory, she wasn't afraid, she wasn't hurt. She didn't have to think about anything and she didn't have to care about anybody. With Patty she knew who she was and where she stood. She was in control and didn't have to try to second-guess anyone. She had a role to play and she liked it. She was untouchable now. She was Raine St. James, and nothing her parents, Kelly, or even Beth could do would change that.

CHAPTER FIVE

August 19

Walking through an academic building, Beth was drawn to the sound of Rory's voice coming from one of the classrooms. It was clear, without the fear or anger she'd heard so often since Rory's return, and instead filled with confidence and passion. It was Wednesday, so the class was Rory's second session of Gay and Lesbian History. Beth barely stopped to think about the fact that she'd memorized Rory's schedule. She closed her eyes and saw Rory at seventeen, sitting on a desk in their Advanced English class holding a copy of Virginia Woolf's *To the Lighthouse* in one hand and gesturing wildly with the other.

"You missed the point," Rory told one of the guys who'd complained that nothing happened in the book. "It's not about what they're doing. It's about what they're thinking. No, what they're feeling." She was so full of life, her exuberance almost palpable, as she spoke with an uncommon eloquence and centeredness. Beth had been in awe of her then, and those feelings welled up in her as she listened now. The bright, vibrant woman she heard now considered herself to be Raine, but Rory had been every bit as captivating.

Beth opened her eyes and peeked around the frame of the open classroom door. Rory gave the impression she was holding court before the group of students arranged in a circle at the center of the room. Instead of standing behind the lectern, Rory sat on her desk.

She held a piece of chalk, though she'd obviously abandoned the board after writing two phrases in big block letters: DAUGHTERS OF BILITIS and MATTACHINE SOCIETY.

"America was at one of its darkest hours as far as diversity was concerned," Rory said. "Women had been pushed back into the home, sometimes forcefully, after World War Two. Segregationists became more violent in the hope of suppressing blacks, and McCarthyism ran rampant, sending the entire country on a witch hunt. In most places, homosexuality was listed as both a mental illness and a crime."

Rory hopped off the desk and walked around the inside of the circle while she spoke, making eye contact with each of her fifteen students. When she reached the desk again, she rested against it and folded her arms across her chest, then looked directly at Beth. Her deep green eyes warmed Beth as they hinted at both defiance and mischief. She was magnetic, she was charismatic, and she was sexy. Beth was drawn to her, and she couldn't deny it.

Rory turned back to her students. "This was not a good time to draw attention to yourself, especially if you were different, yet these men and women not only had the courage to be queer, they were brave enough to put their difference in writing."

She pointed to a young man. "What would you call people like that?"

"Crazy," he said.

Rory laughed and pointed to another student. "What about you?"

"Heroes," the girl answered quickly, in a star-struck voice that made Beth wonder if she wasn't falling in love with her professor.

"What about you, Ms. Devoroux?" Rory's playful tone put Beth at ease. "What do you think of my foremothers and fathers? Were they crazy or were they heroes?"

Beth shrugged and gave the first answer that came to mind. "Maybe they were both."

Rory's smile deepened, causing her dimples to appear. "There you have it, folks. I'm descended from a line of crazy heroes. Imagine the semester you're in for."

The students laughed and began to gather their things. Rory raised her voice one more time to be heard over the shuffle of papers. "Ms. Devoroux, will you please stay after class? The rest of you read the piece by Faderman and the one by Lee Lynch for Monday. Come in ready to talk because I'm tired of the sound of my own voice, folks."

Several of the students stopped to say good-bye on their way out or wish Raine a good weekend. They all called her by her first name and she did the same to them. Less than a week into classes she knew each of them and they all seemed comfortable with her. Rory was likely to become one of the most popular professors on campus, and Beth felt pride knowing she'd been the one to bring her here.

"You're a natural," Beth said after the students were gone. "The students love you."

"I love talking to them. I've been speaking on college campuses for a long time, and I haven't gotten tired of it yet."

"Surely it's different now in a classroom instead of onstage." Beth knew that during Raine's public-speaking career she had toured much of the country, telling her coming-out story and spreading the message of being true to oneself. Her reputation as a charismatic speaker and writer was one of the things Beth had used to sell Rory to the guest-lecturer committee.

Rory continued to pack her books and notes. "It's better this way. More give and take, more interaction, which is always nice. It's also nice to talk about other people's work instead of my own. It's important to draw strength from those who went before us." Rory finally slung a satchel over her shoulder and faced Beth. "But this is still a stage. We're all performers, Beth. You should know that as well as anyone."

Beth was surprised by the poignancy of the statement, but also a little wounded by its conclusion. She knew Rory was referring to her relationship with Kelly. Her defenses rose. "You think I'm a fake."

"I don't." Rory's voice was sincere. "We choose to show parts of ourselves in various situations and to hide others. The real question is how do we live with those choices? You've found a way to make peace with yours. I've found a way to live with mine."

"And how do you live with yours?" Beth wondered if she'd really made peace with her choices. Standing so close to Raine, she felt anything but peaceful.

"I do the only things I know. I fight, I perform, I—" Rory seemed like she wanted to say more but cut herself off, showing the hint of a frown before she continued, "And I write, which is why I asked you to stay after class."

The abrupt change of topic surprised Beth. For a moment it seemed Rory was opening up, but then something made her censor herself and she was back into business mode, all reflection gone. The transition stunned Beth, but she didn't know what to do. "How's that?"

"As you know, part of my contract stipulates that in addition to my teaching load I publish at least one major article during my time at Bramble."

"Ah, the publish-or-perish clause."

"You got it. I need to enlist the help of my friendly librarian to start my research."

"You should come by the library and I'll show you how to log into the college's electronic archives. You can access almost anything from there."

"What about interlibrary loan?" Rory asked. "I'll probably need some things you don't have here."

Beth bristled. "If you need it, we can provide it. We're not the Library of Congress, but I'm not stuck in the Dark Ages either. If you want anything specific, let me know and I'll get it for you."

Rory laughed. "Oh, Beth, always such a worker bee."

"What's that supposed to mean?"

"I mean, you were Miss Congeniality in high school, you're the town sweetheart, and apparently, you are the world's most professional librarian too," Raine teased. "Don't you ever have any fun?"

"I have lots of fun. I sing in the church choir."

"You wild child."

"I'm part of the weekly stitch and bitch with the clerical staff on campus."

Rory feigned a yawn. "Just because you say 'bitch' doesn't change the fact you're talking about knitting."

Beth knew she was being goaded, but she chuckled anyway and threw down her only non-nerdy activity. "I play softball in the women's league."

"Hey there, you might have found a winner. But it's not softball unless you go out for beer afterward."

"We do," Beth practically yelled.

Rory was laughing hard now. "Be still, my heart. Little Beth Devoroux drinking the devil's brew. I won't believe it until I see it."

Beth liked to hear Rory laugh, and even more she loved that she'd caused her to. "You can see it this Friday. We've got a game at the college field, and then we're all going uptown for the fall festival."

Rory sobered quickly. "Sorry, I'll have to take your word for it."

"What? Why?" What had caused Raine's abrupt mood change?

"A night out in Darlington is not my idea of a good time."

Beth rolled her eyes. *There she goes again. She's got to be cool, always reminding everyone she's too good for this small town.* But she was fine a second ago, wasn't she? Beth looked closer at Rory. She'd tensed, her jaw set, and a fierce indifference clouded her green eyes. Beth had seen that expression recently when Rory was talking about her parents. *She's not aloof. She's scared.*

"Have you been into town yet?" Beth asked gently.

"I've driven through it a couple of times."

Beth nodded, hearing that for the non-answer it was. "The other day you mentioned that you needed to go shopping. Did you do that?"

"No." Rory shrugged and stared out the window, avoiding Beth's eyes. "I haven't gotten around to it."

"What've you been eating?" Beth wanted to shout, but she kept her tone level, knowing Rory's pride was on the line.

"I've been going to the campus dining hall." Rory laughed, but the sound was forced. "It's actually pretty good for dorm food."

"I know what you mean. Sometimes it's easier to eat out rather than shop." Beth inhaled a deep breath. This wouldn't be easy, but she couldn't let Rory continue like this. "Well, I need to run to the store after work tonight, and I hate to go by myself. We should go together."

Rory shifted her weight from one foot to the other, seeming to mull over the idea. *Come on, Rory, don't be stubborn. Accept the help.*

"I guess I could if you're going anyway."

"I am."

"Won't it be bad for you to be seen with such an obvious lesbian?" The corners of Rory's mouth crooked slightly upward. "Not to mention what Kelly will say when she finds out."

Beth hadn't thought about that. Word would get around fast, and Kelly would go ballistic, but she couldn't rescind the invitation now, could she? No, she couldn't abandon Rory. Somehow losing Rory's confidence seemed worse than making Kelly angry, though she didn't want to think about why.

Beth tried to summon some of Rory's cockiness. If Rory could face her fears, Beth could face her girlfriend. "I'm a grown woman. I'm free to go to the store with whomever I choose."

The words came more easily than Beth expected. She hoped she could remember that statement when she had to repeat it to Kelly.

At almost five o'clock Beth pulled up outside Raine's apartment building in a Chevy S-10 pickup truck. Raine had hoped Beth would be there earlier so they could get in and out of the grocery store before the after-work rush, but what could she do? It was too late to back out. Besides, she was starved and couldn't stand one more night of cafeteria food. She'd put off her first outing into Darlington long enough, and she'd had three days to recover from seeing her parents, so that excuse was gone too. Taking a deep breath she closed the door and jogged down the stairs before she could change her mind.

Beth was her usual self, beaming and asking benign questions like, "How was the rest of your day?"

"Fine," Raine answered flatly, not wanting to say she'd spent most of her afternoon staring at a blank page on her computer screen because she'd dreaded this trip too much to focus on anything else.

"That's good to hear," Beth said brightly, then switched to an equally mundane topic. "It's sure been a mild summer."

God, what was it with Midwesterners and the weather? Why did they think it was a suitable subject to replace discussing all things meaningful? They were incapable of conversing about politics, religion, or emotions, but they could go on for hours about the weather.

"I'm ready for fall, though. The campus is so pretty when the leaves start to change…" Beth chattered on, oblivious to the tension in Raine's posture. She would've been too annoying to handle if she wasn't so cute.

Cute? Is that what she was? No, she'd been cute when they were kids. Now she was beautiful. Beth's body was soft, not like Patty's firm muscles or Ali's thin, hard lines. No, Beth was completely unlike the other women she'd been with.

She was decidedly feminine, and not in the manufactured, made-up way, but naturally. She had hips, and she had breasts that were full but not flaunted or pushed up. She had lips that didn't need to be painted to make them noticeable. She had a perfect button nose, and her eyes were a pale shade of blue. Okay, so maybe some things about her were just plain cute, but the overall picture was one of a very attractive woman.

"What?" Beth asked.

"Huh?" Raine had been caught staring. "Sorry. Nothing. I was zoning out."

They were in the parking lot of the local Kroger, and Beth got out. Raine steeled herself for whatever she might encounter then followed her inside.

If Beth knew how hard this trip was for Raine, she gave no indication as she pushed her shopping cart toward the produce aisle. Raine perused the small bins of apples and iceberg lettuce. The selection was one-tenth the size she'd grown accustomed to in Chicago. There were no kiwis or pomegranates or plantains. Not that Raine cared for or ever bought any of those things, but noticing their absence made her feel superior.

She grabbed a bag of potatoes and a bunch of bananas while Beth rattled on about cantaloupes. Several people paused to say hello to Beth, and she greeted each of them by name as she walked down the aisle toward the dairy section. Everyone in the store seemed to know and love Beth. She elicited smiles from several of the older shoppers and waves from a few children. Thankfully, no one seemed to notice Raine trailing a few feet behind her and stopping only to search in vain for goat cheese before settling on Colby Jack.

Raine was actually surprised at how few people she recognized. She used to know everyone she passed and, much like Beth, would get a greeting from each of them. Now she wondered if anyone would even say hello if they did realize who she was.

"How you doing?" Beth asked as they reached the meat cooler.

"I'm fine." What had caused the question and the sweet expression that accompanied it?

"Hey, Beth," a man called from behind the butcher's counter. "What can I get you?"

"Hi, Tyler," Beth replied, turning her attention away from Raine. "How about two of those filets, and could you cut a pork loin into two roasts and a few chops for me?"

"You got it," the butcher said as he set to work. "How's the first week of school going?"

The two of them chatted amicably, leaving Raine to study the seafood section. It was more of a lake-food section, really, since it contained mostly catfish, but she hoped for some salmon stuck underneath it somewhere.

Tyler handed Beth her order neatly wrapped in white paper, then turned his attention to Raine and exclaimed, "I'll be damned. It's Rory St. James."

Beth nudged her gently. "Rory, you remember Tyler McKay."

"Wow, yeah, Tyler, how're you?" He'd put on so much weight he was nothing like the baseball star he'd been in high school, but when he rounded the counter to shake her hand Raine finally saw the resemblance.

He laughed and slapped her on the back. "I don't know why I didn't recognize you. You look just like your daddy. When'd you get back into town?"

"Last weekend. I'm teaching at the college."

"Go figure." Tyler scratched the stubble on his chin. "I'd have never picked you for a teacher after all the hell you raised when we were kids."

Raine finally smiled. Tyler had helped with much of the hell-raising he referred to. "It was an unexpected career turn for me too."

"Well, damn, this calls for a celebration. You coming uptown this weekend?"

"I tried to talk her into that earlier," Beth cut in, a silly I-told-you-so grin on her face.

"It's fall festival. You can't miss that. Everyone would love to see you."

He doesn't know I'm gay. That could be the only reason for the warm welcome. "I'm not sure. I'm going to play it by ear."

"I'll work on her, Tyler," Beth said when Tyler frowned at Raine's noncommittal response.

"You do that, Beth, 'cause if she doesn't come on her own I'll have to track her down and drag her out." Tyler laughed and headed back behind the counter. "And you know I'll do it, Rory."

"See you later," Beth said, and steered Raine down the final aisle of the store. Raine grabbed a box of Apple Jacks and a loaf of white bread before she headed to the checkout line behind Beth. She was almost finished and had miraculously run into only one person she knew. The light in the other checkout flickered on. Without thinking, Raine quickly switched lines, so eager to be done that she didn't understand the mild terror on Beth's face until she got a better view of the woman running her carton of eggs over the scanner.

"Shit," she muttered. It was Old Lady Anthony, the choir director at the Southern Baptist church.

Raine kept her head down as she loaded her groceries onto the conveyor belt. When it came time to pay, she looked around for the credit-card machine and pin pad but didn't see one. Darlington obviously hadn't moved into the age of self-scanning. She didn't have enough cash on her to pay for the groceries, so she set her jaw and handed the card to Mrs. Anthony. The woman read the name on the card, then peeked at Raine over the rim of her glasses.

"Rory St. James," she said with a sniff. "To what do we owe this honor?"

Scan the damn card, Rory wanted to shout. "I've moved back to teach at the college."

"Seems the liberal universities of this country are filled with people of your persuasion."

Raine literally bit her tongue while the ignorant old biddy scanned the card and waited for the receipt to print. She then signed her name quickly and turned to go, but Mrs. Anthony wasn't finished.

"Rory," she called loudly, "homosexuals live outside God's law."

The old familiar anger welled up inside her. All those years of hiding, of fearing disapproval, of feeling like she was suffocating roiled to the surface, but as she spun around, unsure whether she'd lash out or cry, a hand rested gently on her shoulder and guided her toward the door.

"So do people who sit in judgment of others, Mrs. Anthony," Beth said, loud enough to be heard by anyone near the front of the store.

Raine stopped once they got to the parking lot, her humiliation melted into shock. "Did you really do what I think you did?"

Beth's cheeks were pink with either excitement or embarrassment, and she seemed astonished too. Her grim smile grew slowly until she broke into hysterical laughter laced with fear and relief, and Raine knew it well. It stirred in her, too, and they barely made it into the car before the giggles completely overwhelmed them. They laughed for what seemed like hours, like two people who'd reached their breaking points and lapsed into a moment of insanity.

When they gradually settled down enough for Beth to drive, she wiped her eyes and started the car. "I wish I could've seen her face," Raine said.

"She was appalled." The humor had left Beth's voice.

"I bet. She's probably not used to people talking to her like that."

"Then she shouldn't have spoken to you that way."

Raine detected Beth's protectiveness and didn't know whether to be embarrassed that Beth had fought one of her battles or grateful that she'd cared enough to do so. In the end she chose the latter.

"Thank you," she said as she got out of the car and grabbed her groceries. Then, turning to look directly into Beth's baby blue eyes, she added, "for everything."

Beth rewarded her with a broad, genuine smile. "Anytime."

Once inside, Raine reflected on her trip to the store. While she'd been at the hub of Darlington's population, she'd had to interact with only two people. Tyler had been welcoming and warm, but he hadn't indicated that he knew she was gay. Old Lady Anthony, on the other hand, made it clear not only that she knew, but also that she disapproved. The whole trip was probably a wash, and Raine hoped she'd bought enough food to last awhile since she wasn't eager to go through that ordeal again.

Then she thought about Beth lashing out at Old Lady Anthony in her defense. That old bigot must have looked like someone had thrown a bucket of ice water over her head. Even better than that was the smile Beth gave her before they parted. That alone was worth the trip. Raine might even start to enjoy her shopping trips if Beth went with her every time.

❖

Later that evening Beth fried one of the pork chops she'd picked up at the store and mulled over her day. Seeing Raine in the classroom brought back so many memories of Rory. She'd seemed so cool and confident whereas Beth was bumbling and awkward. She hadn't been a nerd or been picked on, but she was decidedly average, whereas Rory excelled at everything important. She was athletic, attractive, popular, and passionate. Watching her interact with her students today, Beth knew none of those things had changed.

Yet some things had changed. Underneath her façade Rory had old wounds that had never fully healed. Why else would someone with so much bravado be timid in the face of a bitter old woman like Mrs. Anthony? Why was Rory self-assured in one situation and mousey in another? She hadn't had any trouble mustering up her trademark defiance when Kelly attacked her, but one off-hand comment by a checkout clerk caused her to clam up. It was painful for Beth to watch her withdraw, especially after seeing such a beautiful glimpse of the old Rory in her classroom that morning.

Beth flipped the pork chop and set a pan of green beans on a gas burner. She was staring mindlessly at the blue flame when the phone rang.

"Devoroux residence," she answered, thinking only a tele-marketer would call at dinner time.

"You sure sound chipper for someone who's set the whole town to talking," Kelly said sourly.

Beth grimaced. She should've expected this. She'd told off the town busybody in a public place. She honestly should've been surprised it didn't get back to Kelly sooner. "Hello, Kel. How was work?"

"What the hell were you thinking, Beth? Going around town with *her* is going to cause a stir as it is, and then you give the choir director a lesson on gay liberation on top of that."

Beth laughed. She knew she shouldn't, but something about the statement struck her as too funny to ignore. "Gay liberation? Kelly, I don't know what you heard, but I swear I didn't lecture, and I never even said the word *gay* or *homosexual*, for that matter, which was the term Mrs. Anthony used."

"Mrs. Anthony called you a homosexual?"

"God, no. She called Rory a homosexual."

"Rory is a homosexual."

"Honey, so am I," Beth said, still unable to contain a giggle despite the fact that Kelly was blowing the incident out of proportion. "Last time I checked, so were you."

"That's not—I didn't mean—You know what I meant," Kelly stuttered, anger rising in her voice. "Raine's a flamer. She's a dyke. She brings everything on herself."

"She wasn't like that today. We were grocery shopping like everyone else. No neon rainbows over our heads, no lewd behavior in the cucumber section, no gay agenda whatsoever."

"This isn't funny, Beth, and it's not like you to take part in something like this."

"What exactly did I take part in?" The humor was beginning to wear off, and Beth was losing her patience with Kelly's inquisition. "I went to the grocery store with a colleague, a bitter old busybody made unprovoked homophobic attacks, I pointed out calmly that her behavior was not Christlike, and then we left. Which of those actions was so grievous?"

"It's the implications, and you know it."

Beth did know that. She and Kelly had discussed similar things hundreds of times. Not only did they have to avoid stating they were gay, they needed to avoid anything that implied it. "Fine, what would you have preferred I do in that situation? Would it be enough for me to stand by and watch the attack next time, or should I jump in and attack Rory too?"

"You should stay away from Rory altogether," Kelly snapped.

Beth was stunned. All the exuberance that had filled her since leaving Rory vanished. Kelly's statement hadn't changed only the mood of their conversation. It had altered the tone of their relationship. Kelly often made requests or judged things Beth did or said, but she'd never told her who she could and couldn't be friends with.

"Beth?" Kelly asked after the silence became too much to withstand. "Are you still there?"

"Yes." Beth couldn't bring herself to say anything else. Later, when she'd had time to think, she'd come up with plenty of witty rebukes, but now her mind was blank.

"Well, I don't think we should go to the fall festival together this weekend," Kelly said, her tone more apologetic than demanding.

"Right, because if I'm guilty by my association with Rory, you don't want to associate with me." Beth was devoid of emotion. "And the last thing I'd want is to have my actions reflect badly on you."

"So you agree it's best if we don't see each other for a little bit?" Kelly sounded surprised at Beth's quick acceptance.

"Yes, I do." And she did, but not for the same reason as Kelly. Beth didn't care what others thought of her, but right now she didn't care much for what Kelly thought of her either.

"Good. Let's give this time to blow over. Everyone will forget about it in a week."

I won't, Beth thought, but she said only, "Good night, Kelly."

CHAPTER SIX

August 22

Raine stared out her back window at the fences of the college softball fields. Which one was Beth on? Her game might be over by now. Raine tried to tell herself it was no big deal. Beth had invited her several times, and every time Raine gave a noncommittal answer but implied that she'd try to attend. She *had* tried. She'd tried to will herself to walk across campus, something she'd done every day for the past week, but tonight was different. Saturday night was townie night at the ball fields, which were occupied with various church and recreational teams from throughout Darlington.

Raine flopped onto the couch that came with the apartment. She couldn't face the softball crowds, especially after her previous interactions with townies. While they hadn't been the torch-wielding villagers that had haunted her dreams, she didn't want to repeat the awkwardness of her family dinner and Mrs. Anthony's blatant disgust. She just couldn't stomach their disapproval. Even Tyler, who had been welcoming, would likely change his attitude after he heard what happened in the checkout line.

She had fought so hard to forget this place. Sure, she liked to think she could face it now and stand strong in the face of criticism, but why should she have to? Why would she willingly subject herself to their disdain, to their whispered accusations or outright condemnation? That wasn't her idea of a good time. No, she'd rather spend her night cooped up inside watching the St. Louis Cardinals game. The Redbirds were one of the few things from her childhood that hadn't betrayed her.

Just after eight o'clock Raine heard a knock at the door. Even through the distortion of the peephole's curved glass, she could clearly make out Beth in her softball attire. She opened the door and grinned in spite of her apprehension.

"We won," Beth said with a smile. "I thought you'd like to know since you didn't see any of the game."

"About that…" Raine didn't have an excuse. "Do you want to come in?"

Beth looked around the empty apartment and said in a mocking tone, "I don't know. You seem awfully busy, but yeah, do you mind if I have a quick shower?"

"Shower?"

"Yeah, I'll change here before we go out."

"Out?"

"Is there an echo in here?" Beth asked as she headed for the bedroom. Rory followed her as far as the threshold and then rested against the doorway as Beth tossed a duffel bag onto the unmade bed. "Doesn't make sense to go all the way back to my house when we can leave from here."

"Okay, I'll bite. Where are we going?"

"To the fall festival," Beth said casually, but Raine noticed she didn't meet her eyes. She obviously knew that statement wouldn't go over well. "Now, do you mind if I shower? I don't want to get my clean clothes all sweaty."

"Sure," Raine said with a chuckle and closed the door before she headed back to the couch.

This little drop-in didn't seem like Beth's style. She was sweet, quiet, and well-mannered. Then again, a week ago, Raine thought Beth was straight. Perhaps there was more to little Beth Devoroux than her good-girl image suggested. For one, she certainly didn't come across as a frumpy librarian in her softball shorts and her T-shirt that showed enough of her cleavage to make Raine's eyes wander.

She also wasn't too timid or closeted to barge into Raine's apartment and ask to use the shower. *Holy shit, Beth is in my shower.*

Raine paced around the living room, flashing back to the way she'd invited herself into the shower with Patty. Instead she pictured Beth with her long dark curls dripping wet and cascading down her gorgeous body under the spray. Knowing that dream was only a few feet away made her a little dizzy, so she sat back down and rubbed her face viciously as if trying to wipe away the images.

She had to pull herself together. Despite her recent show of bravado, Beth was sweet and innocent, not to mention in a relationship. She was clearly here to drag Raine out of her solitude, but probably had no other motives for her visit. Raine was the one who'd sexualized her actions. Beth hadn't indicated that she was offering anything more than friendship.

Raine forced her mind back to the central question of the evening. How could she get out of going to the fall festival? If the softball games had been daunting, the fall festival was the fifth circle of hell. The festival, held in the center of Darlington, consisted of everything from craft booths to street vendors to pony rides. It was the epitome of small-town life, and all of Darlington would be there, either taking in the food and festivities or socializing in the bars and restaurants that ran specials to entice them. She refused to subject herself to all of her nightmares magnified by the influence of alcohol and mob mentality.

The shower stopped, and Raine heard Beth moving around in the bedroom. She tiptoed to the door with no intention of opening it, but she couldn't ignore the thought of Beth in there dressing. How was she supposed to concentrate on getting out of the evening's entertainment if she couldn't think about anything but Beth in her bedroom? Maybe that was part of Beth's plan, to be so alluring that Raine couldn't refuse her invitation.

No, that was silly. Raine knew plenty of women who'd use that ploy, but Beth wasn't one of them. Beth was watching out for her, trying to play social director. For some reason she'd put it upon herself to see that Raine got out, and she was attempting to do so right now, but it wouldn't work.

Raine refused to be bullied or pushed or even persuaded to do something she didn't want to. She was strong in her convictions. She'd stood up to stronger forces than Beth Devoroux. Her fortitude had made her famous in the first place. Who did Beth think she was, barging in with her sexy legs, peeks of her cleavage, and her innocent femme persona? Raine wouldn't fold like a rag doll. She didn't let anyone tell her where to go, did she?

If she were being honest, she'd have to admit that Beth had convinced her to go see her parents, and Beth had taken her to the store. *And see how well those things went for you?*

Another knock at the door. "What the hell?" Raine mumbled.

"That'll be Tyler," Beth called from the bedroom.

Raine opened the door. "Are you here to drag me out too?"

"Beth thought she might need reinforcements," Tyler said with a grin and brushed past her into the apartment.

"And does our little doe-eyed Mata Hari have any other surprises for me tonight?" Raine raised her voice so she could be heard through the bedroom door.

Tyler made himself comfortable much the same way he'd done when they were lounging in each other's living rooms as teenagers. "Either we get you to go to the fall festival with us or call people and tell them to meet us over here."

"What the fuck?"

"Yeah, who wants to have a party in family housing, right?"

Raine couldn't believe what was happening. The anger she hadn't quite been able to muster finally welled up inside her. She had to stop this. Beth had crossed the line from busy-body to bully. Good intentions or not, Raine didn't appreciate being pressured into doing something she wasn't ready for.

"You should sit down, buddy," Tyler said, seeming oblivious to the tension in the room. "Women need forever to get ready. I thought you'd know that by now."

Raine started for the bedroom door. She'd had enough of this little charade and planned to stop it, right now. "She won't be getting ready for anything when I get done with—" Raine stopped. "What?"

Tyler yawned. "I thought you were some kind of big shot with the ladies, but you act like you've never had to wait while a woman powdered her nose or tried on seven different pairs of shoes."

"You know I'm gay?"

Tyler laughed. "Only since you were like fourteen."

"What? How?" Raine was stupefied.

"You never wanted to date me, and I was the most popular guy in school. Besides, you were the only girl I knew who could hit my curveball."

Raine didn't know whether to laugh or cry. "Why didn't you say something?"

"It wasn't my place. I figured you'd talk about it when you were ready." He sat up and shrugged. "I didn't think it would take you damn near fifteen years, though."

Raine sank down onto the couch and tried to sort out this new development. She'd assumed Tyler didn't know she was gay and would turn against her when he found out. But not only did he know now, he'd known in high school. The entire time they were friends, he'd been friends with her for who she really was, not the image she tried to project. It didn't make sense.

Beth opened the bedroom door and stood there expectantly. "Ready to go?" Her hair was pulled back in a ponytail with a few stray tendrils framing her face. She wore a tight pair of Wranglers and a blue button-down that set off her eyes. She looked every bit like a farmer's daughter, the perfect blend of sweet and sexy. Raine gulped, but didn't trust herself to speak. So much for being strong and defiant. She couldn't even remember her reasons for not going out, much less articulate them.

"What?" Beth asked. It was the first time she'd shown even a hint of insecurity, and Raine immediately regretted causing it.

"Nothing." She forced a smile. "I know when I'm beaten."

Tyler slapped her on the back. "Good. Let's go before you have the chance to change your mind."

"One beer, then I'm going home." Raine attempted to regain some semblance of control over the situation, but as Beth and Tyler both chuckled, she was afraid she was in for a long night.

❖

Beth was glad for the dim light as Tyler drove them to town in his rusty Dodge pickup. She'd hid her trembling hands by keeping some distance between herself and Rory, but now that they were in such close proximity she feared her lack of confidence would show. She had used all her courage to buzz into Rory's apartment and act like she belonged there, when in reality she was so nervous she'd stood outside the door for ten minutes before she worked up the energy to knock. She'd never been the one to take charge, and she worried that she'd be incapable of doing so tonight, which is why she'd called Tyler for backup.

She wanted to help Rory move past her fear, and that wouldn't happen as long as Rory insisted on staying walled up in that apartment. She felt responsible for bringing her back to Darlington, and she couldn't live with the thought of her being miserable because of it. If that meant Beth had to stretch out of her comfort zone in order to get Rory out of her own shell, then that's what she'd do. And she had. She'd marched in and told Rory they were going out like it was a foregone conclusion, even though she was anything but certain of that herself.

Rory, for her part, was easier to convince than she'd expected. She was obviously surprised at first, but while Beth was in the shower she expected Rory to plan her escape. Thankfully, Tyler had arrived in time to offer some moral support. What had they talked about? When she opened the door, all Rory had done was stare at her. That didn't seem like the Rory she knew, but neither of them had been herself tonight.

Tyler parked the truck a few blocks from the town square, and they joined the steady stream of people heading toward the festival. Rory didn't speak as she walked with Beth beside her and Tyler a few steps in front of them. Tension practically radiated from her, and Beth wanted to squeeze her hand, but that would be pushing it too far. Even as a friendly gesture it would raise suspicions, and while she wasn't as paranoid as Kelly, she wasn't eager to draw attention to her sexual orientation.

Strange, she hadn't thought of Kelly all night. Kelly would definitely disapprove of what she was doing, but that didn't matter. Rory needed a friend, and Kelly said she didn't want Beth's company tonight. Beth was still angry with her. She understood and respected Kelly's reasons for being cautious, but that didn't give her the right to tell her who she should be friends with. Surely Kelly would come around eventually and see that Rory wasn't a threat. Until then, Beth intended to hold her ground, and that included enjoying herself tonight.

Beth snuck a glance at Rory. She was beautiful. Her chestnut hair feathered lightly to one side, and her broad shoulders squared, adding a sense of purpose to her solid gait. She might be shaking inside, but no one would know. She was absolutely stunning.

"Did you eat yet?" Tyler asked when they got to the town square. Rows of booths on either side of them touted everything from crafts to corn dogs.

Rory shook her head. "No, I'm not really hungry."

Beth didn't feel like eating anything either, but Tyler shoved through the crowd before she could say anything.

"No drinking on an empty stomach," he called over his shoulder. "Let's get some chili."

"Right, because mixing alcohol and chili is always a good idea," Beth said, but the comment only made him laugh as he continued his push through the crowd.

They entered one of the restaurants that lined the square, and Tyler secured them a table before heading off to the bar. "You okay?" Beth asked Rory.

Rory scanned the room, her emerald eyes pausing on each face as if checking for threats, then chose a seat with her back to the wall. "Sure, I'm fine."

Beth felt for her. Rory was obviously nervous, and it must be exhausting to always be waiting for the next fight. She needed to relax. She was better company when she was unguarded, and she was definitely more attractive when she flashed her rakish grins instead of the tight line her mouth and set jaw were currently forming. No one in this jovial crowd would try to start a fight tonight. She edged close enough to Rory to smell her cologne and inhaled it deeply.

"You can loosen up. Tyler and I are right here, and a lot of people will be happy to see you tonight."

As if on cue, Tyler came back carrying two beers and two small cups of chili, and following him was another high-school classmate, Chris Bennett, holding an identical order.

"Hey, stranger," Chris said, setting a beer and a container of chili in front of Raine. He hadn't changed a bit. He was still a lanky farm boy, his sandy hair tucked under a ball cap and his faded jeans marked with a Copenhagen ring. "I heard you were back in town, but I had to see it to believe it."

"Hi, Chris," Rory said. "How're you?"

"Not bad, how 'bout yourself?"

"Hanging in there." Rory held up the beer bottle. "Thanks for this."

"It's my pleasure to buy a beer for a local celebrity."

Rory grimaced slightly and took a big swig. She probably wasn't eager to discuss her celebrity status with the people she'd put down in her writing, and Beth didn't blame her. Many of their former classmates read Raine's early work out of the novelty of knowing someone famous, but the stories never reflected well on their hometown.

It was ironic that Rory had such negative memories of her time in Darlington, because everyone Beth knew had nothing but fond memories of her. She'd been almost universally liked, outgoing, athletic, fun, and charismatic. To find out that she didn't feel the same way about people who cared about her stung at first, but the general opinion seemed to be that it was better to be mentioned in a negative light than to never be famous at all.

"How's your mama, Chris?" Beth asked, shifting the subject away from Rory.

"She's okay, but I think she's driving Daddy a little crazy. She got a new knee last month," he clarified for Rory.

"Maybe I'll stop over and see them tomorrow."

"She'd love that, Beth. You know she adores you, and she's going crazy without all the church-choir gossip." Chris laughed. "What about your folks, Rory?"

Beth cursed herself for opening the topic of parents. She should've known it would work its way back around to Rory, and she'd have to explain that she still wasn't speaking to her family. As frustrated as Rory's attitude toward her parents made Beth, a crowded restaurant wasn't the place to readdress that subject.

"They're all right," Rory said levelly, then swallowed another drink of beer. "I had dinner with them the other night, and they were in a tizzy about the dry weather."

Chris and Tyler both chuckled, but Beth could hardly contain her shock. Rory went to see her parents? Even had dinner with them? And on Sunday, the same day she and Beth had fought about them. Why hadn't she mentioned it sooner?

"Your daddy's got to be cursing the drought as much as mine is. It can't be any better on his corn crops than it is on our soybeans."

The conversation turned to crops, with Chris and Tyler doing most of the talking, so Beth took the opportunity to watch Rory, who had a bite of her chili and killed her beer before scanning the room again. With her frown and furrowed brow, she appeared older, like the burdens she carried had actually stolen her youth. Despite her nonchalance about her parents, the topic obviously heightened her paranoia. Maybe the St. James family reunion hadn't gone as well as Rory implied, but why wouldn't she have told Beth? It would've been a great chance to prove that she was wrong. Then again, if it had gone well, why wasn't she happier about it? Something was off. Beth could sense it, but she didn't have time to figure it out now.

The waitress brought another round of drinks, though Beth wasn't even half done with her first. Rory, on the other hand, kept up with the guys, taking a swig of beer with every bite of chili. Maybe the food was too spicy for her, but maybe she was using the alcohol to help bolster her confidence. She had no idea how much beer Rory could handle, but Chris and Tyler weren't likely to stop feeding her drinks anytime soon. The descent into drunkenness was a male-bonding ritual Beth didn't understand and didn't care to witness tonight, especially since Rory had so many unresolved issues in town.

Beth wanted Rory to relax, but not numb herself, and it was up to her to get them out of the situation. Rory needed a clear head to navigate the various social situations over the course of the evening, and if she wasn't ready to acknowledge that, Beth would do it for her.

"Drink up, boys," she said cheerfully. "That's your last one for now. I want to shop at the craft booths."

"Damn," Tyler muttered as he downed his second beer. "What is it with women and your need to buy cheap crap you've already got too much of to begin with?"

"I do it to torture you," Beth said with a grin, and ushered them out the door, making an effort to lay a comforting hand on Rory's shoulder as they exited the restaurant.

The temperature dropped slightly when night fell, and the crowd began to thin as the elderly and families went home, leaving the festival to teenagers and young adults. Raine remembered roaming the streets of town as an adolescent. She and her friends didn't have much to do for entertainment, so they spent a lot of time loitering on the town square. They'd anticipated festivals like this one to spice up their dull routines.

Of course, they were too cool for any of the kiddy rides and only occasionally deigned to play the carnival-style games, but the food, music, and each other always held their attention. They laughed, joked, and soaked up the thrill of the busy atmosphere to hold them over until another event came along. Raine grinned slightly. Not all her memories of home were unpleasant.

She began to loosen up as she followed Beth along the row of vendor booths. Beth knew everyone and stopped to make over the various products for sale. Raine didn't see anything she wanted, but she loved to watch Beth. She smiled so easily as she shared greetings and brief conversations with several people they passed on their way around the square. Beth's company was in high demand, and Raine stood back with Chris and Tyler as she talked to a group of older women at a bake-sale booth.

"This is what you get when you go out with the darling of Darlington," Tyler told Raine while they waited for Beth.

"She's pretty hard not to like," Raine said.

"It's more than that," Chris said. "They all adopted her when her parents died. The whole town took responsibility for her, got her through college, kept her fed, helped her stay in her parents' house, everything. They all think of her as one of their own kids now."

"She deserves it," Tyler said, and Raine nodded. She hadn't considered how Beth survived after her parents' death. She hadn't been a minor, but she was young and totally alone. She wouldn't have been equipped to handle everything she needed to do in order to put her life back together while dealing with that kind of grief.

The thought of Beth scared and sad made Raine's chest constrict. Since she'd arrived in Darlington she'd been too wrapped up in reliving her own pain to consider the events that had shaped Beth's life since she'd last seen her. She'd noticed changes in her, but those had mostly been physical. As far as her character and personality went, Raine still thought of her as the same girl she'd known in high school.

"Are you bored to death?" Beth asked when she finally freed herself from the company of the bakers.

"Yes," Tyler and Chris responded in unison.

"What about you?" she asked Raine. "Are you dying to get back into a bar?"

"It's all the same to me." She was just as likely to encounter someone she didn't care to see there as on the street. Though she was starting to enjoy her current company, this was Darlington, and trouble could find her any minute.

"You're outnumbered, Beth, even with Rory wussing out of giving a real answer."

"Fine." Though Beth acquiesced, she appeared nervous. "We'll stop in Busch's for one beer, then come back out."

The boys made a break for the nearest bar, with Beth and Raine a few steps behind them. The crowd was bigger in the bar than it had been at the restaurant, and the clientele was closer to Raine's age, which put her on the defensive. She scanned the room to see if she recognized anyone, but was careful not to make eye contact. She spotted several people she'd gone to school with, but no one she considered close friends. Most of the girls she'd played sports with were probably married with children by now.

"You didn't become a Cubs fan after all those years in Chicago, did you?" Chris asked Raine when he came back to the table with a beer for each of them.

"Not a chance. That's one thing about that town I never got used to. They've got a beautiful stadium but a truly shitty baseball team. I still follow the Cardinals."

"Then we're all in agreement." Tyler raised his beer and shouted, "To the Cardinals."

"Hear, hear." They all clinked their beer bottles together, and several people around them cheered as well. Raine smiled. She hadn't realized how much she'd missed this kind of easy camaraderie. She loved Edmond, but there was something special about being with people who had known each other since preschool.

"We should go down to St. Louis some weekend and see a game together. They've got a big home stand in three weeks, and my brother can get us tickets," Chris said. "It'll be like old times."

"Sounds good to me." Raine welcomed the chance to get out of Darlington. "Beth?"

Beth stared at the table like the chipped Formica had suddenly become the most interesting thing in the room. "I don't know."

"What's the matter?" Raine asked. They were having fun. She'd even started to relax.

"Nothing," Beth mumbled so low that Raine barely heard her over the noise of the crowd. "I don't know if I'll be free that weekend."

What was that supposed to mean? Raine sat back and stared at her before taking a long drink of her beer. What would she be doing that weekend that would be more fun than a ballgame?

Raine wasn't alone in her confusion because Tyler asked, "You got a hot date you're not telling us about?"

Raine realized Beth's blush wasn't one of modesty, but of nervousness, and her reluctance suddenly made sense. Beth had plans with Kelly, but she couldn't say so in front of the guys. They didn't know she was gay, and they certainly didn't know about Kelly.

Chris jumped in. "Who's the lucky guy?"

Raine grew increasingly uncomfortable as Tyler laughed and said, "I'm hurt, Beth. I thought you were in love with me."

Chris picked up the joke. "No, I thought she was in love with me."

"What about you, Rory?" Tyler asked. "Maybe she's in love with you."

Both guys threw back their heads and roared. Beth finally lifted her eyes. They were so full of fear and pleading that Raine's stomach turned. "No," Raine said a little too loudly. "Beth's way too good for me or a couple of bums like you two, either."

"Damn right she is," Tyler said.

"To Beth!" Chris yelled, raising his bottle again.

"To Beth." Raine smiled as Beth's blue eyes lightened with relief while everyone drank in her honor.

"Time to go back to shopping," Beth said, standing up.

"No." The guys both whined and begged for one more beer.

"You said we could shop more after you had a drink."

"No, *you* said that," Chris reminded her. "We never agreed."

"Cheaters." Beth laughed. "That's no fair. The bars will be open all night. The booths close at ten o'clock."

"One more round, and then we promise to go peacefully." Tyler put on his most innocent face, though it wasn't a very good one.

Beth's gaze fell squarely on Raine, and she arched an eyebrow as if asking if she was comfortable staying in the bar. Raine knew Beth was being protective, but Raine was pushing her luck by staying out this long. Still, everything had been fine so far. What did she really have to be afraid of, anyway? People staring at her or talking behind her back? That fear seemed juvenile after everything she'd been through, though something about being in this town made her feel like a teenager again—afraid of getting caught, afraid of disappointing people, afraid of being different.

But she wasn't seventeen anymore. Who cared what other people thought? She was having fun. She didn't want to be a killjoy for the guys, and she didn't want Beth to think she was incapable of holding her own, so she put on her most confident smile and said, "This round's on me, boys."

The men cheered and hailed the waitress.

"Hey, Rory, remember the time out at the lake when you jumped buck-ass naked off the spillway bridge?"

Raine choked on the beer she'd just taken a drink of, not because he'd called her Rory, but because of the good memory he'd associated with that name. "God, I'd completely forgotten that."

"I haven't," Chris said with a goofy grin.

"Man, that was a wild night." The memory was coming back to her now. Tyler and Chris had been there, with at least ten or fifteen other people. They were all drinking from the same three bottles of butterscotch schnapps that someone had snagged from the back room of a liquor store and smoking a joint that was so weak it could've been oregano. Raine warmed at the memory. She had been the life of the party even then. Maybe Raine wasn't responsible for all her showman tendencies. "The softball team had just made it into the playoffs."

"Because you scored the winning run," Beth added

"That's right," Tyler said. "That's why we were celebrating. You were on fire that night, both in the game and at the party."

"And I stripped down and dove in," Raine explained to Beth. "I don't even know what I was thinking, but these damn fools followed me like I was the Pied Piper."

"I remember." Beth smiled. "We were all young and reckless."

"We? You were there? I don't remember that."

"I do." Chris laughed, and Beth punched his arm.

"No, seriously." Raine couldn't wrap her head around this new bit of information. "You went skinny-dipping with me in high school?"

Beth nodded bashfully. "You and about ten other people."

Raine couldn't believe she'd seen Beth naked and didn't remember it. That couldn't be possible. They hadn't talked much in high school, but surely she would've noticed a body like that if it was naked in front of her. She had an image of Beth standing before her now, like the visions she'd had of her in the shower earlier. In her mind Beth's full, supple body was uncovered and waiting to be touched. Raine took a hard swallow of her beer. "I always thought you were a good girl."

"I didn't think you knew I existed in high school."

"I was stupid if I ever overlooked you." Raine smiled a genuine, unguarded smile at Beth, and for that second they were the only two people in the room. "You've got my attention now, and I wish I'd paid more attention to you back then."

Beth seemed pleasantly surprised, and a blush crept back into her cheeks. "Well, I'm here now."

The comment was so intimate and sincere that Raine's heart skipped like a rock across a smooth pond. She had no idea how long the two of them would've continued to stare at each other if Chris hadn't interrupted the moment by muttering "shit" and slouching down in his chair.

Raine followed their line of sight but didn't recognize the woman walking through the door. She wore khakis and a loose green blouse. "Who's that?"

"Lindsay Kennedy," the other three answered in unison.

"No way." Raine hardly recognized their class busybody with her red hair pulled back tightly and large gold cross on a chain around her neck. "Are you sure?"

"Yeah, she's a real bitch on wheels now that she got Jesus," Tyler said.

"She got Jesus?" Raine laughed. "She slept with half the guys in our class."

"Let's go," Beth said forcefully.

"Why?" Raine was finally having a good time in spite of her surroundings. "Are we afraid of her?"

"Yes," the other three answered quickly and stood up, but Lindsay intercepted them before they took two steps.

"We were leaving," Beth said flatly.

"Then I got here just in time." Lindsay gave them a fake smile. "I wouldn't want to miss a chance to catch up with Rory after so long."

"Actually, I go by Raine now," Raine said defiantly. Tyler and Chris exchanged a quick glance of surprise. She, too, was uncertain why she chose to make that stand now, since she hadn't felt the need to make a big deal about her name with the others. In fact she'd felt eerily comfortable slipping into her old self as the evening progressed.

"Raine. That's original. A new name for a new lifestyle?"

"Lifestyle?" Raine grimaced. "You mean my sexual orientation? Yes, I changed my name after I came out."

"I don't know the lingo of debauchery," Lindsay said dismissively.

"Really? You seemed to have a pretty good understanding of debauchery in high school." Raine heard Chris and Tyler snickering behind her, and Lindsay bristled.

"Jesus has wiped my heart and mind clean. I don't remember any of my previous sins."

"Well, I'd be happy to jog your memory," Raine offered. She expected the Mrs. Anthonys of the world to lambast her, but Lindsay Kennedy was a hypocrite, and Raine had no patience for that.

"That's not necessary," Lindsay answered, clearly flustered. "Anyone can change with the help of the Lord. He can make you a whole new woman."

"What if the Lord made me gay?"

"The Lord does not make people perverts, Rory."

"Whoa, Lindsay," Tyler cut in. "You're going too far."

"It's the truth, Tyler. Rory is sick. She will burn in hell if good people don't convince her to turn her life around." Some people around them stared. "I don't expect you and Chris to understand, but Beth, you're a God-fearing woman. I can't believe you'd subject yourself to the poison of her lifestyle."

"I believe it's God's place to pass judgment, Lindsay," Beth said slowly, as if choosing her words carefully. "Rory's life choices are no one's business but her own."

Lindsay and Raine both stared at her in disbelief, but likely for very different reasons. Raine couldn't believe the hypocrisy in

Beth's statement, but Lindsay was the first to recover. "Beth, I'm shocked at you. I thought you were a better Christian than that."

"And I think it's time you move along," Beth said stoically, and Lindsay stomped off.

"Damn, you told her." Tyler laughed. "Another round of drinks on me."

Beth flopped into her chair, her earlier objections to the drinking gone as she watched the guys head toward the bar.

"*My* life choices?" Raine finally managed to squeak out once they were alone.

"What?" Beth asked, clearly confused.

"My life choices, Beth? What the fuck was that supposed to mean?" Raine's anger was burning again. She was being attacked and Beth looked like a protector coming to the rescue, when in reality she should've been in the line of fire too. Instead, she got to stay safely on the sidelines like Saint Beth and make lofty decrees about Raine's life. Mrs. Anthony had been one thing, but Raine was fully capable of handling Lindsay. She didn't need help from a woman who didn't have the courage to come out of the closet.

"I got her out of your face."

"I was handling the situation fine. I didn't need your backhanded criticism, thank you."

"You were causing a scene."

"Lindsay wanted a fight. I gave her one. That's how you handle bullies. You take what they give you, and you throw it back at them."

"You sunk to her level, and it won't make things any easier for you here if you let someone like her draw other people's attention to you."

"Draw attention to me? Everyone's attention is on me. They already know I'm a freak. You're upset because I was drawing people's attention to *you*." Raine spat the words and then watched as the force of them hit Beth, who sat back in her chair, mouth open. The wound showed plainly in the shimmer of her blue eyes. Raine immediately regretted the words, but her pride made her refuse to admit it.

"How dare you, Rory," Beth whispered. "I've done nothing but go out of my way for you since you got home."

"Well, you can stop." Raine stood and bent closer. "I wouldn't want *my life choices* to put your precious reputation at risk." Then she headed for the door.

❖

Beth watched Rory retreat through the crowded bar. *What just happened?* She was trying to be helpful and thought she'd done Rory a favor. What was wrong with standing up for Rory, giving her the support she'd seldom had in Darlington? Though she didn't jump up on the bar and shout that she was gay too, she was sympathetic to what Rory was going through. What was she supposed to do, come out of the closet because some Bible thumper was impolite? Why couldn't Rory recognize the fine line Beth was walking to even be seen with her?

Kelly was already angry, and this conflict would complicate matters once word got around town, and it would. How would Kelly react when she found out that Beth had not only ignored her request to stay away from Rory but had also repeated the incident that had made her mad in the first place?

Rory thought she was worried about her reputation. Well, perhaps that was partially why she didn't take a harsher stand with Lindsay. But she had a relationship to think of. How was she supposed to protect Rory and Kelly at the same time? She hadn't accomplished anything except to disappoint them both.

"Where'd Rory go?" Tyler asked when he and Chris returned with their drinks.

"She left," Beth said flatly, her energy gone.

"What? Why?"

"I don't think she felt comfortable in here anymore."

"Because of Lindsay?" Chris asked. "Geez, no one takes her seriously. Last weekend she told me I was going to hell. How many times has she told you that, Tyler?"

"At least ten times this year alone." Tyler shrugged.

"Rory's a little sensitive right now," Beth tried to explain. "She expects attackers from every angle, so that's what she'll find."

"What a life, huh?" Tyler drank his beer. "Can you imagine having to watch over your shoulder all the time?"

"It would eat at you," Chris said.

They were right. Beth had always known it. From the time she realized she was different, she'd known the cost of hiding. She was never fully herself. Trying to avoid pain and strife, she never got to fully experience peace or joy either. Was she even capable of feeling any kind of unguarded emotion anymore? Surely there was some permanent consequence for hiding such a big part of herself for so long, and for what? To have friends she couldn't confide in, to lose the respect of the people she admired, to have a partner who didn't want to be seen with her?

"Guys, I'm ready to go home," Beth finally said.

"Damn Lindsay," Tyler grumbled. "That bitch totally ruined our night."

Beth laughed because Lindsay was a bitch, and if she were here right now she might tell her that, but deep down she knew she was the one who had ruined their night out.

They walked back to Tyler's truck and Beth grabbed the keys, as the men were in no shape to drive. When they pulled away from the festival and into the sleepy streets of Darlington, Chris finally asked, "What should we do about Rory? We can't let her lock herself in that apartment. We just got her back."

"I don't know that we have Rory back," Beth said honestly. "She's awfully invested in being Raine now."

"She wasn't Raine until Lindsay showed up. She was fine being Rory when we were talking about skinny-dipping in high school."

Beth smiled in spite of her sour mood. Rory had been fun when they were reminiscing about the good ole days. She was playful, relaxed, and laughed easily. She was sexy all the time, even when brooding, but Rory was absolutely captivating when she laughed. She even got a little flirtatious with Beth.

Beth warmed at the memory of Rory saying, "I was stupid if I ever overlooked you." Beth had almost melted. She'd seen Rory in action before and knew she could be devilishly charming, but until tonight those charms had never been directed at her. The effect was pleasantly unsettling.

"Come on, Beth. Let's try again next weekend," Tyler said.

"I want to, guys," Beth said, "but Rory's made it clear she doesn't want to be in Darlington. I don't think she'll let herself be hauled uptown again."

"Then we'll have to come up with something else to do."

"Like what?" If Beth could think of any way to make Rory feel comfortable, she would, but she was tired of forcing her into social situations that only frustrated her.

"Leave that up to us. Just meet us at Rory's again after your game next Saturday."

Saturday? That at least gave her some time. Hopefully by then Kelly and Rory would settle down, and maybe Beth could sort out her own inner conflicts. Besides, she wouldn't be able to brush off the guys without a good excuse. Saying "I'm secretly gay, so Rory thinks I'm a hypocrite, and my closeted girlfriend is ashamed of my behavior" didn't seem like a good option, so she relented.

"Fine, but that's the last time." Even as she spoke, Beth got the sickening feeling that she'd just uttered the famous last words of a fool.

CHAPTER SEVEN

Raine was too mad at Beth to think about where she was going. When she finally stopped walking, she was a few blocks from Patty's house, which made sense. Patty lived closer to the town square than to the college, and even if Raine was angry enough to walk all the way back to campus, she wasn't ready to be alone with her thoughts.

Patty offered the perfect distraction. She wasn't complicated, she wasn't demanding, she didn't have an investment in Rory the way everyone else in town seemed to. Patty was interested in Raine, and that was exactly what Raine needed right now. Beth had shown up at her apartment like it was the most natural thing in the world, then paraded her through town like they were old friends. She had laughed and joked and even flirted with Raine, but the minute they ran into resistance she hid in the closet. Beth didn't want a fight, she didn't want to make a scene, she didn't even want to stand up for herself.

Raine didn't care. She didn't need Beth. She didn't need anyone. She *did* need to feel far away from this town and its stifling influences. She needed to feel strong and self-assured. She needed to be in control. She needed to drown the only memories of Rory that she'd allowed to surface over the course of the evening and return to being Raine.

She'd let herself slip. She had let down her guard and allowed people who knew her as Rory lull her into relaxing her defenses about her own identity, and because of that weakness she'd opened herself up to more pain. She couldn't go back there. She needed to be strong and angry to make herself impenetrable, and that meant calling on Raine. Rory might've been heartbroken by Beth's hypocrisy or afraid to lose the one real friend she had in town. Rory might even be moved by the hurt in Beth's eyes when they argued, but Raine wasn't. Raine was immune to the past. She cared only for the present.

She knocked on Patty's door and heard her call, "Who is it?"

"Raine." She felt better as the name left her lips.

It was a blur of skin, sheets, and sweat as they collided. Patty's T-shirt and shorts were gone before they were halfway down the hall, and Raine's clothes hit the bedroom floor. They kissed and groped with a ferocity that would've appalled her under other circumstances, but she didn't hesitate now. Raine pushed Patty onto the bed and pinned her hands above her head with one hand while she rubbed her other firmly across Patty's body. She didn't savor the moment or tease or think about her movements. The sex was mind-numbing and purely physical. Patty responded by orgasming quickly and flipping Raine over to return the favor.

Neither of them paused after the first round. They simply had sex again, using a multitude of varying positions and methods. Patty's athletic conditioning provided strength and stamina, and the hours that followed burnt off the excesses of Raine's fear and frustration until she was spent and collapsed into a dreamless sleep.

Raine awoke to the smell of coffee and the bright light of mid-morning. She didn't know how long she'd slept, but it wasn't long enough. Her body was weak from the night's activities, and her head felt fuzzy from the beer. She wanted to close her eyes and drift off again, but her stomach growled loudly. She'd eaten only a small bowl of chili in almost twenty-four hours, and she'd burned off those calories early during her time with Patty. She sat up, relieved that her head didn't throb when she moved.

Patty was at the kitchen table with a mug of coffee and the *St. Louis Post Dispatch*. She wore athletic shorts and a sports bra that clearly revealed her muscled physique.

"Morning," Raine said, resisting the urge to run her hand over Patty's sculpted torso. She needed sustenance before she let her libido lead again, so she headed to the coffeepot.

"How you feeling?" Patty asked from behind the newspaper.

"Mentally, physically, or emotionally?"

Patty chuckled. "Pick one."

"Better on all counts, actually." Raine kissed Patty quickly, then sat down beside her. "Thanks to you."

"My pleasure. You were pretty wound up when you got here." Patty seemed unsure whether she should say more, but chose to add, "I'm up for some conversation if you ever need more than sex."

Raine hung her head. This was the third time in a week she'd barged in on Patty, had sex, and then left. It hadn't occurred to her to feel guilty about that until now.

Patty said, "Listen, I'm not asking for anything more." Perhaps she read the remorse in Raine's expression. "It seemed like maybe you had something on your mind."

Raine thought of her family, Lindsay, Mrs. Anthony, and especially of Beth, but she couldn't even begin to put everything into words. Instead, she chose the theme that united all of them. "I really hate this town."

Patty nodded. "Why do you think I get the St. Louis paper every Sunday? I need a glimpse of the real world to remind me there's something else out there."

Raine scooted her chair closer. "What are we reading today?"

"Job listings."

"Seriously?"

Patty shrugged. "Just dreaming. I never apply for any of them, but I feel less trapped when I know I have options."

"Why not?" Raine was surprised that Patty would want a different life, but she shouldn't be. What sexy, young lesbian would want to live in Darlington?

"I was raised up the road in Oquiendo. My parents still live there. Small-town life is all I know," Patty said wistfully.

"But you hate it or you wouldn't want to run away. Why not apply for one of those jobs?" Raine scanned the classified column and pointed to a listing. "St. Louis University is hiring a coordinator for their aquatics center. You'd be perfect for that."

Patty smiled excitedly. "That's the one I've been staring at all morning."

"What are you waiting for? It's a college, it's athletics, it's in a city, and it's only an hour away from your family. You don't have a thing to lose."

"I haven't been offered the job yet."

"You will be. This job is made for you. They won't find anyone more qualified."

"I could always come back if it didn't work out," Patty said, clearly considering the possibilities more seriously.

"Sure, but I doubt you'll want to." Raine was feeding off Patty's excitement, as if she were the one plotting her escape. If she couldn't get out of this godforsaken town, she could at least live vicariously through Patty.

"I'm gonna do it," Patty said resolutely. "I'll go print my résumé right now."

"I'm proud of you." Raine hugged her. It occurred to her briefly that if Patty left she'd lose her sex buddy, but given Patty's excitement, that didn't matter. Patty wasn't long-term-relationship material, but she'd been there when Raine needed her. Now it was Raine's turn to help her. "Is there anything I can do for you?"

"You can go back to bed," Patty said seductively. "We've got some celebrating to do."

Raine didn't need to say anything else. Body aches be damned, sex was exactly what they both needed to get their minds off the magnitude of their changing circumstances.

❖

August 23

Raine peeked at her watch for the fifth time in ten minutes. She was about halfway through her painfully awkward dinner with her parents and her brother. They had already covered the weather, church, and the high-school football team's big win on Friday. Now the topics came less readily, and Raine's tension level grew exponentially.

Had dinner with her family always been this dull? They'd eaten together every night at six o'clock and had never wanted for conversation. Raine and Davey talked about school, their friends, and anything else going on in their lives. Her father discussed politics, hunting, and plans for the farm. Her mother was an endless source of funny stories and local gossip. Now they only scratched the surface of those topics or avoided them altogether.

Raine couldn't handle it any longer. If she had to sit here staring at her fork a minute longer, she'd pull her hair out. "Daddy, when does hunting season start?"

"October," he answered plainly, and returned to chewing his baked chicken.

"Bet you're excited about that."

"I suppose."

Since Raine didn't get anywhere with her father, she switched targets. "What about you, Davey? Do you still hunt?"

"Little bit. Mostly ducks."

He wasn't much help either. "Well, maybe you'll give me a duck this year. I haven't had duck tips for a long time."

"Sure."

This is ridiculous. Why did they invite me if they won't talk to me? "Dinner's good, Mama," Raine said truthfully of the oven-baked chicken with mashed potatoes and gravy accompanied by sweet corn picked from the garden less than an hour before their meal. It was Midwestern fare at its purest, and she hadn't had meals like this since she left home. Her own kitchen skills were limited, and while she'd frequented the finest four-star restaurants Chicago had to offer, no restaurant could ever capture the taste of home cooking.

"Thank you," her mother said. "I'll pack some up for you."

"Thanks," Raine said, but didn't know where to go from there and reluctantly retreated into silence. The longer they continued with nothing more than the occasional quip about benign subjects like the neighbors' new cat or the large pothole in the street out front, the more frustrated Raine became. Her family hadn't asked her a single personal question. They hadn't inquired about her job, her friends, or, God forbid, her relationship status. They hadn't referred to the fact that she'd been gone for ten years, let alone brought up the reason why. It was as if nothing had ever happened.

No, that wasn't the case, because if nothing had ever happened, they wouldn't feel this awkward. If nothing had happened, they'd talk and joke and tease each other about silly things. If nothing had happened, they wouldn't be distant, disapproving, and disappointed in her. Maybe they thought if they pretended those things didn't exist they would go away. Maybe they hoped *she'd* go away.

Her mother got up, cleared the dishes off the table, and came back a few minutes later with several Tupperware containers full of food for Raine. "So you don't get hungry this week."

Her father and Davey moved to the den to watch baseball. Raine was left at the table by herself, further evidence she was being ignored, like all the other unpleasantness between them.

Fine. If they don't want to have to deal with me, I won't make them. She headed for the door, but before she got there her mother called, "See you next Sunday."

Raine shut the door behind her. She wasn't so sure about that.

Chapter Eight

August 27

Beth strolled deliberately up and down the aisles of the college library, a task she liked to perform several times a day. She could check that everything was in order, no books had been left on the floor, no food or drinks were near the shelves, and no students were using the seclusion of the less-frequented sections as a romantic getaway.

Her patrol wasn't totally a function of her position as head librarian, though. She used the time to unwind from the tension of paperwork as well as to interact with students. As she turned down the last aisle housing general fiction, she found a young woman staring blankly at the shelves.

Beth recognized the girl's befuddlement over the Library of Congress cataloguing system. "Can I help you find something?"

"I'm in Professor St. James's class, and I need to find a gay book."

"A gay book?" Beth smiled at the characterization and the ease with which the girl had said it. This was a new generation, one that gave her hope, but she couldn't resist the joke inherent in the girl's request. "I'm pretty certain none of the books have a sexual orientation."

The young woman bristled. "No, that's not what I meant."

"Relax." Beth chuckled. "I was teasing. We don't have a separate section for gay and lesbian literature, but I'd be happy to point out a few books that might work for you."

"That'd be great." The girl was visibly relieved.

"Let's start here." Beth indicated the shelf directly in front of them. If it was gay books Professor St. James wanted, that's what she'd get. Rory probably thought that Beth wouldn't have the courage to carry gay- or lesbian-themed literature in the library, but she was wrong. "We're standing right by Woolf and Wilde."

"Which would you pick?"

"I'd start with *The Picture of Dorian Gray* and *Orlando*."

The girl skimmed the cover of both books. "Are you sure these are gay?"

Beth laughed. "Queer scholars claim they are. Did you want something with obvious gay themes?"

"I'm not sure. We're supposed to bring in a book with queer characters."

"If you want someone more easily identifiable as queer, we'll move up a few decades." Beth walked up a few more rows into the literature section. *This one will impress Raine for sure.* "Here's *Toothpick House* by Lee Lynch. You won't have any trouble finding lesbians in there."

"Okay, that'll do."

"No, no, we're only halfway through the alphabet." Beth was reveling in her task. It wasn't every day she was able to share her personal favorites in literature and get the satisfaction of working with Rory, even remotely. She loved the idea of opening doors through literature. This girl was obviously unaware of the proud tradition of gay and lesbian writers, and Beth wanted to right that wrong. She was sure that's what Rory was trying to do with the assignment. "Next we have James Baldwin and Rita Mae Brown."

"I only need one." The girl tried to dodge the last two books as Beth held them out to her. "Other people in class might want some of these."

Beth thought about that logic. Students didn't have many other options in town. Still, she didn't want to pick just one. She was proud of her library's selection, but she couldn't force them all on one student in one session. "Baldwin and Brown might be a little radical for beginners. Wilde and Woolf will make you work harder to get to the heart of their subtexts." She grabbed *Toothpick House* and handed it to the girl. "Start here, but promise me if you like it you'll come back for the others."

The girl smiled. "I promise, and I'll tell everyone else in class about them too."

As the girl headed to the checkout desk, Beth resumed her patrol. What would Rory say when the student informed the class about the great selection of gay books and the helpful librarian who knew exactly where to locate them? Would Rory be impressed? Would she rethink her characterization of Beth as not wanting to draw attention to herself? More important, why did Rory's opinion of her matter so much?

❖

August 28

After her afternoon class, Rory stopped by the main academic office to check her campus mailbox. She had already forgotten to do it several times and had received several snippy phone calls from the secretary, so when she did finally remember to stop in, she made sure to do so after the offensive woman went home at three o'clock.

"Hiding from our clerical staff?" Miles called out when he came around the corner from his office.

"Is it that obvious?"

"Don't worry. All the new faculty are afraid of her."

"I bet that's the way she likes it."

Miles threw back his head and laughed. "You catch on quickly."

"Yeah, hey, sorry I missed the GLBT social Sunday," Raine said as she sorted through her mail, most of which was junk or flyers for sporting events and student performances.

"You didn't miss much. We didn't have any fireworks this time around. It was just me, Wilson, and Beth."

"Is that unusual?" Raine hoped she hadn't scared people off. She might not agree with the lengths they went through to stay closeted, but she didn't want to add to their list of fears.

"From what I understand, you and Patty were both recuperating from doing God only knows what." Miles made sure no one else was within earshot before adding, "And Kelly is afraid to be seen with Beth right now, because she's too risky."

"Beth is risky?" Raine laughed. "That's not a word I'd use to describe her."

"Well, you know Kelly. She's a hot paranoid mess. Sometimes she crawls even deeper into the closet for a few weeks until she feels like she's reasserted her heterosexual cover."

"And Beth is supposed to wait around while Kelly freaks out?"

"When Kelly gets suspicious, everyone has to prove their loyalty, especially Beth. Kelly is terrified of offending perfect strangers but doesn't mind insulting her own lover."

Raine rolled her eyes. "Kelly is such a tool."

Miles guffawed. "You're so bad. I love it. Have dinner with me next week?"

"Are you cooking?" Raine didn't want to go out anywhere in town, but she was tired of eating alone. It would be nice to have some company that she didn't have to censor herself with.

"I wouldn't eat anything from the grease pits that pass for restaurants around here. You'd better believe I'm cooking, and on copper-bottom pots."

"You're on."

Raine was so excited about making dinner plans with Miles that she didn't finish reading her mail until she was halfway back across campus. A small note between two flyers read simply, "Call Dean Flores Molina."

"Damn," Raine muttered. That couldn't be good. She'd been on campus only two weeks, and the dean was already summoning her. What had she done now?

❖

August 29

Beth stood at the door to Raine's apartment holding a box of pizza. She'd surprised Rory the weekend before but didn't think she would fall for that again. Besides, she didn't have the energy to be that brazen this time. Simply being herself might be the best option for approaching Rory, so she indulged her need to nurture.

She didn't feel obligated to reach out to Rory or crave her gratitude. She was drawn to her. She wanted to comfort her, longed to offer some kind of respite from the turmoil that always radiated from her. Beth felt a connection to Rory that had only strengthened in the few unguarded moments they'd shared since her return.

She knocked on the door and got an immediate response. "Go away."

Beth laughed. "I brought a peace offering. Let's start over."

"What is it?"

"Open the door and I'll show you."

"You're up to something." Rory's voice was clearer now that she was obviously standing just on the other side of the door.

"Sure, I am, but don't you want to know what it is?" Beth suspected that except for her classes, Rory hadn't been out of the apartment all week. That had to be wearing on her by now. She might not like this town, but she was an extrovert and wouldn't be able to function for very long without social interaction.

"I'm going to regret letting you in here," Rory said as she unlocked and opened the door.

"Probably," Beth held out the pizza, "but at least you'll enjoy the pizza."

"Oh, my God, is that from Encarnacion's?"

"Yup." Beth smiled as Rory perked up. She was barefoot. The tattered hems of her faded jeans dragged the floor. She wore a faded Roosevelt University T-shirt that fit snugly enough to reveal she wasn't wearing a bra. Beth turned away. She wasn't the type of person who ogled women's bodies. She respected them, enjoyed them, of course, but never ogled.

Rory stood back to let Beth though the doorway, then followed right behind her to the kitchen. "I haven't thought of this pizza in years. The stuff we get in Chicago is top-notch, but nothing compares to little ole Encarnacion's."

"I know what you mean." As if to accentuate her point, Rory's stomach growled.

Beth opened the box, awash with pleasure at Rory's excitement as she stared at the pizza like the proverbial kid in the candy shop, almost drooling. "Go ahead."

Rory grabbed a square of pizza and shoved the whole thing into her mouth. "Hot, hot, hot!" She hopped from one foot to the other, her mouth open, and tried to cool it by blowing in and out rapidly. But instead of spitting out the scalding pizza, she swallowed it whole.

Beth laughed. "You act like you haven't eaten all week."

"You sound like my mother," Raine mumbled, her mouth full of pizza.

"Your mother?" Beth was shocked that Rory had brought up her family.

"Yeah, she said I look starved and made me take food home." Rory grabbed another pizza square. "I haven't had pizza like this in forever. I can't wait for it to cool."

Rory seemed so young right now, giddy over something this simple. So lighthearted, in fact, that even the mention of her mother hadn't killed her joy. Beth wanted to hear more about Rory's visit with her parents, but she hesitated. For the moment she wanted to enjoy this glimpse of the Rory she'd always wanted to know.

"I love that they cut the pizza in squares. They cut them in wedges in Chicago. Squares are much easier to handle, especially when I was a kid." Rory continued to wax philosophical between bites. "Do you remember when pizza was a special treat and not food you ate when you were strapped for cash or drunk?"

"We only got pizza occasionally when I was growing up. It wasn't until high school that I started to think of pizza as the fifth food group."

"Oh, yeah, Friday nights at Encarnacion's before the football games. Good times."

"Really?" Beth asked.

"Of course. Why?" Raine gave her a curious expression. "You didn't think so?"

"I did, but I got the feeling you don't have any good memories of Darlington."

Rory pushed back from the table, leaned back in her chair, and clasped her hands behind her head as she appeared to consider the question seriously. "Sometimes it feels like that. I remember hiding who I was. I remember being scared someone would find out. I remember all the times I felt awkward while my friends went off with their boyfriends or at the dances where I tried never to dance with the same guy more than once because I was afraid he might get the wrong idea. I guess the good memories faded behind the bad ones."

"For me it works the other way around," Beth confided, though she'd never put these thoughts into words before. "I felt all of those bad things too—the fear, the awkwardness—but in the end the good times I've had here always overshadowed them."

The gravity of the conversational shift settled on them, and they both grew quiet. Was Rory pondering what caused them to view the same basic situation in such drastically different ways? It was a question that would keep Beth awake at night.

A loud knock on the door interrupted their musings, then Chris and Tyler called to them. "Let's get this party started. No moping on a Saturday night."

Rory's accusatory look made Beth realize she was blushing. "I forgot to mention that the boys were coming over too."

"Yeah, that must have slipped your mind," Raine said sarcastically as she opened the door. Her shoulders were tense again, and her dimples had disappeared.

Beth wanted to say that it really had slipped her mind. She'd intended to tell Rory about their plans for the evening, what she knew of them anyway. She hadn't expected the time to pass so quickly. She hadn't anticipated that a conversation about pizza would lead them where it had. She'd become lost in Rory and forgotten about Chris and Tyler's plan. How was she supposed to know that all it would take to make Rory feel comfortable was a box of pizza and a quiet conversation?

She hoped she hadn't lost Rory's trust completely.

❖

"I guess I got duped again," Raine said as she let Chris and Tyler into her apartment.

She shouldn't have been surprised. She knew Beth was up to something when she showed up with the pizza, but she'd thought with her stomach and then been lulled into a false sense of security, again, when they settled into such a nice conversation. She'd felt comfortable opening up to Beth. She hadn't expected to find an ally in Darlington, much less several of them. It almost upset her to enjoy parts of her time here. She wanted to stay distant and angry.

Of course she'd run into bigots too, but she'd expected that. It confused her to talk to Beth so easily. They shared a common upbringing, job, and sexual orientation, but ultimately they viewed those things in profoundly different ways. When they were alone, though, their differences often faded, allowing moments like the ones they shared before the guys arrived.

"Nobody duped you. We want to hang out," Tyler said, throwing an arm over her shoulder. "We're your friends."

Raine wondered if they really were friends. They'd been close in high school, but that was so long ago. They hadn't spoken since then, hadn't kept in touch or shared any major life events. Could someone be a friend if you didn't know anything significant about the last decade of their life? Still, they'd welcomed her home and accepted her lesbianism, even stuck up for her when she was criticized. That counted for something. Plus, Raine was only two weeks into a sixteen-week semester, and she would be lonely if she spent it in isolation. Perhaps it wouldn't hurt to consider the people in the room right now as friends, as least for the time being.

"What would hanging out entail?" she asked, then quickly added, "And don't say 'going to the bar' because that won't happen."

"Give us some credit. We got the message when you ran out on us last weekend," Chris said, helping himself to the pizza.

"Yeah, we'll be as far away from uptown as we possibly can." Tyler grinned.

"Where's that?"

"The country," Chris and Tyler said in unison.

"You nimrods." Beth groaned. "That's your big idea?"

"You weren't in on this?" Raine thought Beth was the mastermind behind these ambushes.

"No, I was told to show up. Those two," she rolled her eyes at Tyler and Chris, "were supposed to handle the rest."

"We did," Chris said defensively. "We bought beer, gassed up the truck, and came to get you right on time. What else do you need for a night in the country?"

"You want to go sit out in the country and drink beer?"

"And listen to the radio and talk, get caught up with each other," Tyler added. "We used to do that all the time."

Raine didn't think the plan sounded like fun. It didn't sound like anything, really. They wouldn't have much to do, but her other option was sitting in the apartment, and she didn't have much to do there either. At least the guys' plan got her out for a while, around people, and she could relax and not worry about running into anyone she didn't want to see. It wasn't a terrible idea. "All right, I'm in."

Tyler drove out of town, turning from a county highway onto a country road that wound through timber and farmland. After a while he pulled onto a dirt path that led between two cornfields for nearly a mile and stopped abruptly where it met a large irrigation ditch.

Raine got out of the truck and walked around the small clearing. Cornstalks rose all around them, their leaves rustling in the faint night breeze. The moon was nearly full and reflected off the trickle of water in the ditch. She couldn't see streetlights or hear cars, and the aroma of damp earth had replaced the smells of town.

"Wanna beer?" Tyler tossed her a can without waiting for her response.

"It's a long way from Michigan Avenue, ain't it?" Chris propped himself against the open tailgate of the truck.

"Yes and no," Raine said. "In the city you're just a face in the crowd. You don't have to see anyone you don't want to. The place is big enough to hide in plain sight, kind of like this. You can do what you want without having to worry about other people knowing your business. It's the same concept, just a different method of achieving it."

"I'll be damned." Tyler cracked open his beer. "Never thought of it like that."

"I didn't think you liked to be anonymous. I thought you were the famous Raine St. James," Beth said, without mockery or judgment in her voice.

Raine regarded her more closely while she tried to process the statement. Beth was sitting on the tailgate, swinging her feet. Her blue jeans and light blue polo shirt brought out the blue of her eyes, even in the muted moonlight. She was making an honest observation, and Raine adopted her tone. "It didn't start out that way. When I got to Chicago, I wanted to disappear. I was tired of the scrutiny that came with living in a small town. I wanted to be where no one knew me or cared about who or what I did. I didn't start to settle down and connect with people again until I met Edmond."

She hadn't talked to Edmond in two weeks. She needed to call him soon. He probably thought she still wasn't speaking to him.

"Who's Edmond?" Chris asked.

"Her agent," Beth said quickly.

Did Beth remember details about everyone or just her? "He wasn't my agent at first. He was in college, interning at the gay and lesbian center on Halstead in Chicago. That's where we met. When I told him my story, he thought it was great." Raine buzzed over the part about how she'd shared horror stories of growing up in Darlington. "He thought other people might like to hear it too, so he set up a speaking event at the center. Having people offer their support and approval felt good, so when Edmond set up another event at a center in Evanston, I spoke there too, and they paid me. Then everything took off."

"What about your articles?" Beth asked.

"Those started when I was in college. Edmond had been promoting me to college groups, and a women's studies professor at Roosevelt University in Ohio told him about a scholarship for kids who'd been disowned. Edmond did the paperwork, and I was off to college."

The story probably sounded like such a whirlwind. It even seemed a little crazy to Raine, and she'd lived it. "College taught me to research and write. My early articles all came out of my classes, and either Edmond or my professors sent them to magazine and journal editors. Every article I wrote brought more speaking requests and eventually a scholarship to work on my master's degree back in Chicago. Before I knew it, I had a public-speaking career, several published articles, and two college degrees."

"Just like that?"

Raine chuckled. "Just like that." She didn't add that everything fell apart the same way, that her life and career had slipped away from her just as easily as they came, that other people with new stories and younger faces entered the scene, that editors wanted something newer, something better, and the longer she went without a publication, the less she was called for speaking engagements until the phone almost stopped ringing altogether.

"That beats the hell out of my story. I took over the family farm a little bit at a time. My dad hasn't officially retired and probably never will, but I run most everything now," Chris said.

Tyler summed up his career path. "I went to junior college, but all that time butchering our own hogs at home was the only thing that stuck with me. I joined the meat-cutters' union and the rest is history. Nowhere near as interesting as speaking all over the country."

Everyone turned their attention to Beth, who stared at the ground. "Nothing too significant about my journey either. It's hardly worth telling, really."

"I'd still like to hear it." Raine wanted to be closer to Beth in any way she could. If possible, they would've continued the conversation they'd been having back at the apartment. But since the guys had opened the topic of their past, she decided to take advantage of it.

"I went to Illinois State and loved it but couldn't go back after Mama and Daddy died." Beth shrugged as if trying to minimize her circumstances, but Raine could clearly see Beth's sadness under her casual cover. "The church helped me get into Bramble College, but I had a hard time paying the bills after I sold the farm to pay for the house. I was either going to lose my home or be forced to drop out of school, so some people in town pulled a few strings and got me a full-time job at the library. They worked around my schedule so I could finish college. Everyone was so good to me there that I never left."

They were silent after Beth finished her story. Raine's life had been so different from Beth's, yet it had interesting similarities. Neither of them had set out to live the life they ended up with, but their circumstances sent them down different paths. Few of their choices had been their own. The fates spun them in unexpected directions, and all they could do was make the most of what they'd been given.

"Damn, I think that calls for another beer," Tyler said.

"And a happier topic," Chris added. "Anyone got laid lately?"

"I did," Tyler laughed, "in the livestock barn at the county fair."

"I meant with a woman, not a pig."

Tyler pushed him. "It was with Jenny Thompson. I was in the barn checking out some stock, and she came in pissed off at some college guy she'd been dating. You know how she gets when she's mad."

"Oh, yeah, she's a hellcat."

"Well, she got me good, there in the hay, and then again later in the bed of my truck."

Beth hopped off the tailgate. "Yuck, Tyler. God only knows what kind of STDs you've exposed us to."

Raine and the boys burst out laughing. "I don't think you can get STDs from a truck bed."

"Still, it weirds me out to sit in the same spot where Tyler did it with Jenny," Beth said, but now she was laughing too. Raine loved the contagious sound. Beth didn't laugh often enough.

"I don't mind," Chris said. "This is the closest I've been to sex for months."

"A vicarious thrill is better than no thrill at all," Raine said.

"Oh, come on, you've gotten some recently." Tyler nudged her. "You're a stud, right?"

Raine grinned at the characterization, but she wasn't sure that two country boys were ready to see her relationships with women as on par with their own. "I don't know what you've heard about lesbians, but I've never been part of anything resembling your lipstick-lesbian fantasies, so don't even think about it like that."

"Sorry, stud." Chris punched her shoulder. "You aren't the type of woman that shows up in my fantasies. I bet you have your pick of the litter, though. You've got that celebrity thing going on."

Raine shrugged and had another drink of her beer. Her celebrity status had gotten her plenty of attention, too much sometimes. Would the women she dated have been interested in her if they hadn't known her as Raine St. James? Few of them would find her attractive right now, in the middle of a cornfield with a group of people who knew her as Rory, not Raine. She was acting like Rory too—relaxed, unguarded, unrefined—and enjoying herself. "I did okay in Chicago."

"Fuck Chicago," Tyler said. "I hear you've been doing all right in Darlington too."

"What do you mean?"

"Patty Spezio, buddy. Everyone knows she's as gay as it gets, and you've been sleeping over."

"Oh." It hadn't occurred to Raine that people would notice her spending the night at Patty's, and she felt a little sick about it now. The fact that Beth wouldn't meet her eyes only compounded her embarrassment. Apparently she'd figured out her relationship with Patty too. It was nobody's business but hers and Patty's, but Raine had the urge to explain herself to Beth. If she could even put into words what she and Patty were to each other.

"'Oh'? What's that mean? You've had more sex in this town in two weeks than I've had in months, and all you've got to say about it is 'oh'?"

"What's there to say? Patty's a friend." Raine used the only word that seemed appropriate.

"I wish I had more friends like that." Chris prodded her. "How good a friend is she?"

Raine chuckled. It boosted her ego to be seen as a stud, but the further this line of questioning went, the more uncomfortable she became. She didn't mind talking about sex. In fact, under some circumstances it was her favorite subject, but she didn't want to add to the Darlington rumor mill. She'd already been too careless, and while she trusted Tyler and Chris, she didn't want to disrespect Patty.

She should've realized that nothing went unnoticed in Darlington, especially something as scandalous as the town lesbians spending the night together. She suddenly had more sympathy for Beth and the over-the-top measures she and Kelly took. The thought sobered her. "You know, I think that any woman who's good enough to share her bed with me deserves my respect."

"Boo." Tyler threw his empty beer can at her, and Chris gave her a shove. "When'd you become a fucking Boy Scout?"

Raine laughed, but Beth answered. "Maybe it's that type of chivalry, and not Rory's celebrity, that women find most attractive about her."

Her blue eyes were on Rory again, warming her with their beauty. Beth rested against the back of the truck with her elbows on the tailgate behind her. The pose was both casual and sexual, displaying the length of her body without appearing overly provocative. Raine's temperature rose as she returned Beth's slow smile, but Tyler interrupted the momentary connection too soon.

"Oh my God, she turned Beth gay."

"Damn, you're good." Chris gave Raine a high five.

"You two are idiots." Beth's smile seemed forced and Raine could see the fear behind her rebuke. "You can appreciate someone without wanting to sleep with them."

Though the statement was true and probably made out of self-preservation, it stung Raine's ego. She did want Beth's appreciation and was glad to have it, but the added bonus of being told she didn't care to sleep with her reminded Raine that Beth was off-limits. She wasn't sure why that bothered her. She wasn't interested in Beth. Beth was too prim and proper, too closeted, and too taken for her tastes. She was altogether too complicated.

Tyler's eyes gleamed. "Are you saving yourself for marriage, or are you too good to ever have sex?"

"No, I'm not too good to have sex. I'm just too good to talk about it with you," Beth replied.

"Come on," Chris pleaded. "You can't tell us you've had sex and then not share the details. You've shattered my view of you. It's your responsibility to build a new one."

Raine thought about what the guys were asking. Beth obviously couldn't and wouldn't open up in order to protect herself and Kelly. While Raine wasn't interested in helping anyone hide who they were, she decided to stop the conversation for her own sake. If she were forced to think about Beth having sex, she'd have to think about her with Kelly, and that would drive her crazy. It was bad enough that Beth hid who she was, but it was unbearable to think of her wasting her time with someone who didn't want to be seen with her. How could Kelly make love to Beth one day and refuse to acknowledge her the next?

"I don't want to hear another word about it," she said. "I prefer to keep my image of Beth as a perfect angel."

The others stared at her. Perhaps the statement hadn't sounded as teasing as she'd hoped. Raine silently willed them not to recognize her underlying motives.

"I see your point," Chris finally admitted. "Finding out good girls don't exist is like learning there's no Santa Claus."

"Thanks," Beth said, clearly relieved. "I think."

The conversation shifted, and Beth seemed to relax more as the subject of their sex lives faded. The tension slowly eased from her body and the worry lines on her forehead smoothed out. She was beautiful there in the moonlight, and Raine was pleased that she'd helped offer her some safety. However, she wasn't able to shake her own visions of Beth and Kelly together. She'd need more than a change of topic to erase them.

When Beth got home at midnight, the old farmhouse was empty and quiet after the constant chatter of friends. She'd been the designated driver after the guys and Rory killed the case of beer. Her friends safely home, she now put on her worn pair of cotton pajamas and climbed into bed. Sleep should come quickly since she was tired and happy.

It had turned into a good night despite her initial displeasure at Tyler and Chris's plan. Rory had certainly enjoyed herself. She was almost jovial at times, and her dimples had appeared frequently. Beth watched in awe as she commanded the group's attention with stories of Chicago and all the places she'd been. She was funny, entertaining, and open about her past without anger or animosity. She was so much like her old self that Beth barely remembered that she was with Raine instead of Rory.

The only time she clammed up was when they talked about sex. Not her sex life, though. She was charming and debonair discussing Patty. She exuded confidence and laughed easily when the guys called her a stud. She was obviously comfortable with the label. Beth was attracted to Rory's self-assured sensuality yet repulsed at the thought of her fooling around with Patty. That was clearly all they were doing, since Rory wasn't in love with Patty.

Beth knew the signs of someone in love, and Rory had none of them. But did her purely sexual connection to Patty make Beth feel better or worse? Rory deserved to be happy, but Patty wasn't the woman she needed. She needed someone steadier, someone who offered balance.

Beth shook her head. Why was she lying in bed thinking about what Rory needed in a partner? Rory's comment about her being too pure to have sex had made her opinion about Beth's personal life clear. That was Beth's image around town, and she used it to her advantage when she wanted privacy, but Rory knew she wasn't a saint. Why was she so weird when the topic came up? She acted like she couldn't stand the thought of Beth having sex.

She'd probably steered the conversation onto less loaded topics because she respected Beth's desire to remain closeted. At least she hoped Rory respected her need to be discreet, even though she didn't like Beth's decision. Still, Rory didn't have to act like Beth was a nun. Rory had been extremely respectful of Patty without denying her sexuality. It would've been easy to turn their relationship into a tawdry joke, yet she acknowledged that Patty was attractive and desirable without degrading her or their connection.

The phone rang, startling Beth. She wasn't sure who'd call this late, but she was certain it couldn't be with good news.

"Hello?"

"You're home," Kelly said flatly. "I was starting to worry."

Beth flipped on her bedside light as if that would somehow illuminate the meaning behind Kelly's words. "Kel, are you okay?"

"I'm fine. I'm not the one who was out until midnight."

"Did I miss something, Kelly? Was I supposed to stay home tonight?"

"You didn't mention that you had plans. You weren't out in town anywhere that I saw. Nothing was going on at the college or the church, so when I called at nine o'clock I thought it was odd that you weren't home. When I didn't get an answer at ten thirty, I began to wonder where you where. At eleven thirty I started to worry."

"That's really sweet of you, honey," Beth said, though Kelly's words didn't sound sweet, and she could detect their underlying questions. "I went out with Chris and Tyler and some people after the softball game. I didn't know we were going out until we decided to."

It wasn't a total lie. She'd been with the guys and one other person, and she hadn't known they were going to the country ahead of time. The fact that she'd also been with Rory and had made plans to be with her a week ago would only upset Kelly. They hadn't run into anyone else, and there'd been no public scenes like last week, so she wasn't likely to hear about it.

Beth was eager to deflect the conversation away from herself and onto Kelly. "What did you want before you got worried?"

"I missed you. I wanted to hear your voice. Maybe drop by for a while."

Kelly's sincerity made Beth feel guilty for automatically assuming the worst. Maybe she wasn't being accusatory, maybe she was honestly interested in what Beth was doing. Now Beth regretted her lies of omission. Kelly was her partner. Why didn't she trust her to understand? She should've given her the benefit of the doubt and mentioned Rory earlier, but it was too late now without making Kelly suspicious. "I'd have liked that. I'm sorry I wasn't here."

"It's okay," Kelly said. "I do want to see you, though. Will you be at Miles's tomorrow?"

"Sure, and I got a roast to make for us when you come over Tuesday night."

"My favorite." Beth could hear the smile in her lover's voice.

"I know." She'd made the offer as an apology for both the things Kelly knew about and those she didn't.

"I can't wait," Kelly said, then added, "I really have missed you."

"I've missed you too," Beth said. It was the truth. She'd missed Kelly several times throughout the week, just not tonight.

CHAPTER NINE

September 1

Raine nervously approached the dean's secretary. "I have a three o'clock appointment with Dean Molina."

"You're early. You can wait here until she is ready for you," the woman said without looking up.

"Thanks," Raine mumbled, and sat down in the waiting area. She still wasn't sure why she was here. When she had called about the dean's note, she'd been told that the dean wanted to speak with her about some developments that had been brought to her attention. That didn't sound good. Raine was in her third week of classes, and so far things had gone surprisingly well.

She liked her students, and they had responded well to the course material, both in her GLBT history course and her queer theory class. She had only thirty students total, so she'd easily learned their names and why they were taking the classes. A few were gay, but most of them were young, liberal, and eager to learn about something new. She hadn't noticed anyone that seemed problematic, and since both classes were electives, she didn't need to worry that the subject matter would offend them.

But this was Central Illinois. Perhaps someone had complained to the dean or even the board of trustees. What did the college expect when they hired a lesbian teacher to teach gay and lesbian subject matter? *I can't tone down the gayness in a gay class.* Raine's well-honed defensiveness took over. *They should've thought about the conservative backlash before they hired me.* She didn't want to teach at Bramble in the first place, but now that she was here she wasn't about to roll over for anyone.

"Professor St. James, the dean will see you now."

Dean Flores Molina stood to shake her hand, then indicated the chair opposite her desk. "Professor St. James, good to see you. Sorry I haven't kept in better touch, but the start of the semester is always busy around here."

"Quite all right, Dean. I imagine you have got a lot of people vying for your time." Raine wished they would skip the pleasantries and get to the reason for this meeting.

"Call me Flores, please, and my faculty and their students are my top priority. How're you enjoying your classes?"

"More than I expected to. This is my first time teaching, so I have a lot to learn, but I'm catching on quickly." Raine watched the dean for signs of discomfort but couldn't detect any.

She wouldn't have any trouble intimidating anyone. Her business suit was perfectly tailored and accentuated her tall stature even when she was sitting. Every detail, from her manicured fingernails to the way her long black hair was pulled back tightly, conveyed authority and control, but her smile seemed genuine.

"What about your students?" Flores asked. "Do you find them prepared, engaged, and generally up to par?"

Raine tried to decipher any possible subtexts but couldn't think of a single student whom she considered subpar. "I have a good group of young intellectuals. Some are more interested in the subject matter than others, but I assure you I wouldn't ask them to do anything I didn't think they were capable of."

Flores raised an eyebrow questioningly. "That was a very PC answer. Are you sure everything's okay?"

"To my knowledge I've had no problems. If you've heard of any, I'd be happy to address them," Raine said stiffly. She didn't appreciate being toyed with. Whatever the problem, she was ready to face it.

"Professor—"

"Call me Raine, please." She clung to her chosen name and the identity that she assumed with it.

"Raine, from what I hear, you're becoming one of our most popular professors. Your students love you and cannot stop talking about the things they're learning in your classes. If I led you to believe this was an inquisition about your pedagogy, I'm sorry. I wanted to make sure you're happy with your teaching assignments."

Raine relaxed slightly. "I am. Like I said, this is my first teaching job, and I've been surprised at how quickly I've come to love it. I enjoy every day in the classroom, but surely you didn't call me in here to ask that."

Flores's smile widened. "No, I wish I had the time to socialize because I'd love to hear more about your classes, but I need to ask you about something else."

"Okay." Raine set her jaw and steeled herself for the unknown.

"I'm aware that you and Patty Spezio have become friends, and I'm sure you know she's been a valued member of our campus GLBT community—"

Raine tried to contain her outrage. "I don't see how my relationship with Patty has any bearing on my position here at Bramble." She couldn't believe the dean was questioning her personal life.

"Excuse me?" Flores seemed flummoxed.

"We're both consenting adults. Our sex lives should be out of the jurisdiction of college administration. Our relationship doesn't affect our jobs in any way and..." Raine noticed that Flores was biting her bottom lip, seeming to fight back a smile. "What?"

"Raine, I didn't know that you and Patty were intimate."

"Oh." Raine's face blazed. "That's not what you wanted to talk to me about?"

"No." Flores chuckled. "I received Patty's letter of resignation last week. She's accepted a position in St. Louis. Her new employer has been looking for a coordinator for months, and she's the most qualified candidate they've seen in that time. They'd like her to start immediately, and she's eager to give big-city life a try."

"I'm not responsible for her quitting. She's not leaving because of me."

"Okay, Raine," Flores said calmly. "You seem invested in believing you're here to be disciplined. If you keep acting defensive, I'll eventually wonder if I should worry. Why don't you just relax and let me finish."

Raine nodded, too embarrassed to speak.

"Since you and Patty have become friends and the students like you, I thought you might be interested in becoming the advisor for the GLBT Student Association."

"I'd love to," Raine answered honestly. She welcomed the chance to spend more time with her students. She was also eager to redeem herself after the way she'd behaved during this meeting.

"Good. The students loved Patty and we'll all miss her, but this transition may work out well for everyone involved." Flores sat forward. "That wasn't nearly as terrible as you made it out to be, was it?"

Raine finally laughed. "I guess I misread this situation pretty badly."

"Yes, you did." Flores's expression was compassionate. "It's hard to learn the power dynamics in a new place, but it's even harder when you go in expecting the worst."

"Point taken." Raine stood up to go, but before she reached the door, Flores stopped her.

"Raine, we really are happy to have you here."

"Thank you." For the first time she was actually starting to believe that.

❖

September 1

"Hello," Kelly called as she came through Beth's back door. She'd never lived there, but they were past the point of knocking. Kelly placed a bottle of white wine on the counter and kissed Beth. This had been their Tuesday-night routine for years.

Kelly wrapped her arms around Beth's waist and drew her near. "I've missed you."

Beth returned the hug, enjoying the feel of Kelly's body. She was comforting, solid, familiar. "I've missed you too."

They broke contact, and Kelly set the table while Beth checked the pork roast in the oven. Behind her, Kelly rested her chin on Beth's shoulder and nuzzled her neck, mumbling, "Smells delicious."

"It's almost ready."

Kelly kissed her cheek and went back to the table. "I wasn't talking about the food."

Beth flushed at the compliment. Kelly said things like that often enough to remind her that she found her attractive, but not frequently enough to make her expect them. Beth had never considered herself beautiful, so it still surprised her when Kelly said something to that effect.

The meal was a success, and they had two helpings while they caught up on the events of the past two weeks. Kelly told Beth about the cases she was working on as the town accountant. Beth talked about the influx of students at the library. Their conversation continued easily as they cleaned the dishes, Kelly washing and Beth drying. Their routine was set after years of identical Tuesday nights, and Beth found it reassuring that the strain of the past two weeks dissipated under familiar circumstances.

Of course the topic of Rory hadn't come up, and Beth didn't intend to broach it. Her friendship with Rory was likely to remain an issue between her and Kelly, but it didn't need to infiltrate all their conversations. Beth had plenty of friends, as did Kelly, and none of them ever factored into the way they related to each other, so why should Rory? Then again, Beth didn't stay out until midnight talking about sex with her other friends.

Rory wasn't a casual acquaintance. Beth had sought out and continued to be drawn to her despite the fact that Rory seemed to invite trouble. Beth couldn't even manage to stay away from Rory when her lover asked her to.

Perhaps that made their friendship more complicated than others, but right now Beth and Kelly were having a lovely evening reconnecting. Why ruin it by mentioning irrelevant information? Rory had no bearing on what Beth shared with Kelly, so why was she still thinking about her?

Once the dishes were done, Kelly took both of Beth's hands and led her to the bedroom. Now they would make love. It was the culmination of their time together, the rewarding end to their routine. Beth knew it would happen, she even knew *how* it would happen, and still she blushed at the intimacy in Kelly's eyes as she laid her gently on the bed.

"I love you," Kelly whispered.

Beth smiled at the sweet endearment.

They kissed slowly, gently, as Kelly unbuttoned Beth's blouse and peeled it off her shoulders. She ran her hands over her torso and unclasped her bra, pausing to caress her breasts. Kelly handled her body as though it were made of porcelain. She'd always been a tender lover, which Beth needed, especially in the early days when they were learning. Beth was emotionally fragile in the wake of her parents' death, her emotions compounded by the fear and wonder that came with falling in love for the first time. Kelly had been patient and understanding. It'd been her first time as well, and they had both been timid.

Kelly removed her own shirt and pants before she guided Beth's slacks over her hips, leaving only their underwear between them. Beth slid her hands along the length of Kelly's body from her thighs to her breasts and cupped them gently as she guided Kelly on top of her. Over the years their confidence had grown and they'd both become increasingly adept as they learned more about each other's bodies. Still, the tone of their lovemaking never changed. They always handled each other with care.

Nestling her hand between Beth's legs, Kelly lightly stroked her, establishing a slow, steady rhythm. Beth's body responded and she closed her eyes to focus on the physical sensations. She felt Kelly lower herself onto her thigh and rock in time with Beth's motions. Her own wetness increased when she felt the evidence of Kelly's arousal on her leg.

Kelly didn't talk during sex, and she didn't get overly demonstrative even during orgasm. She remained so composed and controlled that at times her body offered the only proof of her desire, so Beth took satisfaction in knowing she was responsible for the hardness she felt against her now as she lifted her thigh to meet Kelly's motions.

Beth clenched in anticipation as she noticed the signs of her own impending climax. Her breath grew shallow and her muscles began to contract on their own. It wouldn't be long now before she had her release, and she wanted to make sure Kelly had what she needed as well. She clasped Kelly's hips and pulled her down harder, their movements losing their rhythm only in the final seconds before they came, quietly shuddering in each other's arms. Then they fell still, their bodies limp against each other, the silence broken only by the sound of their breath as they slowly regained their composure.

Kelly propped herself up on her elbow and kissed Beth's temple. "I love you."

"I love you too." She did love Kelly. She'd loved her even before the first time they made love, and she loved her still after all these years, but hearing the words also brought sadness because it was the final step in their evening. It wasn't a spontaneous "I love you." It was a prelude to good-bye.

Kelly would leave soon. She'd say that she wanted to stay, but the fear of raising suspicions would win out, and she'd return to her own home. This, too, was part of their routine, the part Beth found increasingly less comforting. Kelly wouldn't jump up immediately. She'd stay and cuddle, whisper sweet words into Beth's ear, and make plans to see her again, but their connection had reached its peak for the night. From here on, Beth would be waiting for the moment when Kelly's car pulled out of the driveway and she was left in her solitude once more.

CHAPTER TEN

September 4

Raine knocked on the frame of Miles's screen door and then entered when she heard his invitation to come in. She wandered through the living room and dining room and found him in the kitchen, a cast-iron skillet in one hand and a bottle of white wine in the other.

"Hey," she said, taking in Miles, who was still dressed for work in black slacks and a white button-down shirt. However, he had removed his tie and wore an apron with Michelangelo's David's torso and genitalia across the front of it. Raine chuckled. "Not one for subtlety, are you?"

"I'm the picture of subtlety all week long, but it's Friday night and it's just us bois here. Or are you one of those lesbians who're offended by the idea that men have bodies too?"

"No, men don't offend me, nor do any of their parts, especially when those parts are cooking for me." Raine bent over the stove to peek at what was in the skillet. "Oh, my God, is that *arroz con pollo?*"

"Good eye," Miles said appreciatively, then flipped on the oven light. "Check that out."

Raine bent down. "What's that?"

"Peaches that have been pitted, filled with chèvre, and wrapped in prosciutto to hold them together while they cook."

Raine grabbed Miles's face and kissed his cheek hard. "You're a god."

He laughed heartily and shooed her in to set the table while he finished the meal.

Raine couldn't shovel the food into her mouth fast enough and had to restrain herself from moaning. "Where did you get saffron? Or the goat cheese? I've been in the only store in town, and they didn't even have salmon. Don't tell me I missed the chèvre."

"I don't shop there," Miles said in a superior tone. "My first week in town I went to the grocery store and asked for brie cheese."

"What did they say?"

"I kid you not, the woman working the checkout scrunched up her nose and said, 'You want green cheese?' I thought maybe she was hard of hearing, so I yelled, 'No, brie,' and again she yelled back at me, 'Green?'"

Raine was laughing hard at the thought of Miles and Mrs. Anthony yelling "brie" and "green" at each other. "Did you ever get through to her?"

"I got out a pen and wrote the word 'brie,' and she shook her head and said she'd never heard of it." Miles was obviously still appalled at the encounter. "Can you believe that?"

"I believe it," Raine said seriously. "Meat, potatoes, sugar, salt, milk, and flour. That's the entirety of this town's culinary needs. I'm used to it. I even like the comfort food, but how has someone with your tastes survived?"

"I drive down to St. Louis every two weeks to Soulard Market. That place is not for the faint of heart, but they have everything, and it's all fresh."

"Great idea. More people would do that if they weren't terrified of driving in St. Louis."

"What's with that?" Miles asked cattily. "People around here act like Satan himself is in city traffic."

"They're afraid of anything outside this tiny little box of a town. It threatens their sheltered existence."

"I like small-town life, most of the time. I like the students I work with. I love it that people wave to each other, hold doors, and say 'ma'am' and 'sir,' but what's wrong with injecting a little culture into that way of life?"

Raine thought about that. "I don't know why you couldn't have both. I've always considered small towns and big ideas mutually exclusive. Most people here think the same way. Anything new is dangerous to their way of life."

"Ugh, Kelly said the same damn thing yesterday. She wouldn't even try the hummus I made. She wanted cheese and sausage on saltines."

"I've mentioned before that Kelly is a tool."

Miles laughed. "Don't be shy. Tell me how you really feel."

"In elementary school, she was a tattletale. In high school she was a narc. Now she's a bitch. She was never sweet or innocent, but she thought she was better than everyone else, and she wanted you to know it too. I think she's hated me since before we could even crawl. I was a rule bender, and she was the perpetual hall monitor." Raine was on a roll now. "She must've ratted me out a hundred times over the years. She was one of the ones I knew would love to find out I was gay so she could tell the whole town."

"That's ironic," Miles said, sipping his wine.

"I never thought she'd be a dyke, but don't let her fool you with all her talk about respecting people's wishes. If she could've used my sexual orientation to get leverage over me, she would've." Raine didn't even pretend to know the limits of Kelly's hypocrisy. "If I never saw her again, that would be fine with me, but it pisses me off that she's dating Beth. Why would Beth even waste her time with someone like her?"

Miles's eyebrows shot up. "A little sensitive about our beloved Beth?"

"What? No." Raine was surprised she'd gotten worked up over Kelly and somehow spun all that emotion back around to Beth. "You have to admit, it's a mismatch, right?"

"A little bit," Miles shrugged, "but really, aside from Kelly's need to be so secretive, they seem okay. They were back to their usual happy selves last Sunday."

"They were together Sunday? I thought they were separated because Kelly was freaking out."

"Apparently she got over it. They didn't arrive together, of course, but they were sweet when they were here, and Kelly kissed her good-bye."

The thought of Kelly kissing Beth made Raine nauseous. Beth had such beautifully full lips, and if their appearance was any indication, they would be soft to the touch as well. Why would she share that softness with Kelly, who was hard and unbending? Kelly wouldn't know what to do with a woman like that.

Beth was stunning. She deserved to be put on display, not tucked away in a closet. If Raine had a woman like Beth, she would never be satisfied with a chaste kiss behind a closed door. She'd walk right down Main Street holding her hand, and she wouldn't leave her side, even for one night.

"I don't see how that relationship could ever work, but hey, it's none of my business." Raine had a sip of her wine, hoping the alcohol would quickly cloud the images in her head. It was absurd to think of Beth romantically. She was the darling of Darlington, and other than being gorgeous, Beth wasn't Raine's type at all. Closeted women came with too much baggage.

❖

September 9

Beth was making one of her customary passes though the library when she saw Rory sitting on the floor between two stacks of books. Her back was to the aisle, and she was hunched over a text that she'd opened in her lap. It didn't seem like a very comfortable position, so Beth interrupted.

"The tables and chairs we have in here aren't plush, but they're an upgrade from the floor."

Rory looked up, startled, and then smiled broadly, her dimples peeking out at both corners of her mouth. "Hey, stranger. I spent a whole week without being ambushed. I was beginning to think you were avoiding me."

The comment caught Beth off guard. As much as Rory complained about being pressured to go out with her the past two times, Beth thought she would've enjoyed a weekend without interruptions. It wasn't that she hadn't thought about her. She'd thought about her too much. She'd picked up the phone to call several times and even driven by once, but she didn't want to push.

Rory hadn't indicated that she wanted to be barged in on, and even if she had, Beth was trying to reconnect with Kelly. Spending the weekend with Rory certainly wouldn't help with that. "So you decided to sprawl on my library floor in the hopes of getting my attention?"

"I hadn't intended to camp out here. I got lost in what I was reading."

"You've found plenty to keep you busy. Let's move it someplace more spacious." Beth offered a hand to pull Rory off the floor, but the rush of lightheadedness when their fingers touched made her worry that she'd be the one who needed assistance.

Rory seemed unfazed and got quickly to her feet. "Thanks. Where do you suggest?"

Beth indicated a large table in the corner that offered both space and privacy. She helped Rory carry a stack of journals, reading a few of the titles as she piled them on the table. They were all psychology journals. "Are you changing fields of study, or are you worried that Darlington is affecting your psyche?"

Rory released one of those easy laughs that made Beth feel giddy with the thought that she'd caused it. "I'm sure it is, but that's not why I'm reading. I'm trying to find some research on gay and lesbian identity development for an article."

Beth sat at the table next to Rory. "Sounds interesting. What're you finding?"

"Some standard models that lay out the stages gays and lesbians go through in the coming-out process. They start with people beginning to suspect they're gay and progress until the person is well adjusted, acknowledging their sexuality as a part of them, but not letting it define who they are," Rory explained, pointing to a chart in one of the articles.

She gestured as she talked, and Beth noticed how beautiful her hands were. Her fingers were long and slender, and unadorned, with nothing to distract from the grace of their movement. Rory was probably good with her hands. She seemed to be good at everything.

"So," Rory continued, "I'm researching the stages in the middle."

"And what is this project?" Beth forced her attention from Rory's hands to her eyes, though she quickly realized she wouldn't fare any better by staring into that sea of emerald.

"I want to explore what causes some people to stay closeted in a small town while others fight to break free."

Beth frowned. "Sounds personal. Can you remain unbiased on the subject?"

Rory's half-smile was cocky. "I don't have to. I'm not an academic. I write everything from a personal viewpoint. That's what's made me successful. I don't distance myself from the subject matter. I live it."

It was true. Rory had made a name for herself by giving her side of her story, and when people learned she'd returned to Darlington, they'd want her to extrapolate broader lessons from her personal experiences. But Beth didn't like the sound of where she was headed. "Surely you plan to inject some objectivity, though, or you wouldn't be doing research."

Raine chuckled. "I plan to use the existing models as a springboard for my own ideas, then draw conclusions from my experience and observations as to what drives our responses."

"So you're planning to say that one option is healthier than the other? Dare I guess which one of us you think has chosen the better path?"

"Well." Rory furrowed her brow. "Strictly speaking, if you don't come out of the closet, it's impossible to move toward a full realization of your identity. The research is broad. I'm not attacking you personally."

"I thought you saw everything from a personal viewpoint."

"Touché," Raine said, with forced lightness.

"Rory, I mean Raine." Beth corrected herself because she knew that Raine, not Rory, would be publishing the article. "When you say nasty things about Darlington, you're talking about real people. You're writing about Lindsay and Mrs. Anthony, of course, but you're writing about Tyler and your family and me, too. I'm not asking you to lie, but I hope you think about who your words affect."

Beth wanted to say more. She wanted to beg Rory to open her eyes to all the people who cared about her. Mostly, though, she wanted to tell Rory to stop viewing her as some caricature that she could easily put into a box marked *townie*, *good girl*, or *closeted* and see her as a real woman with her own hopes and desires.

Instead, she left her to her work.

CHAPTER ELEVEN

September 18

Raine wished she'd put on a long-sleeved shirt before she walked down to the college baseball fields in the chilly evening air. She had spent all week working up the nerve to attend this last game of the season, which was likely to draw a big crowd, but she didn't want to let Beth down by missing every single game.

Still, her nerves kept her from arriving on time. She hoped to go unnoticed and stand off to the side of the bleachers, but Chris and Tyler saw her and shouted over the crowd for her to join them.

Raine appreciated the warm welcome in what she worried was an unfriendly crowd, but she wished they would be more subtle. They immediately began to introduce her to a few of the people around them. "And I believe you know this hoodlum," Chris said, grabbing a guy by the shirt sleeve and tugging him around to face them. "He's your spitting image."

Raine smiled at her little brother. "Hey, Davey. Who're you here to see?"

"Your girlfriend, the kindergarten teacher, right?" Tyler asked. "When you going to get a ring on her finger?"

"I'm working on it," Davey mumbled at his feet, a shy habit he'd had since he was a boy.

"Really?" Raine was shocked. Wasn't Davey too young to get married, and to a woman she'd never met? She'd lost track of a lot of things since leaving town, but for some reason this one hit her hard.

"I need to put a little more money away, but she's a nice girl, Rory. You'd like her if you ever met her."

"I'd like to, Davey," Raine said, and seeing the doubt in his eyes, added, "Why don't you bring her to dinner sometime?"

"You weren't at dinner this week," Davey said flatly, looking away again.

Chris and Tyler stepped away when the conversation turned to family matters. "I meant to come by."

"Sure you did."

Davey had seen through her lie, but she didn't know what else to say. He didn't seem interested in her being there anyway. He had no idea what it was like for her to be in that house. "I don't expect you to understand."

"No, you never did," Davey said quietly, his jaw clenched. "You didn't even try to explain. Maybe you didn't trust me enough, or maybe you didn't care what I thought."

Where'd he gotten those ideas? Her parents must have brainwashed him. "Davey, you don't know what you're saying. You don't know what happened."

"That's right, Rory. I don't have any idea what happened. I woke up one morning and you were gone. Then ten years later you come back the same way, with no explanation. I assume you'll leave again someday without telling me why then either."

He hadn't raised his voice, and he still hadn't looked at her, which made the exchange all the more exasperating. This was her little brother. She'd been his protector, his playmate, his best friend, and she'd left him without a word.

She could've handled his anger. Anger was her go-to emotion, what she felt when she remembered the night she left, but she didn't do well with hurt, and that's what Davey was expressing. He obviously felt betrayed also. Raine stared at him, unable to convey the confusion, frustration, and regret that overwhelmed her.

"I promise I'll be at dinner next Sunday," she said. It wasn't enough, but it was all she could offer right now. Repairing her relationship with her brother would take time, but she wanted to make the first step.

She didn't have anything else to say, at least nothing she could say at a softball game surrounded by half the town. Davey just nodded and left Raine to think about how far her life had diverged from the path she would have chosen for herself.

❖

Beth watched from second base as Rory and Davey talked. At least she thought they were talking, but Davey wasn't looking at his sister. Rory moved her lips occasionally, and the dejected expressions on both of their faces indicated a serious conversation, not baseball banter. Whatever wounds were being reopened in the St. James family were likely deep and not quickly mended. When Davey walked away, Raine stared blankly at the field. Tyler and Chris must have read her mood too, because neither of them rejoined her.

Beth wished she could be there with her. Rory and her brother had always been close as kids. Their distance now had to be affecting her. Her proud posture sagged, and the corners of her mouth drooped into a frown. If the external effect was so clear to Beth, even from that great a distance, then surely the emotional damage must be strong.

Beth wanted to hold Rory and tell her everything would get better, even though she wasn't sure that was true. Rory was proud and defiant, and she still let her anger overwhelm her. Beth wasn't certain that, if pushed, Rory wouldn't make the same impulsive decisions she'd made at eighteen. Still, she was capable of so much more.

She was tender when she worked with her students, sensitive when she'd stuck up for Beth in the country, and when she relaxed her defenses, she revealed that old inner light that had been hidden but not extinguished. Beth was drawn to that side of Rory, which was why she quietly left the dugout between innings.

"I was wondering if you'd make it to one of these games." Beth folded her arms along the top of the fence, so close to Rory that their shoulders touched.

"Better late than never, right?"

"Absolutely. Everybody has to deal with things in their own time." Beth hoped Rory recognized that her message applied to more than a softball game.

Rory nodded. "Some of us need longer than others."

"That's okay, as long as you keep at it."

"Why do I get the feeling that we aren't talking about attending softball games anymore?"

Beth smiled and threw her arm around Rory's shoulders, giving her a little squeeze. "My father used to say that baseball is a metaphor for life."

Rory smiled, and this time her dimples appeared. "You'd better get back to your game."

Beth jogged onto the field with her team, but her mind was still with Rory, who had leaned casually against the fence, her long frame stretched beneath her. She was striking, her body nearly flawless, and her expression had softened to one of guarded amusement. Her outward appearance gave no indication of her inner troubles.

At times she could be so cocky and defiant that nothing seemed to be able to touch her. Then in an instant she'd transform into the scared, wounded teenager who had run away from home. Other times, Beth glimpsed the old Rory at the most unexpected moments. It must be exhausting to have three distinctly different personalities warring within her.

The crack of the bat brought Beth's mind back to the game, but only long enough for her to watch the ball sail into right field, where it was caught and lobbed back to the pitcher. She would've welcomed a chance to display her athleticism for Rory. Instead she had to stifle the urge to wave to her. She'd already been invasive enough by going out to see her.

Rory needed to be handled carefully. She was proud and stubborn and a little dangerous. Beth reminded herself that Rory hadn't asked for her help, and aside from her comment about missing her last weekend she hadn't indicated that she wanted company. Beth was risking a lot even to be seen with her.

She forced herself to look away from Rory, scanning the crowd in the bleachers behind the batter, and noticed Kelly sitting in the second row.

Oh, no, she probably saw me hug Rory. It hadn't occurred to her that Kelly would attend the game. She'd already been to two of them early in the season, and she didn't like to show up at too many of Beth's events for fear that it would raise suspicions. Now it appeared that she had some suspicions of her own. She was scowling at Rory. Kelly had surely noticed where Beth was focusing her attention.

This would require a lot of explaining, but how could she tell her closeted girlfriend that she was hugging the town's only out-and-proud lesbian because she felt an irresistible urge to ease her pain? Even if Kelly were willing to hear her out, she wasn't likely to understand something that Beth herself couldn't completely comprehend.

After the game, Tyler and Chris pushed Raine toward the dugout, where they corralled Beth the moment she exited the playing field. She was wearing sweatpants and her uniform T-shirt, her dark curls pulled back in a ponytail. She seemed younger than she did in her work clothes, and yet the casual attire was somehow sexy, or maybe it was the way the flush of her cheeks offset the blue in her eyes.

Either way, Raine had a hard time appearing as though her close proximity wasn't affecting her the same way it had earlier when Beth pulled her close. The hug had been friendly and completely innocent, but she couldn't help the way she'd reacted to the feel of Beth's body pressed against hers. By the time Beth pulled away, Raine's sadness had disappeared. Now she was so aroused she could hardly remember why she'd been upset.

Standing across from Beth while she chatted with the boys, Raine forced herself to think about something other than Beth's body. Thankfully, Chris provided a more neutral topic. "I got four tickets to the Cardinals game next Friday, and we aren't taking no for an answer, Beth."

"I have to check my schedule. I'm not sure if I'm free."

"Sorry." Tyler shook his head. "We know you don't have a softball game, and we'll have you back Saturday, so you can't use the church choir as an excuse. Unless you give us the name of some hot date, we're dragging you to St. Louis with us."

Rory watched Beth try to come up with an excuse. She should step in and help her out, but she didn't understand Beth's discomfort until she noticed her glance quickly over her shoulder. Kelly stood a few yards behind them, pretending she wasn't watching the exchange. She was with another small group of people, and to the uninterested observer she'd appear as though she didn't realize Beth was there, but Raine knew otherwise. Kelly was turned slightly toward her and kept sneaking glances at her girlfriend when she didn't think anyone was watching.

As the guys kept pressuring Beth to go with them next weekend, Kelly's expression grew more agitated. Beth had obviously noticed too and tried to end the conversation by offering to let them know her plans no later than tomorrow afternoon.

She probably wanted the extra time to confer with her girlfriend, and while Raine would love to use this chance to piss off Kelly, she felt compelled to play peacemaker for Beth's sake. "Give her till tomorrow. If she says no, we'll make plans to kidnap her like she did me."

Beth laughed, relief plainly visible on her face. "Thanks. I promise I'll call you then, but right now I need to go talk to some other people."

"Of course she does." Chris chuckled as she left. "Everyone in town will want to say hello to her before they head home."

That was true, but Raine also understood that Beth needed to speak to one person in particular right now, and the thought made her queasy. She didn't want to stay around and watch the awkward dance where Beth and Kelly tried to publicly acknowledge each other while simultaneously pretending they barely knew one another, so she told the guys good night and started back to her apartment.

How could Kelly be so hypocritical and why did Beth put up with Kelly treating her like a dirty little secret? Smart, beautiful, beloved Beth could do so much better than closeted Kelly. Raine might have to respect their right to make their own decisions, but she didn't have to agree with them. And she certainly didn't have to stick around and watch them together.

❖

Beth stopped and talked to several other people before she finally turned to Kelly. It always grated on her nerves that she had to play these games. She'd originally thought Kelly would eventually relax and become more comfortable in their relationship, but instead she'd grown more paranoid as the years passed and their friends began to get married. Now Beth was stuck making small talk with everyone but the one woman she really needed to communicate with.

When the crowd had dissipated enough that Beth could approach Kelly, she noticed that Kelly was already leaving. Was she supposed to follow Kelly, or was Kelly purposely ignoring her? She never knew in these situations, but she decided that it was better for her to try and be rebuffed than to let Kelly go. She had to jog to catch up with her, and when she finally did, Kelly didn't even look up. "I'm glad you came to the game."

"That's not what it seemed like to me." Kelly kept walking. "How was Rory?"

Beth caught her breath. She expected Kelly to be upset, but she wasn't prepared to jump right into unpleasant topics. "I know you don't like her, but she's having a hard time adjusting to being back here."

"Of course she is. She shouldn't be here. She's not like us, Beth. She's not happy unless she's causing trouble."

"I wish you'd stop thinking of her like that. She's had some problems, but she's not a troublemaker," Beth said as they got to Kelly's car, one of the few left in the grassy lot.

Kelly finally looked at Beth. "Whether she means to or not isn't important. She *is* causing trouble between us, and I don't like it."

"What do you mean?"

"God, Beth, do you think I'm blind? My girlfriend is hugging a well-known dyke in front of half the town. Am I not supposed to notice that?" Kelly started to raise her voice but then seemed to remember that they were in public and regained control. "Even if I did ignore the way she watches you, the rest of the town won't. Why don't you see that as a problem?"

"It doesn't have to be a problem if you don't let it get to you. She's a friend. You're my lover." Beth took Kelly's hand and began to lift it to her lips before she registered the shock on Kelly's face.

"What are you doing?" Kelly pulled away and glanced around her, fear and tension stiffening her posture. "This is exactly what I'm talking about. She's getting to you."

Beth shook her head. "No, you were getting to me. Forgive me for wanting to reassure you. I thought you were concerned about our relationship. I forgot that everything comes second to your reputation."

"That sounds like something Rory would say."

"Well, maybe Rory's right about a few things." Beth held up her hands to cut off any further response. She wasn't about to have a fight with her in a ball-field parking lot. "Let's not do this here. Will you please come over tonight?"

"No," Kelly said resolutely as she got into her car, leaving the door open enough to finish their conversation. "We've already become too suspect after your little public display of affection for Rory tonight. I'll call this week sometime and we can talk about it then. Maybe I'll see you next Friday."

"Maybe?" Beth's head spun with the realization that Kelly was once again grounding her for associating with Rory, but this time she wasn't interested in sitting home waiting for Kelly to forgive her. "Kelly, you take your time to sort out whatever you need to sort out, but don't expect me to be waiting by the phone."

With that, she shut Kelly's car door. As soon as she was in her own driver's seat, she flipped open her cell phone and dialed Tyler's number. "Ty, I'm in for next Friday."

She was tired of always being understanding and accommodating for a girlfriend who wasn't interested in returning the favor.

CHAPTER TWELVE

September 25

Raine laughed at the snappy banter from the students who filled her apartment. She'd offered her place as an option for the GLBT Student Association to hold their board meetings. The students were eager to get out of the loud cafeteria, and Raine enjoyed having company in her otherwise silent living quarters. She was in her bedroom now, packing for her trip to St. Louis, but she could still hear the students discussing which gay film to show at the GLBT movie night next week. The gay guys wanted *Hairspray*, but the lesbians were pushing hard for *Bound*.

"The mafia is so overdone," one of the boys said.

"Singing queens aren't?" one of the girls shot back.

"That's a massive stereotype."

"But the lesbian handywoman in her wifebeater T-shirt is a fresh new view of the issues?"

Raine didn't usually jump in on these conversations. Despite the students' cattiness, they always worked their differences out. They were a great group, and while there weren't many queer students on campus, the ones who were out were active. Even some straight students attended meetings on a regular basis to support their gay friends. Raine found them all refreshing, and their energetic attitude toward life was a nice break from her own troubled musings about Darlington. They were so comfortable with themselves and their surroundings that Raine was envious at times.

"Lesbians hate musicals."

"Now who's stereotyping?"

Raine laughed as she dragged her duffel bag into the living room. "How about a truce?"

The students turned to her expectantly and she gave them her one-word answer. "*Rent*."

"It's got lesbians," one of the guys said, "and gays, and trans folks, and straight people."

"And it's a musical," Raine said to the boys. "Not all lesbians hate them."

"You're not a lesbian, Raine. You transcend labels." One of the boys feigned a swoon.

Raine gave him a gentle shove. The students liked to joke about having a celebrity in their midst, and she'd be lying if she said she didn't love such comments. It was nice to have someone recognize her public persona since Patty was gone. The GLBT kids always boosted her ego.

"Now get out of my apartment. I've got a hot date with the St. Louis Cardinals tonight."

Only three of the six students approved her announcement. The others were either Cubs fans or had no idea what sport she was talking about. She walked them out, threw her overnight bag into the trunk of her car, and headed for the library.

Beth was waiting for her in the parking lot. She had on a white turtleneck under a red Cardinals T-shirt. Her dark ponytail was threaded through the back of a baseball cap, and her blue eyes sparkled beneath the bill. She would've been unbearably cute except that her dark blue jeans hugged her hips and thighs, adding a decidedly sexy touch to the sporty ensemble.

Raine was still surprised that Beth had agreed to go on the trip. After her and Kelly's behavior at last week's softball game, Raine was sure Beth would have some making up to do. When Chris called to say Beth would be joining them, he joked that her hot date must've disappointed her, which was probably truer than he knew.

While Raine was sorry that Beth had such a terrible girlfriend, Kelly's loss was her gain. They planned to meet the guys in St. Louis and stay the night. She couldn't wait to spend time with Beth outside of Darlington, and she was eager to see if her good-girl persona would hold true in the big city.

"Hey, you," Beth said, tossing her bags into the backseat and getting in beside Raine. "Ready for some Cardinals baseball?"

"I've been ready all week." Raine pulled off campus onto the state highway that led away from Darlington. She hadn't been out of town in six weeks, and her burdens lightened as soon as she passed that stupid city-limits sign.

"Thanks for driving," Beth said. "I'm terrified of driving in the city. I even hate it on the interstate."

"A lot of people around here are like that. My parents are afraid of the city too." Raine shrugged. "Maybe that's why I loved my early days of zipping around Chicago. There's something liberating about facing your parents' worst fears and surviving. It frees you up to believe they were wrong about other things too."

"Your parents were wrong about a lot of things," Beth said quietly.

"Yeah, they were. They told me I'd never make it if people knew I was gay. I've been proving them wrong ever since." Raine was both proud and sad about that fact. "But that's not good road-trip talk. Why don't you tell me what changed your mind about coming with us?"

"That's not good road-trip conversation either."

"I doubt that. Seems that you've got woman troubles, which is the perfect reason to get away. Distance offers perspective."

Beth smiled weakly. "We aren't going far enough to get the perspective I need."

"We'll be in this car for over an hour, and we have to talk about something. Why don't we take turns? I'll tell you about my last significant relationship, and then you tell me about yours." Without waiting for Beth to agree, Raine began to talk about Ali Suppan, starting with when they'd met at a HRC fund-raiser and ending with her leaving because Raine was poor and boring.

"I have a hard time believing anyone could find you boring."

"Well, I am." Raine laughed. "Women want Raine St. James to be exciting, dangerous, and controversial. They want to be seen on my arm at all the big events. They expect me to always have something witty to say. They want to date a celebrity, and they always end up disappointed when I don't live up to my reputation."

Raine wasn't sure where her tirade had come from. It was true and she'd known it for some time now, but she'd never told anyone. Beth's silence seemed to indicate that the blunt summation had surprised her too.

Finally, Beth squeezed Raine's hand. "Perhaps you should stop dating girls who're only interested in Raine and focus on ones who'd be better suited to Rory."

Raine's throat went dry as Beth lightly caressed her hand. Her smooth skin, paired with Beth's intimate tone, nearly clouded over the fact that Beth was suggesting that Raine should go back to being Rory.

"None of the women I know would've given me a second glance back when I was Rory, and I don't blame them."

"I do. Everything good about Raine stems from Rory. She may not have been as fancy or as polished, and she certainly wasn't as angry. But your charisma, your exuberance, your defiance, your sense of humor were all there before Raine came along. You might not have been able to see it, but I did, and so did everyone else who knew you as Rory."

Beth spoke so confidently that Raine didn't dare challenge her. She was eager to let this conversation drop and just focus on the feel of Beth's hand on her own. Why were they ruining the moment by talking about something she didn't want to think about? She'd spent ten years teaching herself to be Raine so she'd feel confident in who she was and how people saw her. She didn't want to hear that some people liked Rory better.

"It's your turn now," Raine said after a moment. "How'd you and Kelly hook up?"

Beth inhaled a breath and released it slowly. She probably hadn't told many people this story, if she'd ever told it at all, so Raine remained quiet and let Beth gather herself.

"When my parents died while I was in college, I was lost without them. I could hardly get out of bed in the morning, much less focus on their wills, the deeds to the farm, and all the inheritance taxes. I was a mess, and while everyone in town was so supportive, I didn't even know how to start executing my parents' last wishes. I worked with Kelly's dad. He was my accountant and helped handle some of the financial stuff, but I was a basket case, and I took up a lot of his time.

"I was almost ready to give up when Kelly stepped in. She wasn't a CPA yet, but she knew enough to get me through the initial stages of inheriting and selling the farm. She would come over a few nights a week to check on me, and eventually we talked less about the farm and more about ourselves. We became friends. She helped me through the hardest time of my life."

"When did you start going out?"

"It didn't happen all at once. We were each other's firsts, and neither of us was completely sure what we were doing. And Kelly was always afraid of being found out. It was a year before we actually slept together."

"*Kelly* was afraid of being found out? I thought you wanted to remain closeted too."

"I worried about betraying the people in town who'd been so good to me. I wanted to live up to the kindness they'd shown me, but I was also falling in love for the first time. It was hard to hide those feelings, especially after the pain and grief of losing my parents."

Raine was angry again. Kelly had killed Beth's desire to share something so pure as her first love, and the town of Darlington had made her feel like she had to choose between being cared for and being herself. "You've lived like that all these years?"

"I didn't intend to. I thought things would get better, that she'd come around, but instead I've become more like her. Hiding is almost second nature to me. It used to bother me that she never stayed the night, but I rarely think about it now."

"She doesn't stay the night?" Raine was so appalled she barely kept the car from swerving off the road. "I'm not perfect. I've had a few one-night stands, but I always stick around until morning."

"It's not that she doesn't want to," Beth said defensively.

"She just wants to protect her own ass more."

"You don't understand what it's like."

"You're right." Raine let out a bitter laugh. "I have no idea what it's like to lie about the most important person in my life, and I hope I never do. If I ever fall in love, I'll want the whole world to know it."

"Some of us don't need public declarations to feel validated."

"That doesn't mean you don't deserve them, Beth."

Raine thought she detected a tremble in Beth's hand that still rested on hers, but when she tried to meet Beth's eyes, she looked away. "Can we talk about something else, please?"

"Sure." Raine shrugged. The topic upset her as much as it did Beth, and she didn't want to think about what that meant. "Who's your favorite Cardinal of all time?"

Beth smiled. "Stan Musial."

Raine let the baseball talk lift her spirits, but the sadness she sensed in Beth's account of falling in love only to have that joy overshadowed by fear and paranoia would haunt her for a long time. Someone ought to thrash Kelly for putting Beth through that turmoil and shake Beth for letting her.

❖

Beth and Rory arrived early enough to check into their hotel room and walk down to the new Busch Stadium. Rory had never been there and wanted to explore a little before they met Chris and Tyler. As they stepped out of the shadows of the concourse into the sunlight of the stands, Rory abruptly stopped at the breathtaking view. "I've really missed this," she said.

"There's nothing like your home field." Beth was giddy at the pure enjoyment on Rory's face. The view from where they stood was beautiful, but not because of the brilliant green of the grass or the red dirt of the infield. The most striking part was the woman standing next to her.

Rory's eyes were greener than the grass and the natural highlights of her chestnut hair more perfectly toned than the clay. The intricate lines of the stadium's architecture were dull compared to the fine details of Rory's dimples. Beth had always considered the ball field one of the prettiest sights she'd ever seen, but with Rory in the picture, she had no doubt which was the greater work of art.

"Come on. Let's get closer to the field. I want to watch batting practice," Rory said. In one fluid motion she took Beth's hand and turned them toward home plate. They wound their way between other bystanders and around the seats. Beth was amazed that she didn't bump into anything, because she was focused exclusively on the fact that she was holding hands with a sexy, charismatic woman in the middle of a crowd.

The connection probably meant nothing to Rory, who had a childlike exuberance about their surroundings, but Beth couldn't think about anything else. Even when they reached the edge of the field and Rory began to chatter about which players had the best swing, all Beth could think about was the strong fingers that encompassed hers. Rory's skin was softer than she'd expected, and warmer too, or maybe that was the warmth of her own arousal because it was spreading throughout Beth's body now.

She couldn't believe Rory hadn't noticed the physical contact, but that only heightened Beth's awareness of their differences. Rory took casual contact like holding hands for granted. She didn't consider who might be watching or what they might think. For Beth, though, the simple act of enjoying the way Rory absentmindedly ran her thumb gently across the top of her hand, without regard to where they were, was terrifying and liberating, not to mention completely foreign.

"Hey, pretty ladies, can we buy you a drink?" someone called from behind them, and Beth pivoted to see Chris and Tyler coming toward them from the upper concourse. Instinctively she dropped Rory's hand and stepped away.

Only when the connection was broken did Rory seem to notice it had ever existed. She looked down at Beth's hand and then up at her eyes, an unspoken question accompanying her frown. Then with a slight nod, she turned completely away from Beth to face the guys.

"Hey, guys, great day for a ballgame." Rory put on a smile, though this one didn't show her dimples and the spark in her eyes had faded. "Bright sun, the wind's blowing out, and plenty of girls in the outfield bleachers." The transformation was complete. Rory had once again been engulfed by Raine.

"Damn right," Chris said, failing to notice anything wrong, but Beth knew her withdrawal had caused Rory's. She justified her reaction in a number of ways. The guys' arrival had startled her, her years of being closeted made hiding second nature, and most importantly, she had a girlfriend and shouldn't be holding hands with anyone else. But deep down she was sure that she'd let her own fear ruin a beautiful moment.

Raine sat forward with her elbows on her knees, soaking up the expanse of the new Busch Stadium before her. It was the bottom half of the ninth and the Cardinals were down by two. Even as she struggled to fight off the melancholy that had threatened to overtake her since before the game, she was struck by her surroundings. She loved this place, and she loved this game. A collective energy in the ballpark was concentrated on the field, and Raine could practically feel the vibrations from all the good will being emitted around her. It had overwhelmed her the minute she arrived.

Perhaps that was why she'd allowed herself to cross a line with Beth. She'd become swept up in the excitement and the thrill of sharing it with someone she thought felt the same way. Reaching out to Beth to strengthen their emotional connection with a physical one felt natural, and for those few minutes, everything was perfect. They were away from Darlington, away from Kelly, away from fear, and they were together. Or at least she thought so. But obviously Beth hadn't been able to find pleasure in the connection because she was too busy watching over her shoulder for any sign of danger.

Raine sat next to Beth for the entire game, but they spoke rarely. Raine was determined to enjoy the game, and Beth seemed equally determined to ignore what had happened between them as she sat quietly and concentrated on the playing field.

She was beautiful. Raine was getting used to admiring her, even if Beth was closeted, in a relationship, and weighed down by emotional baggage. Their brief hand-holding session had only reinforced Raine's suspicion that Beth's skin was as supple as it looked, and Raine wondered if the rest of her body would feel the same way.

Beth caught Raine watching her. "What are you thinking about?"

"I, um…" Raine feared that her expression would make it clear what she'd been thinking about, so she quickly turned back to the game. "I was admiring the new stadium."

If Beth saw through that cover-up, she gave no indication. "It is amazing, isn't it?"

They both clapped as a Cardinal hit a ball into short right field for a single. "I've seen a lot of ballparks in a lot of cities. None of them compare to our home field."

"How many other ballparks have you been to?"

"A lot. I try to see a game in every city I visit during the summer, and I've traveled a lot. Pittsburgh, Cincinnati, Milwaukee, Cleveland, and of course both of the Chicago stadiums." Raine would rather go to a ballgame than to a busy club or fancy reception, which had always irked her high-class girlfriends like Ali, since the fast crowd rarely appreciated the slow and deliberate beauty of the game. She considered Beth's earlier comments about Raine versus Rory. Was she really happier when Rory surfaced?

During a pause in the conversation, a cheer sounded for another Cardinal hit. "I've always wanted to see every major league ballpark. My father handed that dream down to me," Beth said.

"Yeah?" Raine glanced away from the game to study Beth, who was still facing the field, her blue eyes reflecting the vista before them. She rarely spoke of her parents, but their loss had profoundly altered Beth's worldview. "How many ballparks have you seen?"

"Just this one," Beth replied with a sad, sheepish smile. "This is as far away from home as I've been since my parents died."

"Beth…" Raine didn't know how to finish. She wanted to comfort Beth, to pull her close and soothe her, but she also wanted to shake her and yell that she had to stop hiding and start living.

The crowd's applause distracted her. The bases were loaded. She was still wrapped up in Beth, and she turned back to her to say so, but Beth was no longer looking at her. Along with forty-thousand other fans, Beth was now on her feet, her attention riveted on the man approaching the plate. It was the great slugger Albert Pujols.

The crowd went wild. As he stepped into the batter's box, the tension between Beth and Raine was transferred, or perhaps got sucked into, the tension of the game. Everyone around them had to feel it too. This man had the power to be a hero, to carry them all on the barrel of his bat and out into the night sky. He could also fail them, reveal himself as nothing more than a man, leaving them to contemplate their own shortcomings. There was no in between.

With the pitch, the crowd inhaled and held a collective breath. The crack of the bat caused them all to tense and rise on tiptoes, as if willing the ball to rise with them. Beth and Raine silently clutched each other's arm as the ball sailed into the night sky. A heartbeat passed and then another, the sound of silence echoing throughout the crowd until the ball cleared the outfield wall, leaving an explosive roar in its wake.

The magnitude of what they'd witnessed flooded the crowd, and Raine was swept away with them. A walk-off grand slam, the Holy Grail of baseball, and her excitement was too much to contain. Her disappointment at her earlier rejection forgotten, she threw her arms around Beth's waist and picked her up in a bear hug.

Beth must have been wrapped up in her own exuberance because this time she didn't pull away. She wrapped her arms around Raine's neck and hugged her fiercely. Their bodies came fully together—hips, stomachs, chests—and Raine felt Beth's hands holding the back of her head.

Having Beth's body pressed against hers jolted her senses. She had a woman in her arms, a beautiful, sexy woman. She was clutching

Beth tightly and being held in return. Suddenly the magnitude of the moment had nothing to do with baseball. As she set Beth down and steadied her with her hands at Beth's waist, Raine could feel the supple curve of her hips and the underside of Beth's breasts.

Beth's blue eyes were darker and deeper than Raine had ever seen them, their faces mere inches apart, and their bodies brushed lightly. It would be so easy to kiss her. In fact Raine found it hard not to, but even in such close proximity, her body begging her to acquiesce, Raine refused to cross the line. She had the strange sensation that she'd been careening toward this collision from the second she accepted the job in Darlington, that she was destined to lose this battle. She might have fallen right then if Chris hadn't thrown his arm around her from behind as the sound of his and Tyler's cheers broke the connection.

Raine pulled away as the reality of what she'd done sank in. That was Beth Devoroux she'd been holding. Sweet, alluring Beth, the one woman who could make her feel at ease even in the place that had filled her nightmares for years. Beth, who emboldened and frustrated her, who chose to remain closeted instead of fighting for herself and her relationship, who shared her bed and body with a woman who wouldn't be seen with her. Raine couldn't absorb the contradictions. How could a woman that felt so right be so wrong for her?

As the crowd began to move toward the exits, revelry echoing through the concourses of the stadium, Raine struggled to manage her emotions. She didn't get tangled up with women like Beth. She liked to be in control. She didn't fall for women with girlfriends, women in the closet, or women from Darlington. Ever since she'd returned to her hometown, she'd been out of her element, and it was starting to affect her judgment. She'd relaxed her standards, compromised her beliefs. Her worldview and sense of normalcy had been distorted. She had let Rory creep into her previously cherished identity as Raine.

She needed to get away from Beth before she said or did something they'd both regret. They needed distance between them, both literally and philosophically. Raine had to break her ties with

Beth before she let herself go one more step down the road they were on. She needed to get out, return to her own people, back to a place where she felt at home.

Thankfully, she knew just the spot.

❖

Once outside Busch Stadium, the guys immediately headed toward Laclede's Landing, a strip of raucous low-end bars along the Mississippi River. It was the go-to drinking spot after baseball games, and Beth knew that Chris and Tyler were headed for a steady descent into drunkenness. She wasn't eager to watch them make idiots of themselves.

She was tempted to go back to the hotel, but wasn't ready to be alone with her memories of Rory's hands clinging to her. The feel of Rory's body made her lose her sense of right and wrong. It disturbed her to get swept up in the moment like that. She'd never experienced that all-encompassing need to be close to someone. Even early in her relationship with Kelly, they'd been tempered in their responses to each other.

"Hey, guys," Rory said as they reached a street corner, "this is where I say good night."

"What?" Tyler asked. "You're not coming out with us?"

"Nope, I've had a great time, but a woman's gotta do what a woman's gotta do."

Beth was as surprised as the boys. She'd expected Rory to be immersed in her cavalier attitude and eager to soak up the big-city atmosphere.

"Where're you going?" Chris asked.

"The Central West End." Rory laughed at their confused expressions. "There's more to St. Louis than the riverfront. There're art house theaters and Indian restaurants, independent bookstores, and espresso bars."

"You're really not selling me on this," Tyler said, and scratched the stubble on his chin.

"You probably wouldn't like it," Rory said. "You guys go on and let me go my own way."

Beth had heard of the Central West End, though she'd never visited the gay neighborhood of St. Louis. Rory intended to get her gay fix and the rest of them weren't invited.

"I don't know," Chris said. "We want to hang out with you."

"We can hang out anytime. If I stay with you, your chances of getting lucky are much less than if you're on your own. If I'm in the room, all the women will flock to me."

Beth jumped in. "She's got a point. The two of us will cramp your style." She didn't plan to let Rory leave her with the guys.

"What?" they all asked at once.

"I'll go with Rory. It works out for all of us. You guys get to enjoy your evening without me in your way, and you don't have to worry about Rory being alone."

The guys seemed to agree, and Rory didn't object, though Beth could tell by the hard line of her jaw that she wasn't happy about the change in plans.

Beth had to jog to keep up with Rory's long, determined strides. At least the view from behind was an attractive one. *Did you just check out her butt?*

Beth didn't know what had come over her. First she was holding hands with a woman other than her girlfriend, then she got hot and bothered by a celebratory hug, and now she was checking out a woman's butt. Girlfriend or not, objectifying a woman like a piece of meat wasn't her style.

Once on the MetroLink, they rode in silence to the Central West End. Beth followed wordlessly when Rory exited. At first Beth thought Rory was being reflective, or perhaps a little miffed at the way she'd invited herself along, but now Beth was sure she was being ignored. They reached a bright and bustling intersection surrounded by restaurants and clubs. Rory paused, considering her options, then settled on a building with the sign COFFEE CARTEL overhead. Once inside, Beth finally broke the silence. "I didn't know you liked coffee."

"I don't, at least not the type of coffee you drink in Darlington," Rory said without looking at her as she stepped to the counter and addressed the barista. "I'll have two tall iced, skim caramel mochas."

The little dig registered with Beth, but she didn't let it bother her. She had no idea what a tall iced-whatever was, but if ordering it made Rory feel superior, then so be it.

Drinks in hand, Rory pointed Beth toward a table for two on the patio. When they sat down, she finally leveled her gaze at Beth. "What're you doing here?"

The gravity of the question settled on Beth, and she fought the urge to squirm under its weight. She'd wanted to see the Central West End and be included in the culture. She didn't want to go to Laclede's Landing. She could've listed plenty of reasons for following Rory, but the truest was the only one she couldn't bring herself to say. She'd simply wanted to be close to Rory. Instead, she gave a half-truth. "I've never been down here before."

"Why is that, Beth?" Raine asked, taking a sip of her coffee.

"I don't know."

"I think you've never been down here because it's where the lesbians hang out."

"I am a lesbian, you know," Beth said, with as much confidence as she could summon, though it was hard to form a coherent thought under the intense scrutiny of Rory's emerald eyes.

"You're not really," Raine said flatly. "I've been around you for over a month, and you've done nothing to indicate that you're a lesbian. You say you and Kelly are together, but I've never seen you two touch, or kiss, or even hug. No one knows you're dating. Even your best friends think you're straight. "

Was Beth hearing correctly? "Because I'm closeted, I'm not a real lesbian?"

"You can be a closeted homosexual, but *lesbian* is a cultural identity. It comes with a heritage of brave women who stood up for who and how they loved. They built communities, created art, fought for rights and respect. You do none of those things. You hide, you isolate yourself, and you disrespect the rest of us who're fighting by shying away from anything and everything remotely related to our lesbianism."

Beth had never been so offended. The idea that she was somehow less of a lesbian because she didn't flaunt her sexuality appalled her, and yet when she opened her mouth to object, she couldn't think of anything to say.

She wasn't used to being spoken to like that. Everyone she knew was polite and respectful, which was perhaps why she couldn't express herself now. Maybe the absurdity of Rory's attack had flabbergasted or angered her so much that she couldn't formulate a response. Either of those possibilities was better than the nagging suspicion that she couldn't rebuff Rory's accusations because they were, at least in part, true.

"Excuse me." A woman appeared at Rory's side and stood there shyly, gazing down at her. "Are you Raine St. James?"

Rory flashed her what Beth considered a very contrived smile. "Yes, I am."

"I heard you speak when I was in college. You were wonderful." The girl, who couldn't be much older than twenty, wore a short black skirt and a silver halter top, and every visible limb was as thin as a twig. "Me and my friends are going to Kinney's across the street. Can I buy you a drink?"

"Absolutely. Give me a minute to finish up with my friend, and I'll meet you over there."

The girl seemed almost giddy as she sashayed across the street and into a nightclub.

"You see that?" Raine gave her a cocky grin. "That is a lesbian. She knows what she wants, and she doesn't care who knows it."

Raine rose and hailed a cab, then opening the door, she nodded for Beth, who was so shocked that she complied and started to get into the taxi. Only a flash of anger gave her the fortitude to face Rory and ask, "Is that what you want?"

"What?"

"You're blowing off the people who care about you and know you for who you really are to follow some twig into a bar. Are you sure that's what you want to do?"

"Yeah," Rory practically spat. "That's what I want."

"I don't think you know what you want. You expect people to accept you for who you are, and then you spend all your time trying to be someone you're not. You can go be Raine tonight. You can turn away from the people who've known you your whole life and who love you anyway. You can feel superior for drinking five-dollar coffee and making sure the world knows you're gay. You can go ahead and woo your little groupie to try and convince yourself that you're a superstar, but tomorrow you'll still be Rory and she'll be bored with you."

Rory pursed her lips. "Good night, Beth."

"Good night, Raine," Beth said through gritted teeth. "I'll see Rory in the morning."

Then she slammed the cab door. She couldn't believe she'd exploded, but Rory had pushed her too far. She tried to convince herself that she was justified in attacking her like that, but at the same time she worried she'd destroyed all the progress they'd made over the past few weeks. Maybe they were doomed for disaster from the start.

She'd hired Raine St. James, thinking she might find Rory underneath. Beth had been so sure a brilliant, lively, genuine woman was waiting behind all those practiced defenses, but now she wasn't sure. She'd believed Raine would always be Rory, but the woman who'd dismissed her now was most certainly all Raine. And if that was how she continued to behave, Beth wasn't interested in wasting another minute on her.

CHAPTER THIRTEEN

September 26

Raine stumbled as she entered the hotel lobby. It was five-thirty, and she was in the terrible stage between drunk and hung-over. The bars had closed hours ago, and she'd burned off her buzz by wandering around the city. She was tired, her head hurt, and sightseeing had lost its appeal, but she couldn't bring herself to enter the hotel room. She couldn't be in there with Beth in bed across the room from her. Not after the way they'd lashed out at each other.

Hurting Beth had required all of Raine's strength, mixed with a large dose of fear and frustration. She knew her remarks had stung. She'd even thought she'd seen Beth's eyes become misty with tears, and Raine's own heart had broken. She'd needed all her resolve not to cave and pull Beth into her arms, but she'd stayed steady and said the things she needed to say. She'd needed Beth to know the flirtation between them was over and that they would never agree on the way they lived their lives. She'd drawn a hard line, but they needed to return to their own realities.

Raine obviously wasn't the only one who needed to get some things out in the open, though. Beth had thrown back her own accusations with more venom and accuracy than Raine had thought her capable of. So she thought Raine was a fake, shallow, a snob?

The words hurt, and Raine had spent all night thinking about them. First she'd been angry. How dared Beth presume to know who she was or what she wanted out of life? She'd wanted badly to prove her wrong, to go into the bar and have the time of her life. She'd become even angrier when she couldn't get Beth's words out of her head. Even after three drinks and multiple dances with the woman she'd met on the street, Raine couldn't stop thinking of her as a groupie or a twig.

Then when she left the bar, she began to worry that if Beth had been right about the Twig, maybe she was right about Raine too. Was the woman she'd worked so hard to become just a sad cover for her real self?

She had experienced some disconcerting lapses into Rory since being back in Darlington. She had begun to enjoy her time with her old friends and found herself liking some aspects of small-town life. Even the irrational fears of confrontation had faded to the point that she was comfortable running day-to-day errands around town. Still, it was quite a stretch to assume that meant she should throw away her hard-won reputation and revert to being Rory. She had looped back around to being angry at Beth—who didn't know what she was talking about—only after an hour of wallowing in self-pity.

Still, it was probably best that Beth had also lost her temper. Maybe now she'd stop trying to be Raine's best friend and move on with her life. It would've been nice if they really could have been friends, but the memory of Beth's body against her own caused heat to spread through Raine, reminding her that it wasn't a good idea to think about their physical connection. Even though she felt terrible about hurting Beth, she'd done the right thing. Doubting her decision wouldn't do any good because neither of them could unspeak the words they'd said last night.

Raine slowly opened the door to the room she and Beth had checked in to the night before. She started to tip-toe over to her unopened duffel bag but stopped when she saw Beth sitting fully dressed in a chair across the room.

"Good morning." Beth rose from the chair. "I'd like to get on the road."

"Sure." Raine hadn't expected Beth to be awake. She hadn't known what to expect, but it could've been worse. Raine wanted get home and away from Beth. "You have to drive, though."

"You know I don't drive in the city."

A flash of condescension rose in Raine. This was exactly what she'd been talking about last night. Beth was small-town, small-time, and small-minded. "Grow up, Beth. Do you want to go home now or not?"

"I want to get out of here," Beth snapped.

"Well, I'm in no shape to drive." Raine tossed her the keys. "So you can either stay where you are or do something about it. The choice is yours."

Beth stared at her, her full red lips pursed in anger, but she grabbed the keys and stomped out of the room.

Once in the car, Beth gave her the silent treatment, or maybe she was focused on facing her fears. Either way Raine felt a slight pang of regret. She'd enjoyed their conversations in the car the day before, but now she desperately needed sleep. She lay back in her seat and closed her eyes, giving in to the physical and emotional exhaustion.

She didn't know how long she'd been asleep when she woke and noticed the car was stopped on the side of the road. Beth wasn't in the driver's seat. "What the hell?" she muttered, and checked her surroundings. They were parked on the side of the interstate with no signs of civilization in view.

When she finally turned around completely she noticed Beth sitting on the ground, her face in her hands. In front of her were the remnants of two weather-beaten wooden crosses. Raine's stomach roiled. She didn't have to see the faded names on the crosses to know they read John and Mayleen Devoroux.

"Fuck." Raine purposely knocked her head on the dashboard and her headache multiplied exponentially. She deserved it. She was officially the world's biggest asshole. She'd forced Beth to drive the same road her parents had been killed on and had made fun of her for not wanting to. She'd belittled her and bullied her into reopening a wound that was barely healed. She'd been a jerk to an amazing woman just because she'd turned her on the night before.

What the hell was she supposed to do now?

❖

Beth huddled in a ball, her knees drawn tightly to her chest. Her own thoughts had long ago drowned out the sounds of the passing cars. Her vision was blurry from the tears that threatened to fall, but there wasn't anything to see. Other than the faded crosses, nothing indicated that a crash had occurred here. The grass had returned long ago, the skid marks faded from the asphalt, and years of rain and snow had washed away the shards of broken glass. This was just a spot on the side of the road where a drunk driver crossed the line and ended the lives of a farmer and his wife.

She didn't know why she was here. She didn't feel her parents' presence. She felt closer to them at home, at church, or around their hometown, but lately those connections weren't enough to help her feel grounded. She missed her mom and dad all the time, but now she needed them more than ever. She was confused, frustrated, and lost.

She had a relationship with a woman she cared for but who didn't want to be seen with her. She was drawn to a woman she respected but who didn't respect her. She needed someone to confide in. She couldn't talk to Kelly. She was part of the problem. So was Rory. Miles wasn't someone she could bare her soul to, and none of her other friends knew she was gay. She needed someone who knew her, someone who loved her unconditionally. If only her parents were still alive.

But maybe they wouldn't have known she was gay either. She wasn't out to most of the people in her life. Perhaps she wouldn't have come out to them either. Beth rolled that idea around her mind. Would she have hidden something like that from them? Surely not. She and her mother had talked about everything, and her father had always been a great listener.

Kelly would've fought her since she wasn't out to her own parents, but Beth would have convinced her that her parents would understand. And she was almost certain they would have. They had been small-town people with little education who had probably never met a gay person, but they were good people who loved her. Still, she'd basically described Rory's parents too, and that coming-out story had yet to see a happy ending.

Beth had never really told anyone she was gay. She hadn't had to speak the words to Kelly, and she had an unspoken understanding with other gay faculty like Miles and Patty. Even when Rory came to town, Beth hadn't told her. She had figured it out on her own.

Nothing in Beth's own experience suggested she'd have come out to her parents, and yet she'd always assumed things would've been different if she could've told them. Would she have had the strength to say the words to the most important people in her life, even knowing the possible consequences? If she couldn't tell them, would they continue to be the most important people to her, or would they have joined the long line of people she kept at a polite distance?

The thought broke Beth's heart. Who had she become? If she'd asked that question a few months ago, she could have said she was a friend, a neighbor, a girlfriend, a librarian. Now she wondered what other words she should add. Coward? Fake? Liar? What if she managed to add lesbian to that list? Would she have to give up her other identities in order to fully claim that of lesbian? She'd lose friends, and she'd no doubt lose Kelly. Could she still be the good citizen she'd always tried to be? What about the people who'd given her so much over the years? Would they feel betrayed? And did that even matter?

Rory wouldn't think so. She couldn't understand why Beth didn't shout her sexual orientation every time she entered a room. It wasn't enough for her that Beth was trying to open up or that she'd gone against Kelly's wishes and strained their relationship. Rory didn't even care that Beth had gone to St. Louis and into a gay neighborhood with her. She didn't notice the way Beth lost the ability to control herself when she was in her arms.

In that moment when their bodies pressed together, Beth would've let Rory kiss her, and she would've kissed her back. Beth had shuddered at the flash of warmth that surged through her, but

Rory hadn't been fazed. Rory was so lost in her own self-preservation that she couldn't see past her demons. Where did that leave Beth, other than alone and crying on the side of the highway?

Beth couldn't handle the turmoil any longer. She wouldn't find answers here, but she'd run out of places to look. She covered her face and let tears of frustration fall.

She was so lost in her own unrest that she didn't notice Rory until she put an arm around her shoulders. *God, she feels good.* The thought was out before Beth could process where it had come from. She was upset and exhausted, and a strong, beautiful woman was there to hold her.

She rested her head on Rory's chest, soaking up her warmth and listening to her whispered shushing sounds. Rory offered the comfort she was seeking, and Beth wanted so badly to accept it. Her body begged her to give in and enjoy the moment with Rory, and this was most certainly Rory. Rory was kind, gentle, and intuitive. Beth wanted to enjoy her before she changed back into Raine.

Raine. That thought jolted Beth, giving her the energy she needed to push away and stand on her own.

"What?" Rory asked, surprise and confusion in her deep green eyes.

"It's you, Rory. You make me crazy."

"I'm sorry I made you drive."

Beth laughed. "You didn't make me drive. Raine did."

Rory stared at her as though she'd lost her mind and began to get to her feet slowly, as if she feared sudden movement might spark another outburst. "I *am* Raine."

"No, you're not. You're being sweet. Raine is self-centered. You're being introspective. Raine is brash. You're apologizing. Raine never apologizes for anything."

"I don't know what you want from me."

"Honestly, I don't know anymore either," Beth admitted. "You've done nothing but cause trouble for me since you got here. Every time I reach out to you, you put me down. Every time we get close, you withdraw. Every time I see something genuine, you hide it behind some façade you've created."

"I don't know what to tell you. I'm not Rory anymore. I'm not here to get in touch with my past. I like who I've become." Rory glanced away, as though she couldn't bring herself to look Beth in the eye. "And even if I didn't, I don't know why you'd care."

"Fine." Beth threw her hands up. "If that's really the case, I was wrong about you. From now on I'll leave you alone and focus on putting my own life back together."

She turned her back on Rory and got in the car. It was too hard to watch her close herself off, but obviously Beth couldn't stop her. She needed to move on. She'd been happy before Rory arrived, or at least content. Surely she could go back to the way things had been before, couldn't she?

❖

September 27

Raine was angry that she was back in Darlington. She was angry at Beth for picking fights with her, and she was angry that she was awake at five o'clock in the morning thinking about her. Who the hell was Beth Devoroux anyway? Beth didn't know her. She didn't understand what it was like to be thrown out of her own home. Beth had no idea what she was talking about when she continued to bring up Raine versus Rory. No one wanted her to be Rory—not her agent, not the women she dated, and certainly not Raine herself. Rory was a country girl. Raine was a hero. Rory was boring. Raine was exciting.

Well, maybe that wasn't completely true. She hadn't been exciting lately. Ali had accused her of being dull. It wasn't her fault that she liked baseball games more than the theater. The girlfriend before Ali had called her a fake when she found out that Raine preferred burgers to tabouli. And the woman before that? *Reba McEntire*. Raine chuckled at the memory of that fight. She'd wanted to go see Reba in concert when her ex had symphony tickets.

Raine paced around her bedroom, enjoying the cool hardwood floors under her bare feet. Maybe women didn't like Raine as much as she'd thought, or maybe they just didn't like the residual aspects of Rory that always popped up no matter how hard Raine tried to drown them. Except for Beth. She claimed to like Rory better. How could that be? Why would someone prefer the woman Raine had worked so hard to bury? Beth had it backward. This whole town was backward.

Raine tried not to think about Chris and Tyler, who had welcomed her without question. She didn't let her mind wander to her students or her colleagues, who accepted her without reservation. She especially didn't focus on Beth—the way she smiled, the way she looked in the moonlight, the pain in her eyes when they argued, or the way her body fit perfectly against her own.

She needed to pull herself together. Darlington was hell. She needed to remember that. She was a mess from being submerged in its small-town culture for too long. She had to stay focused on why she was here and what she needed to do to get out. She had to write her article.

The library wouldn't open until noon on a Sunday, but she could work all evening with no chance of running into Beth. She thought briefly of her promise to Davey, but didn't let herself dwell on it. The last thing she needed was to spend another Sunday dinner with her parents. They were almost as confusing as Beth. Still, she couldn't blow them off, so she grabbed the phone book and dialed Davey's number without regard to the time. He was a farmer, and they were always up before the sun.

"Hey, Davey," she said when he answered. "It's Raine. I mean Rory."

"What's wrong?" he asked suspiciously.

"Nothing. I'm going to have to miss dinner tonight."

"Jesus, Rory." Davey sighed. "I told Mom and Dad you'd be there."

"I'm sorry. I just can't make it tonight."

"When will you make it? Or do you plan to keep jerking them around, getting their hopes up and then destroying them all over again?"

"It's not that big a deal. They barely notice I'm there. They won't miss me."

"Pull your head out of your ass," Davey yelled. "If you paid attention to someone other than yourself for one minute, you'd see what you're doing to them. They walk on eggshells around you. You can't buzz in and out of our lives when it's convenient for you."

"Convenient for me? Do you think getting kicked out of my home at seventeen was convenient for me? You think I like feeling like a stranger in my own family? I'm the one on eggshells around them."

"If we're so damn awful, why don't you stay gone instead of hanging around and wrecking us all over again?"

"Fine," Raine shouted, and slammed the phone down only to pick it up again. This time she knew the number to dial.

"Leave me alone," a sleepy voice answered.

"Edmond, get me out of here."

"Raine?"

"Yes, it's Raine." Though she wasn't sure who she was at the moment. "You gotta get me out of this town."

"You signed a contract." He yawned.

"You're my agent. Get me out of it."

"I can't, and even if I could, what would you do?"

"I'll flip burgers."

Edmond snorted. "You're a craptastic cook."

"I don't care. This place is killing me, and apparently I'm destroying everyone's lives."

"Whose lives have you destroyed?"

"My parents', my brother's, Beth's—"

"I should've known there was a trick involved. Who's Beth?" She heard the sheets rustle and knew Edmond was sitting up.

"She's not a trick. She's this girl that I knew in high school. She's amazing and sweet, and she's such a closet case, and her girlfriend is a total douche bag." Raine felt her already high frustration level rise yet again.

"Are you sleeping with her?"

"No. It's not like that."

"Do you want to sleep with her?"

"No," Raine said, but her chest tightened at the images that ran through her mind, images of Beth and her beautiful curves and delicate skin pressing unrestricted against hers.

"So what's the problem?"

"The problem is I have to get out of here," Raine stated again.

"I'll see what I can do, but you'll have to wait awhile. Why don't I come visit for a weekend?"

Raine considered his offer. If she couldn't get out, at least Edmond might help her remember who she was. "Yeah, I'd like to see you, but you have to work on the contract too."

"I promise," he said calmly. "Now let's both get some sleep, okay?"

"Okay." She hung up, but between Davey's accusations about her family being nervous around her and the images of making love to Beth, she'd be awake all night.

CHAPTER FOURTEEN

October 4

Beth sat behind a podium to the right of the communion table. The church choir sang "Here I am, Lord," in the loft above her, and Beth hummed the familiar melody. She couldn't see the congregation from her vantage point, so she scanned the row of stained-glass windows opposite her seat.

They were beautifully intricate and well over a hundred years old. She'd seen them every Sunday for as long as she could remember, and she still noticed something new in them occasionally. As a child she'd searched the pictures for entertainment during the sermons. At her parents' funeral and the months afterward, she searched them to distract herself from the fact that she was there to worship a god who'd taken her family. Now searching was a comfortable habit in this quiet sanctuary away from conflict. The faces of saints and martyrs watched over her and offered messages of peace.

She needed peace. The last week had been an emotional minefield of wanting to apologize to Rory, or Kelly, or both of them while simultaneously feeling hurt and betrayed that neither of them recognized the position they'd put her in.

The choir finished its song and Beth rose to face the podium. She'd been the liturgist hundreds of times throughout her life, but she still trembled at the sight of the congregation turning their attention silently to her.

She cleared her throat. "A reading from the Gospel of St. Matthew. 'When the Pharisees heard…'" Beth read clearly the passage she'd practiced.

She took her task seriously. The Word was a gift from God, and she had been chosen to share it today. She might not be able to please Rory or Kelly, neither of whom had spoken to her since her trip to St. Louis last weekend, but she was up to the task before her now, and it was an important one. "'Thou shalt love the Lord thy God with all thy heart, and with all thy soul, and with all thy mind. This is the first great commandment. And the second is like unto it, Thou shalt love thy neighbor as thyself. On these two commandments hang all the law and the prophets.'"

The pastor rose behind the pulpit. He was a frail man in his late sixties whose white hair and wire-rimmed glasses made him resemble George Burns.

"Love the Lord," he said. "Folks, I hope you're here because you love the Lord." The congregation chuckled. "It's that second commandment we have trouble with. 'Love thy neighbor as thyself.' We certainly hear it enough. People say it, pray it, and cross-stitch it onto throw pillows, but do we ever stop to think about it?"

Beth didn't want to be boastful, but she liked to think she loved her neighbor. She liked to care for the sick, help in times of trouble, and be a good listener. She loved her neighbor to a fault at times, which was clearly evidenced by her disastrous attempts to help Rory.

"The commandment has two parts," the pastor continued. "Love of neighbor and love of self. I bet you've always been told to focus on the neighbor part."

Beth nodded as though he were speaking directly to her. She did focus on her neighbors. She worked selflessly for them. She sang in the choir, she worked at the soup kitchens, she dragged Raine out of her apartment, she hid large parts of her life to protect Kelly. Wasn't that what she was supposed to do? Wasn't that the Christian thing to do?

"We don't like to talk about love of self. For some reason it is seen as synonymous with self-absorption or egotism. But folks, if you do not love yourself, you cannot possibly love your neighbor the way God intends you to. You can't give what you do not possess."

Surely that didn't apply to her. She didn't hate herself. She wasn't depressed. She was happy with her life, mostly. She overextended her energies regularly, but always for people she cared about. She didn't abuse herself.

"If you're not fair to yourself, you cannot offer fairness to your neighbors. If you're not honest with yourself, you cannot deal honestly with others."

Okay, maybe he is talking to me. Beth was being unfair to herself by trying to please everyone but herself, but she didn't want to disappoint anyone. She was a pleaser, a peacemaker, though she hadn't made much peace with Rory or Kelly, and she certainly didn't feel very peaceful. And she wasn't completely honest with anyone. Not with Rory about her involvement in bringing her to Darlington. Not with Kelly about the time she'd spent with Rory, and she wasn't honest with anyone else about her sexual orientation. Did she need to be honest with herself about her own fears and desires before she could be honest with them?

"You can't give what you don't possess," the pastor reiterated.

When he put it like that, it seemed simple, but it would be anything but. Beth had spent a lifetime denying herself and fulfilling the needs of others. When it came to loving herself, she didn't know where to begin.

The pastor closed the sermon by quoting Jesus. "'On these commandments hang all the law and the prophets.'"

Oh, come on, Beth moaned internally. Nothing like piling on the pressure.

After the service almost everyone in the crowd of mingling parishioners greeted her. A few even invited her to join them for lunch at their home. She'd been a member of the church her entire life, and her fellow congregants had watched her grow up. They'd helped care for her when her parents died, and many of them played the role of surrogate family members. She loved them dearly, but today she had too much on her mind to visit with them.

She was tired and confused about her priorities. She needed some time and space to sort out her feelings. Even though she could have helped with some chores at the church, Beth got in her car and headed home, a small step toward showing herself the compassion she had always showed others.

❖

October 8

Raine was going stir-crazy again, and she still had a day and a half until Edmond arrived. She'd been able to focus on her new article for a week and had been extremely productive, stopping only to teach her classes and meet with the GLBT student group. Without Beth or her family interrupting, she'd scratched out a first draft, her own angst fueling her diatribes about self-hating gays and lesbians. She'd used existing models of identity development to paint such people as stunted and unable to reach any level of self-actualization until they freed themselves from their limited worldview. It was a nice blend of sociology and memoir. She'd loved it at first. From the completion of her early draft she knew the article would be well received in her former circles. Now, though, on day eleven, she wasn't so sure.

She was starting to regret her fight with Davey. She'd broken her promise to attend family dinners, so he had a right to be angry. He simply didn't understand what their parents had done to her. He didn't know what it was like to have to choose between being true to himself or his family's values. He'd obviously misread their parents' discomfort for fear. Why would they fear upsetting her? They'd done nothing to stop her from leaving the first time. They wouldn't care if she disappeared again.

Then there was Beth. How had things gone so wrong with her? One minute they were laughing and sharing a real connection; then all those feelings surfaced. The attraction that resulted from her touch, the confusion at her reactions, the anger they'd directed at each other— none of it made sense.

Beth had been a pest since Raine arrived in Darlington, like she was on some mission to prove Raine was welcome there. On some level Raine resented the intrusions into her life, but she'd also come to expect them, maybe even welcome Beth's company. Why did she have to go and muck it all up by falling for her?

Wait. She hadn't fallen for Beth. She'd simply enjoyed having her around. She was a friend, and it wasn't unusual for friendship to be misinterpreted as attraction, especially with a friend as beautiful as Beth. Everything about her was stunning, from her crystal blue eyes to her full hips and sexy curves. Yet if Raine was just lacking the physical, why didn't she go home with the Twig in St. Louis? She wasn't Beth, but she had her finer points too, and she came without all Beth's closeted, coupled, small-town baggage. Why wasn't she enough?

Raine's phone rang. It was the first call she'd received in a week, and she jumped up to answer it. She hadn't even said hello before she heard a barrage of voices in the background. "Scott's parents are coming to kidnap him," someone said from the other end of the line.

"What?" Raine tried to decode the message without any context.

"They found out he's gay and they're coming to get him. They think college made him queer. You have to stop them."

"Who is this?"

Another voice came on the line. "Raine, it's Scott. There's nothing you can do. I have to go with them. They're paying for college."

"Scott," Raine said slowly. The conversation began to make more sense as she recognized the voice of Scott Wainwright, one of her students and a member of the GLBT student group. "What happened?"

"My mom was cleaning my room and she found a letter from a boy. She freaked out and told my dad." The boy's voice was steady but thick; he was obviously on the verge of tears. "They think I fell in with a bad crowd at college and that I'm confused. They're making me come home."

Raine remembered how desperate and afraid she had felt when her parents found out about her. The emotions began to surge inside her, but she forced them down as she tried to logically consider her options. "When will they be here?"

"Soon."

"Stay in your room. I'm coming over. Have one of the others go to the library and tell Ms. Devoroux what's going on. Tell her to bring the PFLAG information."

"Raine, you can't do anything—"

"Maybe not, but we have to try." She hung up and grabbed a picture off her nightstand. She knew Scott was feeling lost, scared, angry, and betrayed because she still felt that way too, only she wasn't seventeen anymore.

❖

Raine was in a stare-down with Scott's father. Attempting to control her terror, she forced herself to notice the differences between him and her own father. He was shorter and his hair was light, though it was the same close-cut farmer's style her dad favored. His eyes were filled with a fury that she imagined was mirrored in her own. Anger was the dominant emotion in these situations, or maybe it trumped all the others.

Beth rounded the corner, a contingent of students clustered near her. Raine's tension level dropped, if only slightly. Beth was striking, her beautiful features etched with resolve as she rushed into the room.

"Beth Devoroux," Raine said as calmly as she could muster, "these are Scott's parents, Mr. and Mrs. Wainwright."

Beth stepped in and closed the door behind her, leaving the students waiting in the hall. She extended her hand to Mr. Wainwright, but he only stared at her coldly.

"I don't know what this is about. We didn't ask for a committee meeting. We're here to pick up our son."

Beth dropped her hand to her side. "I understand. If we could have a moment of your time, for Scott's sake?"

"No," Mrs. Wainwright said between sniffles. She was diminutive, her long dark hair streaked with gray and her dark eyes red-rimmed from crying. "You people can't have any more time with Scotty."

"I understand you're upset—"

"You don't understand any of this," Mr. Wainwright shouted. "How could you know what it's like to work every waking minute to provide for your kid, only to have him throw it all away? You don't know how that feels, do you?"

Beth stood still, as if frozen in fear, as she struggled to answer that question or respond to the anguish in this father's clenched fists and trembling jaw. Instead she opened and shut her mouth mutely.

"I didn't think so." He turned to open the door but stopped at the sound of crashing glass.

They both turned to Raine, who had slammed a picture frame onto Scott's desk. "I know what it feels like." Raine didn't know what had come over her. Maybe her memories of a night like this triggered her outrage. Or perhaps she saw her own fear reflected in Beth, which was even harder to watch in someone she cared about than to experience herself.

Raine squared her shoulders. "I know what it feels like to live your life trying to be what someone wants you to be. I know what it means to sacrifice yourself for someone you love, only to have them turn on you."

They all stared at her, even Scott, who'd previously been sitting on the edge of the bed with his head in his hands. Raine fumbled to free a faded photograph from the broken glass casing. "I was seventeen when my parents did to me what you're doing to Scott."

Mr. Wainwright refused to take the picture, but his wife stared at it, as did Beth, transfixed with the image of the young woman before them. It was Rory sitting on the side of a street, city traffic buzzing around her. She wore a pair of torn jeans and a denim jacket, her hands on her hips and her chin tilted upward in a show of defiance.

"My parents told me I wasn't gay. They told me I was confused and that they wouldn't let me go down that road."

"What did you do?" Scott's mother asked.

"I yelled at them for hours. I cried until I couldn't stand it anymore, and then I left." Raine took a breath and released it slowly. It still hurt to relive that experience, but if she could stop it from happening to someone else, she had to try. "I didn't see them again for ten years."

"Scott wouldn't turn his back on his family."

"You're turning your back on Scott," Raine answered quickly. "You're telling him that he's not good enough for you, that you won't love him for who he is."

"I love Scott more than my life," Mrs. Wainwright said. "I want him to be safe and happy. I want him to get married and have babies."

"We want him to be a good man," Mr. Wainwright added, "the man we raised him to be."

"An honest man? A brave man? A strong man?" Raine asked, but didn't wait for an answer. "He's all those things. It took honesty, courage, and a lot of strength for him to come out to you."

"He's throwing his life away. It's not easy for boys like that. I know what happens to them, what other men say and do to them." Mr. Wainwright's voice cracked. "He's my boy. It's my job to protect him."

"We have dreams for our son," Mrs. Wainwright said, laying a hand on her husband's shoulder. "We're scared to lose them."

"You don't have to let go of those dreams," Raine said gently. "Scott's smart and he's got a bright future ahead of him. Don't miss out on that. Don't make him choose between your love and his own dreams, or you'll lose him."

"Scott?" His father pleaded with his eyes.

"It's true, Dad." Scott finally stood, shakily. "I can't change who I am. If you make me leave here, I'll find another way. I'll do it on my own if I have to."

"I'm afraid, son. I don't know how to help you down this road." His father choked on his words, and Raine finally saw the fear he'd been hiding behind his anger.

Beth stepped forward, handing each of Scott's parents a PFLAG pamphlet. "A lot of people here can help Scott, and some people here can help you too. You can call this group, and you can call me anytime you have questions or concerns."

"You can call me too. I promise that none of you are alone in this," Raine said, still not able to relax completely even as she saw the anger drain from Mr. Wainwright's expression.

"I can't wrap my head around everything at once," Scott's mother said.

"You don't have to." Beth used a gentle tone with her. "You're seeing your son in a new way after an entire lifetime of getting to know him. Scott's had years to come to terms with who he is. You're allowed to take some time too."

Raine was struck by that image, the thought of a mother and father having to go through their own coming-out process. For the first time, she wondered what it would feel like to be on the other side of that relationship. Leave it to Beth to turn her way of thinking around. Raine was learning that she liked her view of the world when she saw it through Beth's eyes.

"It's okay to be scared," Scott said. "Just don't make me leave, okay?"

Mr. Wainwright nodded slowly. "You can stay."

Raine swayed under the weight of what they'd accomplished. She was relieved for Scott, but a new confusion engulfed her. Raine saw echoes of her own past differently because she had seen Scott's father's fear. She was emotionally and physically exhausted, but her night was far from over.

They didn't leave Scott and his parents until after dark. Beth waited while Rory stopped to assure the other students that everything was okay and that Scott would be staying at school. They were all in awe of Rory, and Beth could see why. Rory ran to their rescue and saved their friend. She'd been everything the legend of Raine St. James implied—strong, fierce, and defiant, but what had it cost her?

Could they see the worry lines etching their hero's face? Did they notice that she walked slowly, deliberately, like she had to summon her nearly depleted energy for every step she took? Her eyes had burned brightly as she stood toe-to-toe with Mr. Wainwright, but now they were empty and dark. Her skin paled without the flush of adrenaline. This was what people meant when they said someone looked dead on their feet. The spark had gone out of Rory, leaving only a shell of the earlier warrior.

"Hey," Beth said, her arm around Rory's waist as they crossed the quad. "You must be exhausted. Why don't you go get some rest?"

"Did you notice how scared he was?" Rory asked.

"Scott?"

"No, his dad," Rory replied with a shiver.

It was a cool night, but certainly not cold. The chill came from somewhere deep inside Rory, and Beth pulled her closer, attempting to ease it. But she shouldn't be around Rory, and she certainly shouldn't touch her, not if she was trying to gain clarity about her life. When she was close to her, all Beth could focus on was how good she felt. "You talked him down, Rory. It's fine. He'll be okay and so will Scott."

Rory nodded. "They're through the worst of it."

"You are too."

"Am I?" Rory laughed bitterly. "Or will I keep repeating nights like this until I get it right?"

Beth searched her emerald green eyes for answers to a clearly rhetorical question. This wasn't about Scott and his father, maybe had never been about them. "What do you need?"

"I need to stop doing the same things I've always done and expecting different results." Rory sighed. "It's time for me to grow up and accept responsibility for my future."

Beth wasn't sure what Rory meant, but Rory didn't make statements like that easily. She slowly stepped back and studied Rory. The spark was returning, as was her color, but something was different about her eyes this time. Her motivation wasn't anger or fear. It was purpose.

Rory quickly kissed her cheek. "Thank you."

Beth stifled a gasp at the powerful surge of pleasure that shot through her. "For what?"

"For last weekend, tonight, the future, for everything." Then Rory turned around and jogged toward the parking lot.

Beth raised her hand to the spot Rory's lips had brushed so lightly. Her heart raced as everything she'd seen, heard, and felt over the last few hours—fear, relief, confusion, and now excitement—washed over her.

Rory wasn't the only one who'd been inspired. Beth's own sense of purpose was growing inside her, and she needed to right a few wrongs of her own.

CHAPTER FIFTEEN

October 8

Raine pulled into her parents' driveway and took a deep breath before she got out of the car. She was taking a big chance. Either she'd misread a situation as a teenager or she was misinterpreting one now, and both possibilities held heavy consequences for her past and her future.

She walked around the house to the back door, the door she'd used as a child. It was a small step, but to her it signified that she belonged here instead of being a guest in her parents' home. As she started up the steps, the door opened and Davey came out. "What are you doing here?"

"I need to talk to Mama and Daddy."

"You sure that's a good idea?"

"Nope," Raine answered honestly, "but I've got to do it. Why don't you come too, so I only have to do this once?"

Davey hesitated only a second before he opened the door wide enough for her to enter, then called out, "Rory's here."

Their parents met them in the dining room. Her mother began to wring her hands and headed for the kitchen. "Rory, you look like you haven't slept in days. Let me fix you something to eat."

"No. Mama, I need to talk to you and Daddy. Davey too." Rory motioned for them to have a seat at the table, and when they did, she joined them.

"Is something wrong?" her father asked.

"Yes, sir." She nodded, but when she tried to elaborate, words failed her. She struggled to swallow the lump forming in her throat. She didn't know how or where to start. Perhaps she could talk about Scott and his family, but that would be missing the point. She needed to stop avoiding the issue.

However, years of self-preservation made it hard to admit her own fears and weaknesses. She couldn't even make eye contact with her family, so she focused on the way the grain in the wood table curved and faded, creating a haphazard pattern.

Finally, without meeting their eyes, she mumbled, "I've been thinking about everything we said to each other the night I left."

Her mother gasped. "You can't go back to that. We all spoke in anger."

"Yes and no," Raine said. "I was angry, and I think you were too, but mostly I was scared. I was afraid you didn't love me anymore and afraid that I couldn't make it on my own."

"We never stopped loving you, Rory," her mother said quietly.

"That would've been nice to hear ten years ago, or even two months ago when I got back to town."

"It's not easy to say when you've had your heart broken." Her father's voice was thick with emotion.

"I know it's not, and I know I haven't made it easy for you to talk to me, but I'm trying. It wasn't easy to come over here, but I did. I'm trying to understand your side. I need to know if I'm in this alone."

"You're not alone," Davey said quickly.

"Thanks, Davey." Raine nodded and turned back to her parents. "Can't you try to see where I'm coming from?"

Her mother answered. "I've been trying for ten years, Rory."

"I don't mean to be disrespectful, but I haven't seen that. You had to know I was in Chicago. You could've found me."

Her father hung his head. "We didn't know you wanted to be found. We thought you hated us. We made so many mistakes with you. Sometimes I think about how alone you must have felt. You went through everything on your own. How could you forgive us for that?"

Rory was shocked. Instead of hating and being ashamed of her, were they ashamed of themselves for letting her down? "But even when I got back to town, you could've talked to me. I was right here and you didn't say anything. You didn't ask me about my life, or if I was dating, or even if I was okay. You acted like I didn't matter."

"The last time we talked to you about those things, you left." Her mother began to cry. "We were so relieved that you were safe, and nearby, and speaking to us again that nothing else mattered. We didn't want to make the same mistake again, Rory. We didn't want to lose you a second time."

Tears streaked down her mother's face. As a teenager Raine couldn't imagine her parents being afraid of anything, certainly not her. Even a few weeks ago she would've laughed at the thought. Now Beth's accusations about turning her back on the people who knew her and loved her anyway hit home.

She had hidden her real feelings, her real self, and in turn she hadn't been able to see her parents for who they were. Now after opening up about her own pain, she could clearly see her mother's fear and anguish, mixed with deep regret.

"I'm here now, and I promise I won't storm out again, but I need you to open up too. No more forty-five-minute conversations about the weather."

The corners of her father's mouth turned up slightly. "You'll to have to be patient with us, Rory."

She nodded. "I know. Patience is something I need to work on, but I want to get to know you all again."

"And we want to get to know you too, the real you, Rory," Davey said.

The real Rory? Did she even exist anymore? Or maybe she'd never stopped existing. She'd just been waiting for a chance to emerge. She thought of Beth's comments about preferring Rory to Raine. Raine had run to Chicago and made a name for herself. Raine had cultivated anger and disillusionment into a full-time job. Raine had built a life behind an impenetrable façade of brash individuality. In other words, Raine had gotten her into this mess.

She was beginning to see why more than a few people were tired of Raine and ready to see more of Rory. Perhaps she was becoming one of them.

❖

Beth knocked firmly on Kelly's door and didn't even flinch when Kelly opened it and quickly looked past her to make sure none of her neighbors were watching. The motion reaffirmed Beth's reasons for being there. They hadn't seen each other in weeks, and Kelly was more concerned about what other people would think than why Beth stood there unannounced. Wordlessly, Kelly let Beth inside, then shut the door behind her. "Is something wrong?"

Beth searched the face of her lover. She was grasping for something, anything to hold on to, a hint of connection, a glimmer of understanding, the possibility of a future together. She found none. "Kelly, something's been wrong with us for a long time."

"What?" Kelly asked, clearly shocked.

"We're not going anywhere as a couple," Beth said. She didn't want to hurt Kelly. She'd loved her for a long time and part of her would always love her, but now Beth was learning to love herself too. "We want different things out of life."

"Where's this coming from? Is this about the softball game?"

"No," Beth said, then added, "not really. That was a symptom of a bigger problem. Neither of us is getting what we need from each other anymore."

"What do you think we need?"

"You need to feel safe, secure, and in control. I need to feel open and loved for who I am, not some perfect image people have of me."

"I do love you, Beth, I don't know what more you want."

"I want a future, Kelly, a future where I give myself the same consideration I give other people. Where I can say and do what I want to without worrying what someone else will think of me. I want to stop hiding and start living my life."

"You want to be with Rory," Kelly said flatly.

"What? No." Beth struggled to adjust to the sudden change in direction. "I didn't even mention Rory."

"You didn't have to. You sounded just like her."

"This isn't about Rory," Beth said, but was that the whole truth? She saw Rory with her green eyes burning brightly as she confronted Scott's parents, and she felt the gentle caress of Rory's lips against her cheek. Wasn't it Rory who'd first mentioned the future?

"You didn't feel this way until she came along, and you won't feel this way when she's gone." Kelly paced around the room. "And she will leave, Beth. She's using you while she's here, and then she'll disappear again and say God knows what about us all."

"She's not using me, and she's not the issue here."

"She's not?" Anger laced Kelly's words. "I've seen the way she looks at you, the way she stands a little too close, the way you two always find an excuse to be around each other."

"I don't know what you're talking about."

How did Rory look at her? They were friends, and sometimes less than that. Was Kelly lashing out or had Beth missed something? She shook her head, wishing she could wipe away her questions.

"It doesn't matter what Rory wants or does. This is about us, Kelly. This is about whether we have a future together."

"Of course we do." Kelly reached for Beth's hand and pulled her close. "We've spent eight wonderful years together. Nothing has to change."

"You're right. Nothing will ever change between us. We'll see each other twice a week and pretend we don't know each other the rest of the time. Don't you want more than that?"

"I don't know what you expect from me, Beth."

"Think about what a future with me will entail. Does it involve us ever living together? Will we ever have friends over, go out on dates, have babies? Or will we be eighty-five and sneaking around the nursing home?"

Kelly sunk down to the sofa, hanging her head. "You're asking me to choose between you and my friends, my family, my clients, my church, everything I've worked for."

Beth sat down next to Kelly and held her hand. It hurt to see Kelly so distraught. "I'm not asking you to choose. You can't give those things up for me. You have to make those decisions for yourself, the same way I have. I'm letting you go, Kel. I want you to be happy in whatever life you want. I hope you want the same for me."

"I do want you to be happy. I never wanted to hold you down, but I think you're making a mistake."

"You didn't hold me down. I was content to put everyone else before me. At least now if I make a mistake, it's my mistake."

"If you come out, there's no going back, Beth. You can't undo that. We'll never be together again, even if Rory does leave you."

"This isn't a decision I've made lightly, and it isn't about Rory. For the first time in a long time, I am doing what I want."

Kelly shook her head skeptically. "I don't believe that, but I don't seem to have much of a choice."

"I'm sorry you feel that way," Beth said, and kissed Kelly's forehead. "Good-bye, Kelly."

She didn't let the tears fall until she closed the front door behind her, and even then she didn't release the body-shaking sobs she'd cried at the loss of her parents, or even the steady stream of tears she'd shed on the side of the road two weeks earlier. She felt sadness for a past relationship and had bittersweet memories of a first love outgrown and love faded into platonic caring.

Beth had closed a door on part of her past and she mourned what could have been, but only for a moment before she focused on what she wanted next.

CHAPTER SIXTEEN

October 10

"Damn, it's good to see you." Raine hugged Edmond, then slapped him on the back before he had a chance to get through the door.

"Down, boi." Edmond laughed but hugged her back with equal ferocity. "I may have missed you a little bit too."

Raine let him set his bag down and surveyed him as he looked around her small apartment. He was pretty. There was no other word for it. His brown hair was short and spiked with highlighted tips. His flawless complexion was tanned—from a booth instead of actual exposure to the sun—but the tone set off his deep brown eyes. He hadn't changed since she left Chicago, but she couldn't get over seeing him in Darlington. He'd clearly tried to dress the part for his country vacation, but his jeans were designer and his brown button-down shirt still held the stiffness of the store hanger. His attempt to fit in would only make him stand out more against the brick and rust of her hometown.

"When does the tour begin?" he asked.

"There's no real tour. It's a two-room apartment."

"The tour of the town," he clarified. "I can't wait to see it."

"That's not a good idea," Raine said seriously. This wasn't what she'd had in mind. She wanted Edmond to get her mind off where she was, not force her to face it. "I thought we'd veg out, watch trashy movies, eat junk food. Look, I've finished my article for you."

"Not a chance." He shoved the article into his briefcase, then pulled her out the door. "I'm dying to see the place that made your career. I've taken ten percent of everything you've made off it, and I'm entitled to a proper look around."

By this point he'd dragged her halfway down the hall, so Raine relented. Maybe she could get the tour out of the way quickly and they'd be home before they ran into anyone.

"All right, this is the main drag," Raine said as they pulled onto the town square. "You loop around the square and then go down to the edge of town, turn around in the church parking lot, and come on back. We called it cruising, and we used to do it every weekend."

"Why?" Edmond asked, clearly intrigued.

"Because there's nothing else to do."

"So you'd drive around in circles all night?"

"I used to, yeah. Sometimes we'd sit in a parking lot and wait for someone else to stop and talk, then cruise with them for a while."

"Sounds enthralling."

"It's not, but it has a certain charm. There's no cost, no start time, no dress code. Everybody's out to have a good time with good friends and go wherever the night may lead."

Raine pointed to a large brick building. "There's the high school. And over there are the softball fields."

"Oy, what is it with you lesbos and softball? It's like the sport is catnip for you people."

Raine laughed. "If you don't get it, I can't explain it, but I was good in high school."

"I believe it. I bet you were the kind of dyke who barreled through players."

"Yeah, I got us into the playoffs like that." Raine smiled at the memory. "I got a big hit that game, but I was prouder of my base running. I went from second to home on a single down the line and the relay beat me to the plate, but I hit the catcher so hard she dropped the ball. I was the toast of the town that night."

Edmond eyed her suspiciously. "You never told me that."

Raine shrugged. She hadn't let herself relive her glory days until recently. It was hard to feel homesick if she focused only on the bad parts of home.

She turned onto a blacktop road heading out of town, though she didn't know why. Edmond wouldn't have known any different if she'd ended their tour at the city limits. She waved to an old man in a pickup as he passed them going the other direction, and he tipped his hat in return.

"Who was that?" Edmond asked excitedly.

"I don't know."

"Then why did you wave to him?"

"That's what you do here," Raine answered, though until that moment she hadn't realized she'd picked up the habit again. Everyone waved or nodded to each other in passing, and they made eye contact too.

It had been really disconcerting when she first arrived in Chicago and no one looked at each other when they passed on the street, but she learned that doing so added to her anonymity. When she got back to Darlington, she'd purposefully avoided the people she passed, but somewhere along the way she must've readjusted. She didn't even get nervous when she went to the store anymore.

She turned down a gravel road that wound between long rows of apple trees and rolled down the window to breathe in the crisp smells of autumn.

"Where are we?"

"This is an apple orchard. I used to work here in the fall."

Raine parked her Prius near a red barn that had been converted into a store. She smiled at an old man in overalls and work boots. "Hello, Mr. Hancock."

"Well, if it isn't little Rory all grown up." He threw an arm around her shoulders. "Your daddy told me you were teaching at the college."

"Yes, sir, and this is my friend, Edmond. He's come down from the city to see how we country folk live. I thought we'd pick a few apples."

"Well, you know where the sacks are. Go ahead and a pick a peck as a welcome-back present." He patted her gently on the back. "We're awfully glad you're home."

"Thank you." Raine smiled, knowing the old man didn't give away freebies often. His fruit was his livelihood, and times were tough for farmers in this part of the country.

She grabbed a small burlap sack and headed down a row of Gala trees. "These are the best for eating out of hand." She plucked an apple from the tree, smelling it briefly before she bit into it. The juice ran down her chin, and she laughed as she wiped it off with the back of her hand. "God, that's good."

Edmond watched her with an amused expression. "Country folk?"

"What?"

"Back there you said 'we country folk.' You wave to the strangers you used to be afraid of. Now you're tromping through the mud revealing your secret apple expertise. What gives?"

Raine laughed nervously. She hadn't realized she'd let her guard down. It was happening more often now. She was finding more of Rory and less of Raine, and she wasn't sure what that meant. But she was enjoying herself. "I don't know, Edmond. Don't you feel different out here? No traffic, fresh air, sunshine, and a whole lot of memories running free."

Edmond seemed skeptical. "For someone who hates this place, you sure have an abundance of good memories about it."

Raine was too surprised to answer. She ducked under a low-hanging branch and grabbed an apple. "Come on," she said, tossing it to Edmond. "We'll pick up some local cuisine on the way home. It'll be a real down-home experience for you."

The gray-haired woman working the register at the local watering hole and chili restaurant greeted her warmly. "Hey, Rory, it sure is good to see you. You know you're the spitting image of your daddy?"

"Yes, ma'am, I hear that a lot," Rory said, ignoring Edmond's raised eyebrows. "We'll have two large chilis and a super nacho to go." Raine stressed the last part of the order. She didn't want Edmond to sit in a place like this for too long. He was already getting loopy from the novelty of it all.

"What's a super nacho, and is it cooked in a room as dirty as this one?" he asked incredulously as he examined the peeling linoleum floors and the dingy wood-paneled walls.

"Shh. You wanted local flavor. This chili is a local delicacy. I ate it every week for the first seventeen years of my life, and I'm not dead yet."

He shrugged and looked around. "There's a guy checking me out."

"There is not," Raine said, without looking up from the ticket she was signing. "You're paranoid."

"No, he's coming over. Am I about to get gay bashed?" Edmond asked in a high-pitched whisper.

Raine grabbed the sack of to-go containers, but before she could turn around, someone grabbed her shoulder. "You'd best not be trying to sneak out of here with that," Chris said.

"Hey, Chris. Actually, we were just leaving." Raine tried to duck out from his hold on her.

"Not a chance, woman. We haven't seen you in weeks, and now that we've got you and Beth in the same place, there's no way we're letting you go."

"I don't mind staying," Edmond quickly interjected.

Raine let Chris take off with her food toward a table in the back of the bar. "Why do I keep letting you drag me into these things?"

She started to follow reluctantly, but Edmond stopped her a few yards from the table as his eyes fell on Beth. "Is that the Beth whose life you're ruining?"

"That'd be her," Rory confirmed out of the corner of her mouth.

"She's gorgeous." Edmond had a stereotypical gay man's fetish for all things feminine, and he was nearly swooning at the sight in front of him.

Beth was breathtaking as usual in jeans that hugged her subtle curves and a purple V-neck sweater that looked as soft as the swells beneath it had to be. Her hair was pulled back away from her face, and she flashed them a heartbreakingly sweet smile. "Yes, she is," Raine said, "and she has a girlfriend."

"Is that why you're not sleeping with her?"

"That, and she's as closeted as they come, so shut up about it."

They took their seats, and Raine introduced Chris, Tyler, and Beth to Edmond. She could tell he was pleased with their welcome and their curiosity about his role as her manager.

"So you're the one who got her to come back here?" Chris asked.

"I wrote the contract, but someone here asked for her to come. What was that woman's name?"

"It doesn't matter," Beth said. "You talked her into it."

"I suppose so."

"Then your drinks are on me tonight. It's about damn time she came home," Tyler said.

"You're the third person to say that in the last three hours," Edmond mused as Chris ordered them a round of beer. Raine stifled a laugh when Edmond swallowed his first swig and nearly sputtered it back out

"You okay, Ed?" Tyler asked.

"Yeah, just went down the wrong pipe." Edmond coughed. He had probably never had a beer before, and if he had, it certainly wasn't a Budweiser. He generally stuck to frillier drinks like cosmos or appletinis. *If he thinks that was rough, wait till he tastes the chili.*

"Where the hell have you two been?" Tyler asked Beth and Raine. "You disappeared after the ballgame and we haven't seen you for two weeks."

Raine shrugged and tried to act casual. She didn't want to bring up memories of her behavior after the ballgame or her reasons for hiding from Beth. She was ashamed of the way she'd acted, and she needed to tell Beth that. She needed to tell her a lot of things, actually, but now wasn't the time. "I was working."

"Working on who?" Chris chuckled at his own joke. "You got a woman somewhere we don't know about?"

"No." Raine involuntarily looked at Beth. "I haven't slept with anyone in months." Beth eyed her skeptically. She probably assumed Raine had spent the night with the Twig in St. Louis. What would she think if she knew Raine really spent all night trying to rid her memory of the way Beth's body felt pressed against her own?

Thankfully Edmond choked on the spice of his chili just then. He didn't try to contain himself this time. He blew out deep breaths like a woman in Lamaze class before downing half his beer. "God, that's hot."

The others stared at him in shock and Raine laughed. "You wanted local flavor, and the flavor here is spicy."

"You'll get used to it, Ed. You just need more of a chaser," Chris said kindly.

"That sounds great. This round's on me." Raine took the opportunity to stand up and bolt for the bar. She needed to move around, to put some space between her and Beth, and hopefully clear her head. She couldn't keep depending on someone else to change the subject whenever her attraction to Beth flared up. Beth had been good to her and she'd set clear boundaries. Raine needed to respect them.

❖

Edmond tried another bite of chili and this time followed it with a big swig of the beer Rory handed him. He gave them an obviously fake grin. He was clearly out of his element, and Beth felt sorry for him. The boys must have too, because they ignored his decidedly unmanly grimacing and turned their attention to her.

"So what's your excuse for ditching us?" Tyler asked. "And don't say work. Rory already used that excuse."

Beth sighed and stared down at her bowl of chili mac, wishing they'd focus on Edmond again. "I've been working some things out in my personal life."

"Uh-oh, sounds like guy trouble to me," Tyler said. "Do we need to go knock some sense into that secret boyfriend of yours?"

"No." Beth weighed her words carefully. She'd been playing this conversation over in her mind all day. She knew what she wanted to say. She'd been working up the courage to say it, but years of self-restraint were hard to unlearn. "There's no boyfriend, and there never has been."

"What do you mean?" Tyler asked as he absentmindedly ate his chili. "Are you trying to tell us you're a virgin again, 'cause I think that ship has sailed."

He clearly didn't grasp the magnitude of what she was alluding to. She would have to say the word out loud, and she wasn't so sure she could. Her stomach tightened and a wave of dizziness surged through her. She lifted her eyes to catch Rory's questioning expression and forced a smile.

Beth couldn't decide if having her here made what she was about to say easier or harder, but it felt appropriate. At least she'd have one supporter in the room if this went badly, and knowing that it was Rory bolstered Beth's confidence enough to continue.

"I mean," she took a deep breath, "I'm a lesbian."

Chris froze with his beer almost to his lips, Tyler's spoon fell to the table with a clatter, and people at nearby tables turned to stare, but Beth focused on Rory, whose dancing green eyes and broad smile caused exuberance to wash over her. Coincidentally, the guys also turned to Rory first.

"You converted Beth," Chris said, his voice filled with awe.

Rory laughed. "I didn't convert Beth."

"She wasn't gay before you got here," Tyler said, before turning back to Beth. "Were you?"

"Yeah," Beth said. "I've been gay for a long time." This wasn't where she expected the conversation to go. Then again, she hadn't known what to expect. Why had the boys immediately suspected Rory's influence? Kelly had jumped to that conclusion too. Didn't anyone think she was capable of making her own decisions? Or did they think she was making her decisions with Rory in mind? She wasn't sure which option troubled her more.

"You've been lying to us for years?" Tyler asked, hurt evident in his voice.

• 186 •

"Not intentionally." Beth wasn't sure how to explain her closeted past. She couldn't give too much away because she still needed to protect Kelly's privacy. She hadn't thought about how she'd explain the last decade of her life, and it hadn't occurred to her until now that part of her might never be completely free from the lies of omission. "Everyone was so good to me after my parents died. The whole town stepped in and saved me. I didn't want to disappoint them."

"Jesus, Beth." Chris stared at her like she'd wounded him. "Did you really think we'd turn on you for something like that?"

Rory cut in. "Guys. I'm sure Beth didn't mean you two, but other people in town will be upset about this. The Lindsay Reyeses and Mrs. Anthonys of the world will treat her differently, and they'll suspect everyone she comes into contact with from here on out. She wasn't just protecting herself. She was protecting the people around her too."

Beth searched Rory's face for any sign of condescension or sarcasm. Surely Ms.-Out-and-Proud St. James hadn't just justified staying in the closet. She'd expected Rory to be disappointed or even disapprove, but instead she seemed proud.

"Do you have someone else, someone special you need to protect?" Tyler asked. "Is that why you disappear and don't tell us who you're with?"

"Beth has put herself out there an awful lot today," Rory said. "It took a lot of courage for her to come out. She might not be ready to answer a bunch of questions yet."

Beth frowned. Did Rory really think she came out without considering the ramifications? Then she realized that Rory wasn't being patronizing. She was being protective. She was defending Beth and Kelly by honoring their wish to remain private.

What had it cost Rory to defend something she so clearly disagreed with? Over the past few months Rory had been a better friend to her than Beth had realized, and she'd have to thank her for that when they got some time alone. But for now it was time for Beth to take responsibility for her own life. "There was someone special in my life."

Chris looked confused. "You mean all this time we've been teasing you about a secret boyfriend, you really had a secret girlfriend?"

Beth smiled at his characterization of the situation. "It's not something I have to worry about anymore. I'm now Darlington's most eligible lesbian."

Beth saw the surprise Rory tried to hide by taking a long drink of her beer. When she finally set her bottle on the table, her smile was less than convincing. A long silence stretched between them while Beth searched Rory's eyes for some clue as to what she might be thinking.

Was she glad Kelly was out of the picture? Did she see it as an opening for herself? Did she even care? And why did it matter? It wasn't like Beth was hoping for a reaction, but she'd expected more than the politely blank stare Rory was currently giving her.

Edmond shifted in his seat, drawing Beth's attention away from Rory. "I guess it's my turn to buy the drinks."

Rory jumped up like that was the break she'd been waiting for. "I'll go with you."

Beth watched them walk toward the bar. Surely she was imagining Rory's weird reaction. It had to be paranoia that caused her to suspect Rory of having a vested interest in her breakup with Kelly. Or was it wishful thinking?

CHAPTER SEVENTEEN

October 10

"Geez, he's drunk," Raine said a few hours later when Tyler helped her drag Edmond to her car and stuffed him into the backseat.

"I'm not that drunk," Edmond mumbled before curling into a fetal position.

"Sorry we didn't cut him off sooner." Chris chuckled. "We were having so much fun with him."

Edmond had tried to keep pace with Chris and Tyler and was woefully outmatched, but he seemed to enjoy being included in their manly games, and Raine was too distracted to stop them.

How was she supposed to focus on Edmond with Beth looking so good sitting across the table and suddenly single? She needed to find out what happened and know what this meant for herself, if it meant anything at all, but she would to have to wait. She shut the car door and turned to the others.

"Will you be able to get him up the stairs to your apartment?" Tyler asked.

"I'll go with her," Beth answered quickly, then added, "I left my car on campus."

The guys seemed happy to accept her explanation and get back to the bar, but Raine's head spun. Despite her earlier desire to talk to Beth, she wasn't ready to face her yet. She wasn't completely sure what she was feeling about the shift in Beth's attitude and her breakup with Kelly. She didn't want her emotions to get the better of her.

Raine watched Beth out of the corner of her eye as they drove toward the college. She seemed to be dealing with a completely different person now. Beth was an out and single lesbian, no longer hiding who she was. She was a whole new woman—but she wasn't. She was still beautiful, still heartbreakingly sweet, still smart, sexy, and caring. She was still Beth. But now Raine had no excuse not to face her own feelings.

They rode in silence until Raine pulled into the parking lot of her apartment building. When they both got out of the car, Beth finally asked, "Are you mad at me?"

"What? No." Raine tried to laugh off her own tension as she opened the door and pulled Edmond to a sitting position.

"Really? It kind of feels like you're not speaking to me," Beth said as she hooked one of Edmond's arms around her neck. Raine did the same and they stood him up.

"She'd tell you," Edmond slurred, "if she wasn't speaking to you."

"He's right. If I were mad, you'd know it." They steadied him as he shuffled toward the door.

"You've barely said anything to me since I told you I broke up with Kelly."

"I've got a lot on my mind, with work, and my students—"

"She's lying," Edmond said clearly. "She's emotionally constipated."

"Shut up."

Beth laughed loudly, the sound of it warming Raine. "I kind of like having him around."

"I kind of hate it," Raine mumbled as they half helped, half carried Edmond up the stairs.

"You love me." He tried to kiss her on the cheek, but she pushed him fully into Beth's arms while she dug her keys out of her pocket. "She thinks you're gorgeous. She told me so."

Beth laughed. "What else did she tell you?"

"That she'd be sleeping with you if you weren't a closet case with a girlfriend."

"Damn it, Edmond," Raine said. "Why don't you pass out?"

"I told her I wasn't that drunk," he said to Beth.

They pushed through the door and carried him right to the bedroom, where Raine dropped him hard onto her bed. "Go to sleep." Then she shut the door more loudly than necessary.

Beth was waiting for her in the living room with a little quirk of a smile. Raine knew she was blushing. "What?"

"You think I'm gorgeous?"

Raine sighed. "Of course I do." She put as much distance between them as she could, choosing to brace herself against the kitchen counter. The apartment had never felt so small.

"You say that like it's common knowledge, but that's the first I've heard of it."

"Beth, it's not that easy. I'm—"

"What? Emotionally constipated?"

Raine smiled, despite her frustration. "Yes."

"Why? What do you have to be conflicted about? You're the picture of self-assurance."

Beth moved to the kitchen area, her presence sending Raine's body into overdrive. Something about being this close to her without the boundaries she'd formerly clung to made it hard for her to think logically. Raine gripped the counter and hung her head. "I've recently realized that I've based most of my life on a horrible misunderstanding, and now I'm not sure who I am anymore."

"Rory..." Beth laid a hand lightly on her shoulder.

The touch was sweet, friendly, altogether innocent, but Raine's skin burned underneath it. She needed to pull away, she needed perspective, she needed to run. She always ran. Raine St. James was famous for running, and yet that hadn't exactly worked out well for her, so why was she still doing it? But if she didn't run, if she didn't detach herself, what would she do?

"Look at me, Rory," Beth said. "What are you afraid of?"

She willed herself to make eye contact with Beth and hold it even when she felt as though she might drown in the deep blue depths. Beth smiled at her, and Raine's knees went weak. She'd thought that was just an expression, but she honestly felt like her balance shifted beneath her. "I'm out of excuses."

"Excuses for what?" Beth whispered.

"For not doing this." Raine closed the distance between them and touched her lips lightly to Beth's. Beth gasped, then clutched her shoulders, pulling their bodies together. They pressed against each other, the fullness of Beth's hips melding to the length of Raine's planes. She rested her hands on Beth's hips, massaging the softness below them with her fingertips. It wasn't enough. She might never get enough of touching Beth, but Raine's sense of awe kept her from taking more too quickly.

They parted their lips, slowly, hesitantly, and let their mouths mingle, tongues tentatively exploring each other as their pace increased. Heat flared between them, consuming Raine and causing her to burn in ways she'd never imagined. Beth ran her hand up Raine's shoulder and cupped the back of her head, holding her close as she threaded her fingers through the short hair at the base of her neck. Every part of her sang out in release, but relief eluded her. She craved more.

Raine had a flash of awareness amid the physical sensations that overloaded her system. This was Beth—holding her, urging her on with her tongue, her fingers, her whole body. A wave of pure pleasure mixed with reverence hit Raine.

She didn't know how long they stayed like that, but it wasn't nearly as long as she wanted.

A loud crash came from the bedroom, and they both jumped, startled back into the moment, and heard Edmond swearing loudly.

"You'd better go check on him," Beth said.

"I'm going to go kill him."

Beth grinned and touched her forehead to Raine's. "I'll come by tomorrow."

"Are we...okay?" Raine asked.

Beth kissed her again, lightly, before stepping away. "Absolutely."

Raine flopped onto the couch as soon as the door closed. Kissing Beth hadn't made her any surer about who she was or what she was doing, but she knew one thing. Whatever they'd just done, she'd like to do a lot more of it.

❖

October 11

Beth was propped against the wall outside Rory's door. She wanted to see her, but knocking would require more fortitude than she had at the moment. She'd been reeling since their mouths had met the night before. She'd never been kissed like that. Rory's desire had pulsed through her and crashed into her own. The memory, or maybe because she hadn't been able to sleep with the feel of Raine's body imprinted on hers, made her weak. She had to get a grip on herself. Things were moving too fast. A week ago she'd been closeted and in a stable, if dysfunctional, relationship. Now she was making out with a well-known lesbian heartthrob.

What if the kiss hadn't meant anything to Rory? She was used to women throwing themselves at her. She'd probably been with more women than Beth could imagine. What if she kissed them all like that? Maybe these emotions were common in Rory's world. Beth felt queasy. Could a kiss like that really not affect Rory?

No, Beth had seen her reaction in her eyes. She'd felt Rory's desire, watched her wrestle with the temptation to give in. Rory had surrendered into her arms. She hadn't held Beth like someone playing a practiced role, but rather clung to her like a woman in need.

The door to Rory's apartment opened and Beth jumped, then Rory gasped and dropped a bag of trash. They stared at each other before dissolving into laughter.

"How long have you been out here?" Rory reached for Beth's hand but stopped short of touching her.

"Awhile." Beth closed the gap between them by intertwining her fingers with Rory's.

Rory stared at her feet, seemingly unsure of herself. "Should I go back in and wait for you?"

Beth ached to pull Rory into her arms and kiss away all her uncertainties. "No, I was being silly. Let's go for a walk."

Rory's expression brightened, and she nodded. "Great idea. Edmond is up, and it's not pretty."

"Is he hurting?"

"I've seen him worse." They stepped out into the cool autumn air. The campus was quiet at eight on a Sunday morning with only the sounds of a gentle breeze rustling the brightly colored leaves beginning to fall around them. "It serves him right for all the shit he stirred up last night."

Beth laughed. "Without him, who knows when you would've gotten around to kissing me."

"You say that like I was the only one capable of doing it." Rory stopped and ran the back of her fingers along the line of Beth's jaw. "Or did I misinterpret your reaction?"

Beth leaned into the touch, bringing their lips together in the only answer she had left in her.

They didn't hesitate this time, but fell together there in the middle of the quad. Beth briefly realized that anyone could see them, but she couldn't stop herself. They opened their mouths greedily, taking as much as they could handle while remaining upright. Beth ran her hands up the bare skin of Rory's arms and under the short sleeves of her shirt. She scraped her fingernails along lean muscle and breathed in the scent of Rory, a mix of soap and light cologne. She wanted to soak her up with every one of her senses.

"Good morning, Professor St. James, Ms. Devoroux," someone said as they walked past.

They pulled apart quickly and Rory's face flamed crimson. She was absolutely adorable.

"I'm so sorry," Rory gushed.

"Don't be sorry. I'm not. Perhaps we need to be a little more discreet, but this," Beth took Rory's hand again, "feels nice. Better than nice. It feels liberating."

Rory smiled broadly, and Beth's heart rate increased again. "I'm glad you're enjoying all this. You deserve to be shown off..."

"But?"

Rory brushed her lips against Beth's ear. "I don't know if I can be this close and not hold you."

Beth groaned. "Follow me." She held tighter to Rory's hand and led her across the quad. The library wouldn't open until noon, but Beth used her keys to unlock the door and didn't turn on any lights when they went inside. The long rows of books were illuminated only by the light from the outside windows, leaving the middle of the room in shadow.

Beth turned to Rory. "It's not perfect, but it's private."

"It *is* perfect," Rory whispered as she nuzzled Beth's neck. "You're perfect."

Beth captured Rory's mouth with her own. It was the only way she could respond to how Rory made her feel. Their kiss quickly disintegrated into something more primal as they clutched each other. Rory's hands were on her hips, her back, her arms, and still she wanted more. She played at the hem of Rory's shirt before she slid her fingers upward, over her chest. She used Rory's collar to pull her even closer until she stumbled backward under the pressure of her own desire.

Her back hit a stack of books, and she heard a few of them fall to the floor. Beth almost laughed at destroying her precious cataloging order, but instead she reached for Rory again, this time catching her hands and intertwining their fingers.

"God, I want you," Rory panted in the second before their mouths collided once again. She raised Beth's arms and pinned them to the shelf above their heads. Rory freed one of her hands and ran it down the length of Beth's arm and side before touching bare skin where her shirt had come untucked. Beth gasped at the feel of Rory's hand against the exposed skin of her midriff. Rory dragged her mouth across her cheek and up her jaw to nibble on her earlobe.

Beth sagged under the weight of her arousal. She'd had moments of need, but they'd never been so out of her control, so unrestrained, so all-consuming. She grabbed Rory's shirt again, twisting it in her fist before she tugged it over Rory's head and tossed it to the floor. Beth touched her mouth to the skin of Rory's shoulder, tasting and kissing her way along her collarbone and into the hollow at the base of her throat.

Rory trembled and Beth was overwhelmed with her own power. She'd never felt alluring, and certainly not sexy, but when she met the deep green of Rory's eyes she could see that Rory found her to be both. Rory clearly needed and wanted her, but she saw something more.

"Beth, I…" Rory seemed to choke on a word. Beth felt the word too, but the realization made her step back and bump the bookshelf again.

Rory started toward her again but froze when Beth placed a hand firmly on her chest. "What's wrong?"

"I can't," Beth panted.

"Why? What did I do?" Rory reached out to her, agony mixed with confusion visible on her face. "I thought you wanted—"

"I do." Beth nodded. "I want you, all of you, but it's more than that. I could fall in love with you."

"That's," Raine ran her hand through her hair, "a good thing?"

Beth sighed. "I don't make love to someone with the possibility that it might lead to love, or even because I'm in love with her."

Rory shook her head, clearly trying to understand Beth's ramblings.

"It's only making love if both people feel the same. Otherwise it's just sex, and as appealing as that is right now," Beth looked at the beautiful body before her one last time, "I'm not sure I could survive it in the long run."

Summoning all her strength she turned from the most gorgeous thing she'd ever seen. Beth strode away before she could wonder what a horrible mistake she'd just made.

CHAPTER EIGHTEEN

Raine wandered back to her apartment, dazed. What had happened? One moment she'd held everything she wanted literally in her hands, and the next, Beth was gone. It'd been hard to focus on Beth's words through her lust-induced haze, but she thought the conversation had turned very quickly from sex to love and she hadn't sorted that out yet. She knew only that she was cold, confused, and empty, not to mention topless.

"Where've you been?" Edmond asked when she walked into the apartment. "You look like shit."

"Great. That means a lot coming from the guy with the hangover."

Edmond regarded her more carefully. Whether it was her wrinkled shirt and tousled hair, the way she was pacing aimlessly, or the glazed-over expression she couldn't hide, he must've realized something wasn't right. He patted the spot next to him on the couch. "Spill it, girlfriend."

"Beth and I kissed last night," Raine said, flopping onto the couch. "Then we made out this morning and she ripped my shirt off."

"Beth? The Beth I met last night? Girl-next-door Beth?"

Rory nodded.

"Sweet little just-came-out-of-the-closet Beth?"

"That's the one."

"Gorgeous, dark curls, with blue eyes like Elizabeth Taylor's?"

"Are you trying to kill me?" Rory groaned and buried her face in the couch cushion.

"She doesn't seem like the lady-on-the-streets, freak-in-the-sheets kind of girl."

"I know, right?"

"So this is a postcoital haze you're in?"

"No. She stopped halfway between second and third base and started talking about how she doesn't have sex without love."

"Women," Edmond said emphatically.

Raine threw a pillow at him. "What the hell do you know about women?"

"I watch LOGO. I know how your people are, always pulling the U-Haul behind them. One kiss and she wants a commitment ceremony and a trip to Cambodia to adopt a baby that you'll name something absurd like Mullet or Xena."

Raine rubbed her face. "What am I going to do?"

"Find a different sex buddy." Edmond shrugged, then laughed. "Unless you love her."

Raine's stomach dropped. She couldn't be in love with Beth. That wasn't the feeling she'd been trying to put into words in the library, was it? It didn't make sense.

Then again, what was not to love about Beth? She was smart, sexy, and easy to talk to. Beth challenged her, but she also let her be herself. Beth wasn't after Raine's fame, she wasn't invested in her public image, and she didn't suffer her pretentious side. She'd stood by her when it had been dangerous to do so, even when Raine mocked her for it. Beth had never given up her faith in her.

Also, there was the way Raine's heart beat faster every time Beth entered a room with her captivating eyes, her sinful body, and her devastating smile. Raine was frozen, her throat too dry to speak, but Edmond must have sensed her turmoil because he jumped to his feet.

"Holy shit. You're in love with her."

"No," Raine finally managed to croak. "That won't work at all."

"I don't think it's about working or not. When it comes to being in love, you either are or you aren't."

"Not for me." Raine couldn't be tied to someone who was bound to Darlington the way Beth was. That wasn't how her future was supposed to be, although at the moment she wasn't sure why.

Beth had hoped to leave church quickly today. She didn't feel particularly religious after the way she'd yanked off Rory's shirt in the library. She wasn't sure what had come over her, but kissing Rory was clearly a dangerous activity. It was a miracle she'd found the fortitude to walk away because, remembering the sight of Rory standing there, bare-chested, with desire and longing in her eyes, she wasn't sure she could do it again.

Thankfully she wouldn't have to. Rory must think she was a crazy woman for getting her all revved up and then going on a rant about love and sex. Beth had confirmed that she was still an old-fashioned, small-town farm girl, and no amount of coming out of the closet would change that.

Oh, God, I came out of the closet, Beth thought with horror. Now she'd likely scared off Rory and had certainly alienated Kelly. As soon as word got around she'd lose more friends. Where did that leave her? Sure, she could sleep better at night without the fear of being outed, but she probably was destined to sleep alone. *What a trade-off.*

Her life was changing too quickly, and she had no idea what to do about it. The last thing she wanted was to make small talk with her fellow congregants. She'd almost made it out the door when a woman caught her arm.

"Hello, Mrs. LaRussa," Beth said, forcing a smile for the pastor's wife. She and her husband had been good to Beth, never failing to invite her to holiday meals or remember her birthday. What would they, like so many others who had tried to be her surrogate family after her parents died, think of her recent actions? Would they feel shocked? Betrayed? Disappointed?

"Beth," Mrs. LaRussa said, "would you like to join us for lunch?"

"Actually, I have other plans." It wasn't a total lie. She'd promised Miles she'd be at his house for their gay and lesbian group that afternoon, but that wasn't for another hour. In the meantime she needed to rest and try to clear her mind.

"Another time then?"

"Of course," Beth said, and turned to make her get-away, but Mrs. LaRussa didn't let go of her arm. Beth could see the woman was unsure if she should say what she was about to. She even opened her mouth and shut it before giving another weak smile. Beth sighed. "I guess word gets around fast in this town."

"It does, dear," Mrs. LaRussa said.

"And?"

"And you, my child, are fearfully and wonderfully made by the hand of God. He has a plan for each and every one of us, and He doesn't make mistakes."

Beth threw her arms around the woman in front of her and fought to hold back the tears that filled her eyes. "Thank you."

"No thanks needed. We all love you, Beth. We want you to be happy."

Beth nodded. That's what she wanted too, but she wasn't sure what that meant for her. She had to love herself, but what if she also loved someone else, someone who might or might not love her back?

She was still pondering that question at Miles's later in the afternoon as she pulled a pan of chocolate brownies out of the oven.

"Those smell almost as good as you do," Rory murmured in her ear.

Beth jumped and dropped the pan onto the stove with a yelp.

"Sorry." Rory chuckled. "I thought you heard me come in."

"No, I didn't," Beth said forcefully, then mentally added, *I was too busy wondering if I should let myself fall in love with you.* Seeing Rory now with her hair feathered lightly across her forehead, her green eyes sparkling with delight, and that rakish grin that made her so damn irresistible, Beth wondered if the more appropriate question should be, *Could I stop myself from falling in love with you, even if I wanted to?*

"I'll try to give you more warning from now on." Rory stepped closer. "For instance, I'm going to kiss you now."

Beth relaxed as soon as Rory's lips touched hers. She fought the urge to reach up and touch her because if she did, she'd lose control and begin tearing at her clothing again. Unfortunately, she didn't need to worry about the fire starting to spread through her body, because Kelly's voice saying, "Well, that didn't take long," quickly cooled it.

❖

Raine and Beth jumped apart like guilty teenagers whose daddy had caught them rolling around in the hayloft. Raine had been so wrapped up in seeing Beth again that she hadn't stopped to consider the other members of the group.

"Kel…" Beth seemed lost for what to say. Faced with Kelly's dejection and Beth's sadness, Raine glanced quickly from one woman to the other. In that moment it was clear there was a loser in every game. She knew how it felt to see Beth in someone else's arms, and despite her animosity for Kelly, she didn't wish that kind of torture on anyone.

"Kelly, can we talk?" Raine finally said.

"It's a little late for you to grow a conscience, don't you think?"

Beth cut in. "She's not the reason we broke up."

"Doesn't look that way to me," Kelly said through clenched teeth. "She's been after you since the day she got back to town."

Raine heard shuffling outside the doorway to the kitchen and realized they had an audience. "Kelly, I think we should move this outside."

"Oh my God, Raine's going to fight Kelly!" she heard Miles say from around the corner.

"No," Raine said, loud enough to be heard in the other room. "That sounded bad. I meant we should go somewhere and talk out of earshot from the peanut gallery in there."

Kelly scowled but headed toward the back door. Raine motioned for Beth to stay there. Then, reading her nervousness, she kissed Beth's cheek. "It'll be okay."

They stood on a small deck that descended into a square of dead grass that comprised Miles's backyard. Of course a gay man would have an immaculate house and pay no attention to his lawn. She smiled fleetingly at another stereotype, but her amusement faded as she noticed the sharp chill in the air. The weather was turning cooler, but it didn't compare to the frosty vibe Kelly was sending her way.

"Kelly, I know what you were insinuating in there, but I never pursued Beth while you were together." Even as the words left her mouth she reconsidered them. She had a flash of memories—she and Beth laughing over pizza, locking eyes in a moonlit cornfield, her hand in Beth's at the baseball game, Beth in her arms after the homerun. She'd never purposefully come between them, but if she was honest with herself, she'd been attracted to Beth from the moment she saw her standing in the library.

"You projected your agenda into our lives, Rory. You filled her head with ideas about coming out. What did you think would happen to our relationship when she did?"

"I didn't think about—"

"That's right. You didn't think about anyone but yourself."

Raine's anger built. "What about Beth? Did you ever think about what living in the closet was like for her? Did you consider how much it hurt her to lie to the people who've loved her like a daughter?"

Kelly hung her head.

"No? I didn't think so. Sounds like I wasn't the only one thinking of myself." Raine leaned against the porch rail. Was it possible that she and Kelly were more alike than either of them cared to admit? And if so, where did that leave Beth?

"What are your intentions with her?" Kelly asked more calmly.

Raine stifled a laugh.

"You think this is funny?" Kelly's voice rose again. "She doesn't have a father or a brother to interrogate the people she brings home. Somebody has to watch out for her, and nobody loves her the way I do, so it might as well be me."

Though the logic was convoluted, somehow it made sense. When the tables were turned, Raine had been the one to ask the tough questions about Kelly.

"I don't know what my intentions are," she answered honestly.

Kelly shook her head. "She left me because she wanted a future I wouldn't give her."

"We've only been together for a day."

"Are you still going back to Chicago?"

"Yes," Raine said automatically. She'd never wanted to come home in the first place.

"So you'll either leave her or tear her away from all those people you mentioned earlier. You know, the ones who love her like a daughter?" Kelly was circling now, and Raine felt claustrophobic. Her future seemed to narrow before her. Beth couldn't leave her home, and Raine couldn't ask her to, but the possibility of never seeing her again caused a sharp pain in her chest.

Raine exploded. "I don't know. I haven't thought about how she'll fit into my life. I don't even know what my life will be like a year from now."

"You'd better start thinking about it," Kelly said as she headed for the door.

Raine didn't follow her. She stood at the porch rail, staring blankly at the brown grass below her. She didn't feel the cold or hear the voices from inside. Everything was spiraling out of control. The great cosmic joke that was her life continued. She was working a dream job in her nightmare of a hometown and being forced to realize that she was at least partially to blame for the family tragedy she'd built her career on. Now she had to deal with the fact that she was falling in love with a woman who embodied everything she'd worked so hard to create her identity against.

Could Raine St. James, the boi who survived, really fall in love with the darling of Darlington? What did that mean for her? Could they have a future together? If so, who would that make her? Surely not the woman she'd worked hard to become. But if she lost Beth now—after holding her, kissing her, letting her into her heart—would she even want to be the person she'd become?

❖

Beth pretended to focus on the conversation around her, but she kept stealing glances out the window. Kelly and Rory had a lot of animosity between them, and Beth's actions had only compounded the situation. Still, she cared for them both and hated the way they constantly insulted each other. That's surely what they were doing outside, and it appeared as though Kelly had won this round. As she came back inside and sat across the room, her mouth was set in a hard line and her dark eyes were resolute, while Rory stayed behind on the porch, her back turned to the house and her shoulders slumped.

Beth fought the urge to go to her, to hold her and protect her from whatever demons she was fighting now. She'd had this instinct since Rory had arrived in Darlington two months ago, lost and defensive. Beth felt an unexplainable need to soothe her fears.

At first she thought she was being a good friend. Now she realized her connection to Rory ran deeper. Maybe she'd started falling in love with her from the very beginning. Perhaps Rory had been tugging on her heart as soon as she walked into the library that first day.

Whatever the case, she'd been swept up in the rip current of emotions that always swirled around Rory—with her magnetism, her charm, her passion, but also her uncertainties and her sullenness, as well as her distrust. Beth wondered which side Rory was considering now. What if she chose to run again? Would Beth be able to see the signs and protect herself from getting burned, or would she keep dancing ever closer to the flame, knowing even as it consumed her that she'd be left in a pile of ashes when Rory moved on.

"She's not easy to love," Edmond said quietly as he sat beside her on the couch.

"I don't know if…I'm not in…" Beth sighed. "Is it that obvious?"

He smiled. "Yeah, sugar, but don't worry. I won't tell her."

"Thanks." She liked him. Despite his flashy and polished appearance, he was someone she'd probably enjoy spending more time with. He'd taken good care of Rory all those years ago when she was a lost teenager in a strange city, which carried a lot of weight with Beth. "Are you having a good time on your country getaway?"

"I am," he answered enthusiastically. "It's not what I expected."

"What, you didn't know there were such devilishly handsome gay men in the middle of cornfields?" Miles asked from across the room, where he'd been chatting with Wilson.

"I didn't expect to find gay men at all." Edmond laughed and let his eyes linger a little longer on Miles. "Especially not such handsome ones."

"I'm surprised Rory hasn't been singing my praises." Miles pretended to pout, despite being clearly pleased with the compliment.

"I'm sorry," Rory said, stepping in from the porch and casting a weak smile at Beth before she sat down in an armchair across from her. Rory joined the conversation, obviously trying to ignore Kelly's presence. "You're not my type, Miles."

"She didn't do any of you justice. From the way she's talked all these years, I expected torch-wielding villagers."

"I wasn't that bad." Rory laughed nervously, which led Beth to believe that was probably exactly how she'd described them. Did she still feel that way?

"You told me about some old lady accosting you in the store, and some religious convert verbally attacking you in a bar and—"

"All right, they get the picture," Rory said. "I'm sure they all have similar stories."

"I don't," Wilson said. "Everyone on campus has been very supportive."

"I've never had trouble on campus either, and when I go into town, people are always absurdly polite," Miles added.

"I've noticed that," Edmond said. "Everyone's gone out of their way to welcome me. They act like Rory's the freaking homecoming king, and it's obvious we're as gay as the day is long."

"Not everyone pegs us as gay right away," Rory said defensively, but everyone chuckled.

"Are you serious?" Edmond snickered along with them. "You'd have to be blind not to see how gay we are. Some drunk Cubs fan who'd stumbled into Boystown after the game a few weeks ago called me a fag. The man was so plastered he didn't even know where he was, and he could still clearly see that I was a fag."

Rory laughed. "It's funny when they do that. Cubs fans aren't the brightest."

"Why?" Beth asked seriously. "Why is it funny when you get called a fag in Chicago, but when someone in Darlington says something similar, you condemn the whole town?"

Everyone was quiet as Rory considered her answer. "I guess it's easier to ignore in the city because you're surrounded by people who think like you. The homophobes are in the minority."

"They are here too, Rory," Beth said. "I came out to Mrs. LaRussa today."

"Oh, God, Beth," Kelly groaned. "You didn't."

"She'd already heard the rumors, but I confirmed them. She told me God made me who I am and that He doesn't make mistakes."

"There are good people all over," Rory admitted grudgingly. "But I wouldn't say that the majority of Darlington residents are gay rights activists."

"The majority of Chicagoans aren't activists either. They're normal people who want to live their lives and don't care what you do with yours." Then sitting forward and searching Rory's green eyes, desperately trying to make her understand, Beth added, "But the good people in the city are strangers. Here, they're people who love you."

The room was quiet as Rory sat back in her chair, arms folded across her chest, her brow furrowed in concentration as she appeared to mull over that thought. Was she angry? Maybe Beth had pushed too far, but she wouldn't apologize. She'd spoken the truth, and if Rory was hell-bent on viewing everyone the way she had as a petulant teenager, that was her right. However, Beth wouldn't sit around and help her bash the people who had been so good to her.

Finally, Rory rubbed her hands over her face as if scrubbing away her brooding and asked, "Beth, would you have dinner with me and my parents tonight?"

Beth grinned despite her confusion at Rory's quick change of subject. She wasn't sure what sparked the invitation, but Rory was reaching out to her. While it wasn't a complete acknowledgment of Beth's points, it showed that Rory was trying to make peace with her two worlds and she was including Beth in those endeavors. "I'd love to."

CHAPTER NINETEEN

Raine pulled into Beth's gravel driveway and found her waiting on the porch. Her simple black skirt flowed loosely from her hips down to the middle of her calves, and her cerulean tunic made her eyes shine the color of cornflowers. Her dark curls were pulled back from her face and flowed gently in the breeze as she bounded down the front steps.

Raine faltered at the sight. She'd had plenty of practice with women. She'd dated many, most of them on the sexier end of the spectrum. She'd been with athletes, actresses, and models, all hot enough to singe anyone who stood too close, but nothing could've prepared her for this pure, natural beauty. Raine's stomach started to flutter and the sensation radiated throughout her body. Her throat went dry and her limbs shook as she opened the passenger-side door for Beth.

"Thank you." Beth smiled and kissed her on the cheek. "I've never had a woman open a door for me before."

The sweet greeting made Raine feel like a bumbling teenager in the presence of a fairy-tale princess. "You're welcome."

They drove the few miles into town with their fingers intertwined. She had plenty to worry about. Raine was about to take Beth into her parents' home, as well as being totally uncertain about what her future would hold and how the beautiful woman beside her would fit into it. She should've been a wreck, but she couldn't shake the silly grin she'd had since Beth gave her that little peck on the cheek.

She parked in front of the house. "Are you ready for this?"

"I'm not sure what I'm in for," Beth answered, plainly nervous. "I've never been to meet anyone's parents."

"We're even, then."

"I didn't know you'd seen them often, much less been ready to do something like this."

"I've been having Sunday dinner with them off and on since the first day at Miles's when you yelled at me." Beth looked surprised and Raine chuckled. "I didn't say anything because I didn't want to admit you might've been right. I didn't even admit it to myself until last week when we finally had a conversation that was ten years overdue. Things are getting better with them, and I owe that to you."

Beth held her hand and kissed it. "I know how much courage that took, Rory. I'm so proud of you."

"Don't go overboard. We've got a long way to go, and you might not be so happy with me after the awkwardness tonight."

Beth squeezed her hand. "You're trying, you're opening yourself up, and you're risking a lot. No amount of awkwardness will take away from that."

Raine's mother met them at the door and turned from Beth to Raine before she looked at their joined hands. She smiled radiantly. "Beth, it's so good to see you."

"It's good to see you too, Mrs. St. James."

"Rory's here," she called into the living room, then practically gushed, "and she brought Beth Devoroux with her.'"

When her mother bustled off back into the kitchen, Raine glanced at Beth, who gave her a little shove. "You didn't tell them I was coming?"

"I mentioned that I might bring a friend. If I'd known you'd get a warmer welcome than I did, I'd have brought you months ago."

"Hello, Beth," Raine's father said when he came into the room. "It's nice to see you again."

"Thank you, sir. It's good to be here."

"I was about to set the table," Rory's mother called from the kitchen. "Can I get you girls something to drink?"

"I'm fine," Beth said graciously, "but I'd love to help you get dinner on."

"You don't have to do that, dear." Rory's mother brushed off the offer, but the way she beamed at Beth said she loved the idea.

Beth continued toward the dining room. "I don't mind at all."

Raine watched her go, wanting to follow yet content to simply enjoy the view.

"Ahem." Davey gave her a nudge.

"What?" Raine hoped he hadn't caught her admiring the finer aspects of Beth's backside.

"Are you dating Beth?" Davey asked, and her father muted the TV.

Raine hadn't put a label on what she and Beth were doing. Everything had happened so fast. They'd only kissed for the first time last night, yet it felt like they'd been building up to this moment for months. They hadn't really dated, not formally anyway. Beth had been an amazing friend, yet they were clearly more than friends. They'd flirted and argued, fought and surrendered, hidden and collided. Beth frustrated her, challenged her, excited her, and aroused her.

Was it too early to call her a girlfriend? No other woman had ever had this kind of effect on her. Beth exhilarated and terrified her all at once. Raine wanted to run from her, protect her, hold her, and make love to her. What did you call that?

"Sort of." Rory knew it was a cop-out, but she didn't know how to explain it to herself, much less convey an accurate picture to her father and brother.

"Beth is a good girl." Her father shifted uncomfortably as if he wasn't sure he should go on or not, but his fatherly side won out. "I'm not a young man, and I'm sure a lot of things are different these days, but women like that don't come along very often. And when they do, they don't wait around for long."

"Yes, sir." She knew what her father was saying, even if he hadn't been comfortable giving his recently returned lesbian daughter advice on women. Though the tone was different, the message was similar to Kelly's. Beth deserved someone who would deal with her honestly, with care and respect, and if Raine didn't offer that, someone else would.

Raine wanted to be that person for Beth, the one who could make her dreams come true, the woman who treated her right and reaped all the rewards. Was she capable, and if so, what did that mean for her own future plans?

Raine's mother announced, "Supper's on the table."

Beth sat next to Raine at the table, and Raine silently prayed that she would be able to navigate this dinner, her feelings for Beth, and her future at large with grace. She hadn't expected her time in Darlington to turn out like this, but Beth's hand on hers under the table quieted her mind immediately, though her heart rate increased drastically. Was it time to start thinking less and feeling more? She smiled as she echoed her family's "Amen" after the blessing.

"What's new and exciting out at the college these days?" Raine's mom asked as she passed a bowl of mashed potatoes.

Raine froze. It was the first real open-ended question anyone had asked her since she began coming to these dinners. She immediately censored herself as she ran through all the topics she feared would offend her family, including her course material, her work with the GLBT students, and her making out with Beth in the library.

"Everyone's preparing for homecoming," Beth said, saving Raine. "The library is doing a float for the parade this year, which is pretty funny since parades and libraries are about as discordant as you can get."

"Do you remember that year your junior class made their Halloween-parade float in our barn?" Davey asked.

"I'd forgotten all about that." Rory laughed as she recalled her and her friends stuffing napkins into chicken wire shaped like a giant football. The memory was sweeter than any speaking engagement she'd had or any symphony she'd attended. "We worked on that silly thing every night for weeks."

"I remember," Beth said with a shy smile. "You were the only girl I knew who could weld. I was so impressed."

"Really?"

"Of course. I always wished I could do stuff like that."

"I can teach you." Rory could already feel her arms around Beth's waist, steadying her with one hand on her hip and the other on the blowtorch. She had no doubt the heat between their bodies would rival any metal-melting flame.

"You could use my equipment." Her father was oblivious to where Raine's mind had wandered.

Between bites of steak, Davey said, "I'll haul it over tomorrow."

"You should go help them with their float," her mother added.

Raine couldn't believe how quickly her family had jumped into the event. Did she want them getting this involved? How did people do this? What would she have done if her parents had been this accommodating in high school? It would've changed her whole life. Would she have even left? Would Raine ever have come into existence, or would she have lived happily ever after as Rory? Would she and Beth have connected sooner? Would all her Sunday dinners have included Beth by her side, maybe a couple of kids running around the backyard?

It didn't sound as scary as it would have two months ago, but did she want this? Her high-school friends simply grew into this life without thinking about it. Then again, she hadn't stopped to plan where her life was headed in Chicago either. It had just happened.

She was certainly enjoying tonight's dinner more than any other Sunday she'd spent since her return. It beat her past anger and awkwardness, and the way Beth's eyes danced with light and laughter was charming. Raine wanted more of the same.

The dinner conversations flowed easily, and Raine enjoyed not feeling out of place. Beth was the missing puzzle piece that fit perfectly in this part of her life. Would she be the same in other areas as well? Raine was still pondering that question as she cleared her dishes from the table. Lost in her own thoughts, she didn't notice her mother standing close beside her until she asked, "Is Beth a special friend?"

Raine tried not to laugh at her mother's lack of a term for her relationship with Beth, since she'd had the same problem defining it earlier. In fact, if "special friend" didn't sound absurdly puritan, it would be pretty accurate. Beth was an amazing friend, and undeniably special, but Raine wasn't ready to explain all that to her mother, so she grinned and said, "Yes, she is."

"I'm very glad you brought her over tonight." Her mother wrung her hands, a nervous habit she'd had as long as Raine could remember. "I used to be upset because I didn't think you'd have what your father and I had. I worried you'd never know the happiness that comes from loving someone and having them love you back."

Raine tried to swallow the lump in her throat. "Thank you, but don't get ahead of yourself. Me and Beth, we're…" She didn't know what to say.

"I know. We all come to things in our own time, but when you look at her, it's like the world's been lifted off your shoulders. And she looks at you the same way. It's good for a mother to see, even if you don't see it clearly yet."

Raine could hardly believe she was having this conversation with her mother. It would've been surreal if it hadn't been so genuine. Then her mother handed her a stack of Tupperware containers filled with food, the quintessential Midwestern display of love.

As Raine drove Beth home, she couldn't help but steal glances at her. She was sweet in a way that disconcerted Raine, but she was also sexy. Raine couldn't get the feel of Beth's hands and lips off her mind, and she hungered for more even as she struggled to do right by Beth. She wanted to hold her, touch her, kiss her, but honestly she'd settle for being near her.

"What are you thinking?" Beth asked, gently laying her hand on Raine's knee.

"I don't want this night to end."

"It doesn't have to. We could go back to your place," Beth said with a mischievous grin.

Raine raised her eyebrows questioningly. Was she getting the green light?

Beth rolled her eyes playfully. "Don't get ahead of yourself. I was going to suggest that you invite me over for coffee, and we'll take it from there."

"Oh. Coffee," Raine said with a fake pout. She wouldn't pressure Beth. In fact, she'd accept whatever stipulations Beth had at this point.

❖

Beth watched Rory move back and forth aimlessly across the apartment. It was funny to see such a usually self-assured woman fiddle and fumble. Her cheeks flamed bright red when she spilled the coffee grounds all over the floor. Then when Raine bent over to wipe them up, Beth glimpsed her backside with her usually loose blue jeans stretched tight, highlighting her perfect form. She hadn't lost any of her athletic figure from high school. Instead she'd grown into her limbs and filled out her torso.

Beth knew from earlier that Rory's abs and stomach lightly rippled up into small, firm breasts, and it was her turn to blush when she realized Rory had caught her staring. "Why don't I find us some music?"

As she crossed the room to put some distance between her and Rory, she tried to focus on the rows of CDs under the small boom box. Hopefully, the lists of names and titles would interrupt her lustful thoughts. Rory had the standard lesbian repertoire of music—Melissa Etheridge, Indigo Girls, Jill Sobule, and Mary Chapin Carpenter—but Beth was silently delighted to find an equal number of country CDs. She selected *Reba McEntire's Greatest Hits*.

When the first song started to play, Rory laughed. "I can't believe you picked that."

"Why?" Beth worried she'd broken the mood. "You don't like it?"

"No, I love it." Rory turned the volume up. "Most of the women I've dated were disappointed when they found out I like country music."

"I guess I'm not like the other women you've dated," Beth mumbled. She didn't like to be reminded that she wasn't Rory's type. She was too country, too small-town, too plain to hold her attention very long. Why was she here, falling for a side of Rory that didn't exist under usual circumstances?

Rory hooked a finger under her chin, lifting it gently until their eyes met, and Beth gasped at the tenderness that blended into more subtle shades of desire. "I love that you're not like them. They were all disasters, and I never let them see who I really was. I couldn't trust them to understand that the high-powered, high-energy, chic lesbian they saw onstage had left the country but never got the small town out of her heart."

"Oh, God, Rory." Beth covered her eyes and shook her head. "How am I supposed to think clearly when you say things like that?"

Rory chuckled, taking Beth's hands and wrapping them around her neck before she slid her hands down the curves of Beth's body until they rested delicately on her hips. "Okay, I won't be smashingly romantic again until you give me the go-ahead."

They swayed slowly to the music. It felt so comfortable, so perfect, like they were made for this. Beth rested her head on Rory's shoulder, enjoying the scent that was uniquely Rory's. She was falling and she couldn't stop herself. Rory was too charming to resist, and if she kissed her again Beth wouldn't be able to restrain herself. She felt terrified yet liberated.

"Can I talk yet?" Rory asked with a teasing lilt.

"That depends on what you plan to say."

"I was going to ask what you were thinking."

"How charming you are." Beth didn't see any reason to put off the inevitable. Rory had her. She might as well know it. "What about you?"

"Ironically, I was thinking the same thing."

Beth pulled back to search Rory's deep green eyes for any sign of mockery and found none.

"What?" Rory asked. "You wooed my whole family tonight. Two weeks ago they barely acted like I was there. This week they're practically begging me to marry you."

Beth rolled her eyes, trying to downplay the way her stomach tightened at the mention of marriage. She'd never even let herself consider such a dream. "Your family is wonderful. I had a good time tonight."

"I did too." Rory sounded surprised. "I never thought I'd enjoy an evening like this."

"Really? It's all I've ever wanted." Beth smiled through the wave of sadness that threatened to overwhelm her. "A family around that cares what happens between me and the beautiful woman by my side."

Rory gasped and her eyes clouded over. "I never let myself wish for that. If you don't let yourself want something, you can't be sad that you don't have it."

"What about now?" Beth held her breath. What would she do if Rory said she still wasn't interested?

Her fears, however, were short-lived because Rory held her closer and whispered, "You're teaching me to believe I can have it all."

Beth tried to hide her shudder, but Rory had to have felt it. "There you go being devastatingly romantic again."

Rory's lips still hovered near Beth's as she mumbled, "I can't help it. You inspire dramatics in me."

"Then you better stop talking before I fall apart completely." Beth cupped the back of Rory's head and guided their lips together. As their kiss snowballed from tender to passionate, Beth wondered if she'd ever get her fill of Rory. Right now she couldn't imagine being able to tear herself away. She couldn't conceive of the night ending without them making love.

Beth could barely be angry with herself for being a foregone conclusion, but her resistance had begun to melt the moment Rory asked her to dinner with her parents. Seeing Rory in a casual family setting was like watching the final grain of sand slide through an hourglass. Beth could no longer cling to her modesty. She wouldn't be able to hold off now, and she didn't even want to. Rory was everything she'd dreamed of—charismatic, open, attentive, respectful, and so very sexy.

The way Rory was running the tip of her fingers under the lining of Beth's bra drove her insane. She wanted to beg her to rip it off but couldn't pull her mouth away long enough to do so.

She clutched at the hem of Rory's shirt and started to lift it, but Rory pulled away, leaving Beth feeling empty and exposed. "What is it?"

"Are you sure you want to do this?" Rory said between panting breaths. "I don't want you to do anything you'll regret later."

Beth stared at her in disbelief. Was she serious? "You don't want this?"

"God, no, that's not what I meant," Rory stammered. "I want you so badly I can hardly stand up, but earlier today, you were, well, you did this, and then you said all that stuff about, you know…"

Rory was trying to be chivalrous. Even now, she was genuinely concerned about Beth. Could she be any more perfect? "Forget what I said earlier."

Beth pushed Rory onto the couch and lowered herself on top of her. She'd never been like this before. No one had ever made her lose control. She'd always followed Kelly's lead, but now her need drove her to assert herself. She wanted every inch of Rory naked and pressed against her. Everything about her was intoxicating. Beth wanted to see her, feel her, taste her all at once.

She didn't know where to start. She ran her hands under Rory's shirt and cupped her firm breasts. They felt even better than they'd looked earlier, and she pushed the shirt up over Rory's head to get a better view. Their eyes locked for a moment, the green in Rory's darker than ever, her desire evident. Beth exhaled slowly and lowered her head to take one hard nipple between her lips.

The shrill ring of the phone cut through the sounds of heavy breathing. Beth raised her eyes without lifting her mouth off Rory's chest.

"Ignore it," Rory said through gritted teeth.

Beth was all too happy to return her attentions to the woman arching up beneath her, but after two more rings the answering machine picked up and Edmond called out, "Raine St. James rides again."

"Damnit, I'm going to kill him." Rory propped herself up on her elbows and reached for the phone, but she bumped the table and sent the cordless receiver flying halfway across the room.

"You're brutal, girlfriend," Edmond continued. "I read your article. If your plan was to say anything to get out of Darlington, it's worked, because it will certainly get you the attention you need to get back on the public-speaking circuit."

Beth sat up, not sure she'd understood correctly. Rory struggled to get off the couch, terror evident on her face, but Beth held up a hand. She wanted to hear the rest of this.

Edmond kept on talking. "If you really want to go through with this, I'll get you out of your contract and back on the road at the end of the semester. You'll never have to set foot in your hometown again."

The message ended and the walls began to close in on Beth. She honestly felt like the room was getting smaller and even starting to spin, which would account for the queasiness in her stomach.

"Beth," Rory said finally, putting a hand tentatively on her shoulder.

"Don't." Beth jumped up and moved out of reach. She couldn't let Rory touch her right now, not while she was trying to make sense of so much new information.

"Please let me explain," Rory pleaded.

"You're planning to leave. You want to break your contract. You're going to walk out on your family, your friends, your students." Beth wanted to add, *you're going to walk out on me,* but her heart broke at the thought. She wouldn't be able to say it aloud. "What more is there to explain?"

"Nothing is certain yet."

"Yet? Jesus, Rory," Beth shouted. "Because the deal isn't sealed that makes it okay to lead me on, to lie to me?"

Rory stood up quickly. "I never lied to you, Beth. You knew I didn't come here to stay. You always knew how I felt."

"No, Rory, I obviously didn't know how you felt or I wouldn't be here tonight." Beth's eyes wandered to Rory's bare chest and a flame rose in her cheeks. What might have happened if Edmond's call had come an hour later? "You invited me to dinner at your parents', you brought me home with you, you were going to let me make love to you, for God's sake. How was I supposed to know you were secretly planning to make a break for it as soon as you could?"

"It's not like that, Beth."

"What's it like then?"

"I was putting some feelers out there," Rory said weakly, "exploring my options."

"Options?" Beth blew up again. "And what am I, one of those options? Was I supposed to wait around and hope you picked me? Did you even intend to tell me, or were you planning to sleep with me until you decided to run away again?"

"I'm glad to see you have such a high opinion of me," Rory said, anger rising in her voice as she grabbed her shirt off the floor and pulled it over her head. "If you remember correctly, you're the one who ripped this off me twice today, not the other way around."

"You're right. I fell right into your hands, but I'm sure you're used to that by now. You played me perfectly." Beth cringed at the thought but could find no other explanation.

"You really think that's what happened here? You think I played you? That I misled you to get you into bed?" Rory sounded incredulous.

"What other reason is there?"

"Did you ever stop to think that I was still trying to figure things out? That maybe I was scared and confused because my life wasn't turning out how I'd planned? Or maybe I was falling for you too, and I was trying to figure out what that meant to my career."

"Excuse me. When you put it like that it sounds much better. You like me, but you don't want me to damage your public persona? You don't want the country girl to get in the way of big, bad Raine? I might ruin your image?"

"I didn't mean that." Rory pushed her hands roughly through her hair, causing some of it to fall lightly across her forehead in that disheveled look Beth couldn't help but find a little sexy even now. "I meant that I haven't figured out some things yet, and I haven't decided what I need to do."

"Let me make it easy for you." Beth finally stepped close enough to catch the scent of Rory's cologne, but this time it wasn't intoxicating. Nothing but a seething calm overwhelmed her. "Choose your precious image, because I'm no longer an option. I just got out of one relationship because it had no future and I was tired of being a doormat. I'm not going there again."

"Beth, please don't do this. Please don't give up on us before we even get a chance to see where this is headed."

"We were never headed anywhere together." She sighed heavily as she tried to come to terms with that fact. "I was falling in love with Rory, but you were always thinking about Raine. I told you a while ago that you needed to choose between the two. You've clearly chosen Raine, and I don't like her. In fact, I hate her. I want Raine St. James out of my life for good."

"You don't mean that."

"I do. I wish I'd never brought you here."

Rory cocked her head to the side as though she'd misheard. "You mean you wish the college had never brought me here?"

Beth shook her head. She'd put off this conversation long enough, and she didn't know why. "No, I was the chair of the committee. I lobbied for the position, I pitched you to the board, and I contacted your agent. It was always me."

Rory stared at her in shock. "But why?"

"I read your writing, and you sounded so miserable. I knew you were running out of options. I felt drawn to you, and I wanted to help."

"How dare you," Rory whispered, pausing for a moment before she found her voice again. "What right did you have to put me through this? You set me up to endure all the hell I've faced here, and you knew all along that it was your fault. Who was lying then? Who was misleading who all this time?"

The words hit Beth like an icy wind, chilling her through. "You're right. I overstepped my bounds."

"You're damned right you did," Rory shouted as she charged across the room and opened the door. "You wrecked me."

Beth stared at the door. If she walked out now it would be the end—the end of her time with Rory, the end of their potential as a couple, the end of all her secret hopes and dreams for their future together.

Beth stopped in the doorway to look back at Rory one last time before she closed the door to her completely. "Then we're even, because you've broken my heart."

CHAPTER TWENTY

October 15

"What should we do for our class project?" one of Raine's students asked.

"We should do something for homecoming next weekend," another answered. Raine wasn't paying enough attention to the conversation to notice who said what.

"We could gay up the parade, get some dykes on bikes and some go-go boys."

They all laughed. "What do you think, Raine?"

"That sounds great," Raine said absentmindedly as she stared out the window. She could just barely make out the front doors of the library from where she sat in the classroom. She hadn't been able to force her eyes off the view for the last forty-five minutes. She was dying to see Beth, to make sure she was okay and that the haunted look had left her beautiful blue eyes, but she was also praying she wouldn't see her, for fear of how she'd react. She'd felt volatile the last few days and never knew when she'd get the urge to cry or throw something.

"Earth to Raine," Scott said. "Did you hear any of this conversation?"

"Yeah, go-go boys," Raine repeated before the phrase sank in. "Wait. What?"

The students chuckled, this time more nervously. "We're talking about our end-of-the-semester project."

"Right. Well, it's up to you, but if you want to change minds I'd stay away from turning Homecoming into a Pride parade."

"What do you suggest?"

"How about a Day of Silence? It's a program where students who support LGBT rights take an eight-hour vow of silence to symbolize the way society has silenced gays and lesbians throughout history."

"But our voices are our strongest weapons. Why would we willingly give them up?" one of the girls asked. "Did Harvey Milk or Margaret Mead stay silent?"

"I think that's the point," Scott cut back in. "What would the world be like today if they *had* been silent? We wouldn't have the plays of Oscar Wilde or the poems of James Baldwin."

"And where would the civil-rights movement have been without Bayard Rustin or the feminist movement without Rita Mae Brown?" The idea began to pick up and names began to be thrown out from all corners of the room.

It was hard to believe this was the same group of students she could barely get to say two words six weeks ago. They'd come so far, and their enthusiasm seemed to grow daily. Raine felt energized after every class. In fact, this week her students were the only thing that had kept her from crashing completely.

"But the National Day of Silence isn't until April," one of the students said. "We want to make an impact now."

Raine smiled at his impatience. She could identify. "Sorry, it doesn't work that way. Sometimes we don't feel the effect of our decisions for years, even decades. Many of the great pioneers never lived to see the dreams they set in motion come true."

As she spoke, she realized the same was true of her own career. Every now and then she heard from audience members after the fact. She got the occasional fan letter, but most of the time she gave her speeches, signed a few autographs, and moved on to the next town. This was the first time she'd been able to watch her effect on a group of people long-term.

Her mood lightened. At least her time in Darlington hadn't been a total waste. She'd clearly made a difference in the lives of her students, and no matter what Beth thought, Raine did care about people other than herself.

Why did everything always come back to Beth? Raine couldn't get Beth's accusations out of her head. How could Beth think Raine only cared about her career and getting laid? Why couldn't she see how hard Raine was trying? Didn't it mean anything that she'd reconciled with her parents or that she'd opened up to her? What about the fact that she'd summoned all her willpower to consider Beth's feelings when they'd started making love? What kind of sex-crazed maniac did that?

She was trying to make sense of all the changes, trying to figure out who she was now, trying to do right by her. What more did Beth want? More importantly, why should Raine care? Beth hadn't given her that consideration when she had dragged her back to Darlington.

"We can always get together next semester," another student said, as if that was the simplest answer in the world. He had no idea that the words cut through Raine's inner monologue like a dart to her chest, reminding her how she'd let everyone down if she broke her contract.

"I think we should table this discussion for now," Raine said, rubbing her eyes. "Go home, think it over, and we'll pick this up again next week."

The students looked at her and then glanced at the clock, no doubt confused that she was hurrying them out the door ten minutes early. She'd never done that before, and often many of them lingered to chat with Raine about whatever was on their mind.

Today Raine didn't have the energy. She was too busy maintaining her anger at Beth while trying to forget the crushing hurt she'd last seen on her face. She couldn't think about disappointing her students as well.

Raine packed her things and began to trudge across campus. The crisp breeze blew through her hair and she suddenly envisioned Beth standing beside her, her dark curls windswept and her cheeks rosy. "Damn," she muttered under her breath. Her mind had been playing tricks like that on her all week. Why couldn't she get Beth off her mind? Why couldn't she summon up enough anger to burn away the hurt?

She had every right to be furious with Beth, and intellectually she was. She was angry at being pulled back into her past. She was livid that Beth hadn't been up front with her sooner. She was upset that Beth basically called her self-centered and phony. She was infuriated that after all she'd done to open up to Beth, after all the risks she'd taken, Beth had the nerve to push for more. With all those reasons to be pissed off, why did she still long to be with Beth, to hold her, kiss her, wipe away her pain?

"Raine?"

She turned around to see Flores Molina hurrying to catch her.

"You're in your own world," Flores said with her usual bustle of energy. "I've been chasing you halfway across the quad."

"Sorry," Raine mumbled. She should probably be more social with the dean of the college, but she wasn't in the mood for small talk. "What can I do for you?"

"Our Homecoming speaker canceled on us for next weekend, and I was racking my brain trying to come up with an idea when I saw you."

"You want my ideas?"

"No, I want you." Flores laughed. "I bet women tell you that a lot, but in this situation I mean I want you academically."

Raine forced a grin. She did enjoy working for this woman. "I'm not sure I follow."

"I want you to give the opening address at Homecoming next Friday."

"Oh, well—"

"Don't 'oh well' me. The theme is Expanding Horizons. It's perfect for you, and I know you don't have any problems with public speaking."

Raine quickly tried to come up with a logical reason to refuse, but Flores interpreted her silence as acceptance, or at least as resignation, and gave her a quick hug. "You'll be great."

Raine stood, stunned as Flores hurried off again, stopping only to call "thank you" over her shoulder as she went. What the hell had she gotten herself into now? She couldn't even focus on her classes. How would she be able to keep her mind off Beth long enough to prepare a speech for the entire campus? Then again, maybe a project was what she needed to prove to herself there was more to her existence than Beth Devoroux.

❖

October 19

Beth pushed her shopping cart through the grocery store. She needed to eat, but nothing appealed to her. It was unusual for her to lose her appetite. She'd barely been able to choke down a few bites of food a day since last Sunday at Raine's parents' home. She'd always had the stereotypical farmer's stomach, and the last time she'd been too upset to eat was when her parents had died.

How could losing Rory compare to her parents' death? She'd only had Rory in her life for the past two months. So what if she had hoped for much more than that? It was a silly dream.

What hurt the worst was that the dream had felt so close. Last Sunday when Rory picked her up for dinner, Beth could practically feel forever in the air. Rory's smile when she opened the car door and the tenderness in her eyes as they'd stood on her parents' doorstep were so endearing. The ease with which they'd settled in around the St. James dining table made Beth feel like she was meant to be there. Then the fire that consumed her and Rory that night stirred an ache in Beth's chest that she'd never known could exist. Everything had been perfect, too perfect.

No matter how possible the dream felt that night, Rory wasn't even real. No, that wasn't true, and even in her hurt and anger she knew that Rory was the truth and Raine was the illusion. Unfortunately, she could spend the rest of her life trying to convince Rory of that fact and never succeed.

Beth felt like a fool. She'd been pouring her heart out, and Rory had only been killing time. She supposed she should have been flattered that Rory was willing to go to such great lengths to bed her. She obviously didn't invite just anyone home to meet her parents, but Beth had misread that event as suggesting she wanted something more than a few nights of hot sex.

The sex would've been hot, Beth was certain. She could still feel the way Rory's skin burned under her touch and the complete abandon it inspired in her. She'd never been so consumed with desire. She'd practically tackled Rory when she asked if she wanted to go through with what Beth had thought would be a long night of lovemaking.

And what was that? A perfect act? Did Rory ask all the women that question, or was it one final ploy to give Beth a false sense of security? She was so smooth, and Beth had fallen for her act. She groaned aloud.

"Hey, stranger, you okay?" Tyler asked as he stood up from restocking the meat counter.

Beth blushed, ashamed to be caught agonizing in the deli section. "I'm fine."

"You sure?" Concern filled Tyler's normally jovial expression. "You look like shit."

"Thanks." Beth grimaced. That was how she felt, but at least everyone at work had been polite enough not to mention that it showed.

"I'm serious. What happened to you?"

How could she tell him that she'd let herself fall for one of their mutual friends and got her heart broken? That would put him right in the middle of everything, not to mention the embarrassment of telling him what a fool she'd been. But she couldn't go on much longer with all this angst locked up inside. So, without giving any thought to her surroundings, she threw her arms around him and allowed the tears to fall.

She blubbered, "I almost slept with Rory, and she's running away again after we had dinner with her parents, and she wasn't going to tell me. I think I fell in love with her."

"Oh, Jesus," Tyler murmured, and ushered her back into the storeroom. "So you fell for Rory and she rejected you?"

"Yes," Beth said with a sniffle. "Not exactly. She kissed me, we went to dinner at her parents', and she wanted to sleep with me, but she doesn't want to be with me."

"She said that?"

"No, but she's leaving. She wrote some big article, and her agent found a way to break her contract so she can go back on tour."

Tyler rubbed the stubble on his chin. "Isn't that what Rory does for a living? Goes on tours, talks to crowds, writes articles?"

"Not when she's under contract with the college," Beth said in a huff. She couldn't believe she'd poured her heart out to Tyler and he was siding with Rory. "And not when she's leading me on."

"I didn't mean that she should leave. I didn't even know you two were dating."

"We just started." Beth paused. Were they dating? They'd had one date and a couple of make-out sessions. "She took me home to meet her parents. What does that mean to you, Tyler?"

He nodded solemnly. "That's pretty serious. You don't generally do that with someone you plan to leave in a few weeks."

"Right," Beth said emphatically.

"So maybe she wasn't planning to. Maybe she wants to date long-distance or have you go with her."

The thought hadn't occurred to Beth, but she dismissed it quickly. "She should have talked to me about that before she tried to get me into bed."

"Well, yeah," Tyler blushed a little, "but some of us forget the details when we see a pretty girl."

Beth cracked a bit of a smile. "Rory knows exactly what she's doing with women."

"Maybe," Tyler admitted, "but we both know Rory's not as confident as she wants everyone to believe, especially with everything she's been through in the last few months."

"Don't make excuses for her." Beth didn't want to sympathize with Rory. She recalled Rory's expression when she told her she wanted Raine out of her life completely and realized grudgingly that perhaps Rory was a little wounded too, but she didn't care about that now.

"I'm just saying that a lot has changed in her life. She's got to be confused."

Beth found it strange that Tyler was using the same words Rory had used. "What about me, Tyler? I've come out of the closet, been through a breakup, and fallen head over heels for someone who wanted to get as far away from here as possible."

"That'd be confusing too. You two are about as different as they come, and neither of you is likely to have a personality transplant anytime soon."

"What am I supposed to do?"

Tyler shrugged. "Hell if I know. When's the last time you saw me in a serious relationship? I'm more of a buy-you-beer-and-make-you-smile kind of a guy. I'm not the person you ask for love advice."

Beth sighed. She hadn't really expected answers from Tyler. She hadn't expected so many questions from him either. She'd wanted him to be outraged on her behalf, not make her consider Rory's side of things.

"Can I do something to make you feel better?"

"No. I thought only Rory could make things better, but after talking to you, I'm not even sure she's capable of that."

Tyler frowned. "Glad I could help."

As Beth left the store without buying anything, she felt even worse. Now not only was she brokenhearted, she might be at fault. Had she pushed Rory too hard? Had she tried to make her something she wasn't? She'd always thought she was helping Rory by bringing her home. But perhaps she'd really been forcing her own agenda all along. She'd worried she was falling in love with someone who *wouldn't* love her, but maybe Rory simply *couldn't*. The prospect seemed even more hopeless now.

❖

October 23

Raine startled awake and tried to make sense of her surroundings. She was slumped at the bar that divided her kitchen from her living room. She'd fallen asleep sitting up for the third time that week. She'd given up on her bed, hoping to avoid the vivid dreams of her and Beth together.

The couch was equally haunting; she couldn't even sit there without memories flooding her—Beth on top of her, their lips pressed together while they allowed their hands to roam freely over each other's bodies. Raine could still feel Beth's supple figure and the tantalizing bit of skin that she'd been able to caress before they were interrupted.

She'd replayed that horrible moment in her dreams every night, and now it was happening during the day too. In its current variation Raine had been making out with Beth on the very bar where she was currently sitting, but all that was left now was a small puddle of drool.

"That's sexy," Raine groused, and picked up her pen. She had to finish this speech. She was due at the auditorium in two hours to speak to the entire student body, the faculty and staff, and a large group of alumni. She'd been writing all week, but nothing had any spark. Expanding Horizons should have been the perfect topic for someone who'd made a name for herself by leaving a small town for the big city. She'd traveled all over America and met people from so many different backgrounds that she couldn't even remember them all. Speeches like this were usually simple for her. Why was she having such a difficult time with this one?

Her deep depression didn't help. Her sadness over hurting Beth had infiltrated every aspect of her life. She'd missed a meeting with the Pride students because she couldn't focus on her schedule. She hadn't gone to Miles's on Sunday for fear of seeing Beth, and she'd skipped dinner with her parents because she didn't want to answer their questions. She'd called and told her mother she wasn't feeling well, which wasn't really a lie. Now she couldn't even do the thing she was famous for—woo an audience with stories of her life. Most disturbing, though, she couldn't muster up her trademark anger.

Rage had always been her standby. When she was scared, she got angry. When she was lonely, she got angry. When she was confronted, she got angry. Now she was all of those things, and she merely felt sad, though not the simple kind of sadness that came from life's little disappointments. Raine's sadness was deep, bone-aching, and mind-numbing. Every time she thought of Beth, her chest literally throbbed. She'd hurt Beth. She'd let her down. Raine had broken Beth's heart, which in turn broke her own, but what could she do?

She'd tried to explain her reasoning, but Beth wouldn't listen. Beth had never listened to her. Beth had a vision of what Raine's life should be and she didn't stop to hear Raine's protests. She'd brought her here against her will. She'd dragged her out with Chris and Tyler. She'd browbeaten Rory until she met with her parents. Beth did nothing but push her from the moment she arrived back in town, and Raine had nothing more to give.

Not that Beth expected anything from her now. She'd made it clear that she wanted Raine out of her life for good. It was probably better that way, so why did it hurt so badly?

The phone rang and Raine snatched it. It couldn't be Beth, but a part of her was still disappointed to hear Edmond on the line. "Where have you been? You haven't returned my calls all week."

"I've had a lot on my mind," Raine mumbled. She didn't want to go into it, but Edmond wouldn't give up until he got his fill of her dirty laundry.

"Did you already fuck it up with Beth?"

"Why do you assume I messed it up?"

"Honey, it's what you do when someone challenges you. You lash out. It's your MO, but I thought she might be the one who'd give it right back to you."

"You don't know what you're talking about." Raine ignored the inner voice that told her he'd been brutally accurate. "She'd been lying to me this whole time."

"Really? Miss Sweet-Down-Home is a great deceiver? That doesn't sound like her."

"She was the one who brought me here, Edmond. She's the one who put me through this hell, and she never told me."

"That's why her name sounded familiar. She called to ask about you." Edmond sounded like he'd just remembered what he forgot to pick up at the grocery store, not like someone who'd been told a revealing secret.

"Did you hear what I said? Beth's responsible for me being stuck in Darlington."

"That's one take on it."

"Are you going to tell me another way to look at it?"

"How about you were broke, got evicted, and she gave you the only job you'd been offered in months?"

"Damnit, Edmond." Raine jumped off the bar stool and began to pace around the apartment. "She orchestrated the whole thing. If she'd stayed out of my business I wouldn't—"

"What?" Edmond asked sharply. "You wouldn't have a place to live? Wouldn't have a job? Wouldn't have reconciled with your parents? Wouldn't have finally met the one woman who doesn't let you act like a sullen teenager?"

Raine was glad he couldn't see her with her mouth stretched open. Edmond had never talked to her like that, and she couldn't think of a single rebuttal. "You make it sound like she's the best thing that's ever happened to me."

Edmond sighed wearily. "I didn't say that, but maybe you should think about it."

"It sounds like you like her more than you like me."

"Don't be such a twit, Raine. I like her because I love you." He chuckled. "And you were happier down there than I've ever seen you. You're the only one who can't grasp that."

"What about my career?" she asked weakly as she sank to the floor. All her energy drained out of her at the daunting shift she was facing.

"You've reached a dead end," he said sympathetically. "You need to revise your act or find a new one. No one wants to hear from a twenty-seven-year-old who's still pissed off at her parents."

"I'm not pissed at my parents. I'm not pissed at anybody," Raine finally admitted aloud. "Being back here has changed me."

"That's a new spin on things." Edmond paused. "Actually, redemption is big right now. I could sell that."

"You think being back here redeemed me?"

"I don't know, has it?"

Raine reached back to steady herself even though she was already sitting on the floor. She thought of Chris and Tyler, of her students, her parents and brother, but mostly she thought of Beth.

Beth smiling at her in a cornfield under the moonlight. Beth holding her while they danced in her apartment. Beth's pride in her the night they helped Scott. Beth's hand in hers under the table at her parents' house. Beth kissing her and making all her uncertainty disappear. That was why she wasn't angry anymore. Beth had soothed something inside her. Beth had changed the way she viewed the world. Beth had changed the way she saw herself.

"Damn, Edmond, I did fuck it up."

"You better fix it," he said flatly.

"I don't know if I can." That thought sank in slowly, and Raine felt like she was sinking too. How was she supposed to be what Beth needed? How could they possibly work through this? Was Beth even willing to give her another chance?

"I can't sell this story if you don't get the girl, and you'll be miserable without her."

"I'm hanging up on you now."

"Wait."

"What?"

"Did Miles say anything about me after I left?"

Raine rolled her eyes and dropped the receiver. She'd deal with that problem later. Right now she needed to figure out if she could salvage the greatest thing she'd ever thrown away.

CHAPTER TWENTY-ONE

Beth tried to smile as she led a group of distinguished alumni to their reserved seats in the auditorium. She'd volunteered to usher for the homecoming address before she knew Rory would be the keynote speaker, and by then it was too late to find a replacement. She would simply put on a happy face and sneak out unnoticed before Rory spoke. She was being childish but wasn't sure how she'd react to seeing Rory, and she didn't want to find out in a room filled with the entire population of Bramble College.

Beth was ashamed of the way she'd fallen apart. She'd been a wreck for the last twelve days, not that she was counting. She hadn't thought it possible to be more upset than she'd been during the first week, but after she talked to Tyler on Monday, she began to question her own involvement in her estrangement with Rory. Had she demanded that Rory be someone she couldn't be or asked more from her than she could give? Had she fallen for an imaginary woman, and if so, could she ever settle for anything less than the Rory St. James she believed existed?

The overhead lights dimmed, signaling the crowd to settle down. Beth scanned the room one more time to make sure no one else needed a seat, though she wouldn't be much help since the auditorium appeared to be filled to capacity. She wasn't surprised to see so many people turn out for Rory's speech. She was born to command an audience, and Beth knew she'd be stunning under the spotlight, which was exactly why Beth had to get out of there.

Beth sighed in relief when the last member of the board of trustees was seated and the lights dimmed completely. With everyone's attention focused on the stage, she'd be able to make her getaway. The only thing to stop her was Dean Flores Molina, who was walking down the main aisle right toward her.

"Beth." Flores clutched Beth's shoulder. "Come sit with me up front."

"No." Beth shook her head vehemently, then realized how dramatic she was being and tried to control her fear. "I mean, I'm ushering. I should wait in the lobby for late arrivals."

"Nonsense." Flores looped an arm around her waist and nudged her down the walkway. "There are plenty of ushers here. This is your big moment too. Raine wouldn't be here if it hadn't been for you."

The words hit Beth with unexpected force, leaving her breathless and unable to reply as Flores dragged her the rest of the way to their seats in the front row.

The president of the student body began to introduce Rory, but Beth couldn't hear a word over the roar of her own pulse pounding through her ears. The dull throb emanating from where her heart should be coursed through her body from the knot in her stomach to the tension in her neck. Rory had always affected her on a physical level, but this was not the pleasant tingle of anticipation Beth had grown used to.

A round of applause signaled the end of Rory's introduction, and despite wanting to close her eyes and cover her ears with the futility of a child hiding from a storm, Beth watched as Rory strode onto the stage in a charcoal suit that was obviously custom-made. From the way the slacks clung to her hips to the subtle intake of the short jacket along her sides, every stitch accentuated the peaks and hollows that Beth had so recently caressed. She craved to reach out and touch Rory but flamed with longing when she gazed upward past the deep green oxford shirt that set off the emerald in Rory's eyes. They were hollow and searching, red-ringed and unsteady as Rory scanned the crowd before her.

The audience waited patiently while Rory shifted some papers, then looked up and shook a wayward tuft of hair from her forehead.

She regarded the crowd with her rakish grin, and Beth could practically feel the people around her fall in love with Rory, even as her own heart broke again. Despite appearing tired, Rory had presence. She was magnetic. She was stunning and she hadn't even said a word.

"Students, faculty, staff, alumni, and distinguished guests," Rory began, "welcome to your Bramble College Homecoming weekend. I'm Raine St. James."

She paused for effect as she made eye contact with several audience members. Beth held her breath as Rory's eyes met her own and tried desperately to read the roiling emotions that flooded across Rory's face. Certainly she was surprised, but Beth also detected pain and perhaps regret, or was she simply projecting her own feelings? Rory stepped backward and shook her head. "I'm sorry. I need to start over."

The audience chuckled as though this was a joke, some narrative ploy or rhetorical strategy to keep them interested, but Rory was apparently struggling to keep her composure. *I shouldn't be here. She's still mad at me.* Rory shuffled some papers before she set them aside and exhaled forcefully. She looked up once more, her uncertainty fading under a growing resolve. "I'm not Raine St. James."

Again, a burst of laugher from the crowd, which obviously misunderstood the gravity of the words they'd heard, but Rory continued. "I'm not really Raine. I'm Rory St. James. Just Rory."

Beth fought to suppress the wave of joy rising in her. This woman had hurt her before. Beth had to be cautious, but hearing Rory say those simple words cracked her resolve because she knew Rory hadn't said them lightly. Rory's next words confirmed that understanding.

"That's not easy for me to say because I've worked hard to become Raine. To abandon that identity after so long takes a lot out of me. It takes a lot away from me too. So much of the way I view myself and the way I view the world was tied to the identity I'd created for myself.

"When I was Raine, I knew where I stood. I knew where I was headed and how to relate to people. There were no shades of gray. I was secure in who I was, and I was known for not compromising." Rory stopped and pushed her hands through her hair, then cracked a smile. "I wasn't just known for it. I was famous for it, and that's why I'm up here today."

Rory faced Beth again. "I put myself in this position through the choices I made during the last ten years. I've traveled the world, and I was supposed to bring all my radical knowledge to the students of this little college and expand their horizons." She spoke with enough self-deprecation to get a chuckle from the crowd.

"Expanding Horizons, developing a broader worldview and a stronger sense of how we fit in it, that's the theme of this weekend. It's been more than that, though. It's been the theme of my last few months. I thought I understood what it meant to expand my horizons, but recently I've come to realize that as important as it is to meet new people, see new places, and do new things, it can be even more life-altering to face old things in a new way."

Rory was in her groove now. She had the audience's full attention. She made the large space feel intimate, like she was having a conversation over drinks instead of making a formal presentation to hundreds of people. For that's exactly what Rory was doing, Beth realized. Rory was speaking directly to her. Despite the crowd she continued to bring her attention back to Beth every time she made a point that related to their relationship, and each time she did, a little piece of Beth's heart fell back into place.

"Before I returned here, I had a lot of ideas about what it meant to be gay and what it meant to live in a small town. I thought I knew what it meant to be a friend or part of a family. I even thought I knew what it meant to be loved, but only when I was forced to move past all my preconceived notions did I realize what I'd been closing myself off from."

This time when their eyes met, Beth sensed several other people turning to see her too, but she didn't care. Rory's gaze never wavered as she delivered her next line. "In all my worldly wisdom, I missed out on the most essential human experience of loving and being loved."

Beth's tears began to fall. A few minutes ago she couldn't conceive of a way for her and Rory to reconcile. Now she couldn't imagine not spending the rest of their lives together. Beth mouthed, "I love you," and a smile spread across Rory's face. This time the expression reached her eyes, sparking them back to life as she returned her attention to her audience.

"You can go anywhere and try anything, but until you're open to new outcomes, your life will remain limited to the same lonely confines that have always boxed you in. My advice to you, whether you're seeing a new continent or driving a familiar road, is to be open. Open yourself to new experiences, new people, and new understandings, because when you open your heart, you open your mind, and by extension you expand your horizons."

The crowd was on its feet before Rory had even taken her bow. The round of applause seemed to last an eternity while Beth fought to keep herself from jumping onstage and wrapping Rory in her arms. She waited while a line of admirers formed to congratulate Rory. The college president, every member of the board of trustees, and a large group of students all wanted a moment with Rory. Beth didn't blame them. She was still processing everything she'd heard, but her heart pounded in response to Rory's words. Rory had let go of Raine. She was facing life with a new attitude. She loved her.

She loves me. Beth flopped back into her seat. Rory loved her, and she loved Rory. How had she missed that? Through all the talk of careers, families, and futures, they'd overlooked the fact that they'd fallen in love. Apparently Rory wasn't the only one who needed to expand her horizons.

Rory glanced over again and weakly smiled before she turned back to the woman she was talking to. Beth settled in for a long delay. She'd waited for Rory for ten years so a few more minutes wouldn't kill her, but Rory obviously wasn't adding patience to her new list of virtues. She abruptly cut off whatever the woman was saying by taking her hand and shaking it emphatically and walking away. The woman stood with a puzzled expression as Beth watched Rory approach.

"Come on." Rory grabbed her hand and led her out a side door of the auditorium. They continued to push past several groups of people on the way out. Rory ignored them all, and a thrill rose in Beth.

"All those people wanted to talk to you," she said as they hurried across the quad and into Rory's building.

"I don't want to talk to them. I want to talk to you."

Beth blocked the door to Rory's apartment with her body. "You dragged me all the way back here because you want to talk?"

"I do want to talk," Rory wrapped her arms around Beth's waist and kissed her thoroughly on the mouth, "among other things."

Once they were inside with the door locked, Rory made a big show of unplugging the phone. She then turned back to Beth. "I was an idiot."

Beth laughed. It was hard to argue with that statement. "I wasn't on my best behavior either, but I think we can do better in the future."

"The future? I was afraid I'd mucked it up too badly for you to ever trust me again."

Beth's heart ached at the uncertainty in Rory's eyes, and she clasped Rory's hand. "I want a future with you in whatever form it may take. We're facing big changes, but I want to face them together."

"Together." Rory kissed Beth's hand, then worked her way up her arm, placing a kiss every few inches until her lips were near Beth's ear. "I like the sound of that."

Beth let her head loll back, luxuriating in the feel of Rory's lips against the sensitive skin of her neck. The warmth in her stomach flared into a burning tide that spread rapidly through her. Her love and attraction for Rory melded into a force she couldn't contain. She ran her hands up Rory's back, squeezing their bodies together as she kissed her.

Beth's lips parted, offering access to Rory's tongue, which quickly swept across her own, but instead of fulfilling her need, the kiss only increased it. She ran her hand inside Rory's suit coat and pushed it from her shoulders. As they continued to kiss, Beth fingered the buttons on Rory's deep green oxford. She popped the top button, then another, before Rory clutched her hands.

"No," Rory mumbled. "I'm not doing that again."

"What?"

Rory stepped back. "Every time you tear off my shirt, you run away, leaving me half naked and completely confused."

Beth laughed. "Okay, do you want me to go first?"

The hunger in Rory's eyes as she nodded was all the encouragement Beth needed to grip the hem of her sweater between her fingers and lift it slowly over her head. Then she reached back and unclasped her bra, dropping it onto the growing pile of clothes at her feet. Rory swallowed audibly and Beth blushed at Rory's expression, but the heat in her cheeks wasn't from embarrassment. It was from desire.

She pulled Rory against her, connecting their bodies and mouths once again. This time when Rory ran her hands up Beth's sides, she caressed bare skin. Beth wasn't sure which of them groaned when Rory cupped her breast, and she didn't care. Consumed by the feel of Rory against her, Beth knew she wouldn't last long and began to guide Rory toward the bedroom.

They fumbled across the apartment with Beth unbuttoning Rory's shirt and Rory unclasping Beth's belt while somewhere along the way they both kicked off their shoes. Beth slipped her hands inside Rory's shirt and tugged it from her waistband. Then sitting on the edge of the bed, she unbuttoned the pants and placed a kiss on Rory's stomach as she slowly unzipped the slacks. She pushed them down over Rory's hips, leaving her in only her boxers.

She was stunning, her body everything Beth had imagined. Rory had subtle muscles blending into firm abs, and her stomach was only slightly less firm. Beth wanted to touch her, all of her, and she began to remove the boxers, but Rory stopped her by laying her back on the bed, gently cupping Beth's head as it fell onto the pillow.

"You're the most beautiful thing I've ever seen," Rory whispered. Beth wanted to protest. Surely Rory had been with plenty of gorgeous women. She wanted to ask how a plain, simple farm girl could ever compare, but the words died inside of her when Rory lowered her head and traveled slowly down the length of Beth's body, placing a mix of kisses—some soft, some sexy—along her chest, arms, and stomach. Beth raised her hips, allowing Rory to pull her khakis off and continue her trail of kisses down one leg and back up the other. Beth gasped as Rory neared her inner thigh and breathed against the pulsing between her legs.

"God, Rory, I want you so much," Beth said even as she realized words couldn't express how she felt. More than a want or even a need, she craved the feel of Rory inside her, desired her in every way, emotionally and physically. If Rory didn't touch her soon, she'd pass out or perhaps disintegrate. She'd spent a lifetime putting others first, but now in Rory's arms she wanted what she wanted. Mercifully, Rory didn't make her wait long before she lowered her head and sucked Beth into her mouth.

The sensation of Rory's insistent stroking sent Beth into overload. Her head lolled back on the bed and her hips rocked involuntarily to the rhythm of Rory's tongue on her clit. The tension inside her coiled quickly, but Rory must have sensed how close she was and slowed down. She continued to lightly caress Beth while easing first one finger, then two, inside her.

Beth was dizzy at the ecstasy that coursed through her, and her body began to act on its own, arching up to meet each of Rory's thrusts. As Rory increased her pace, Beth's thoughts and movements became erratic. No longer able to control herself, she surrendered to the explosion of pleasure that surged from every nerve ending. All her muscles tensed in unison, and she shuddered under Rory until her body gave way and collapsed completely.

She felt like weeping at the overwhelming sense of completion that swept over her. She'd never lost control like that. She'd never wanted to, but Rory made her feel safe, even cherished, as she wrapped her arms around Beth and drew her up against her own heaving chest. She placed light kisses along her forehead and temples and murmured, "I love you, Beth."

It was true. Rory loved her, and Beth loved her in return. She wanted to tell her that, show her, make her feel it too, but how could she give Rory what she'd just given her?

❖

Rory held Beth closely. She couldn't get enough of this woman, and she doubted she ever would. *We made love.* The thought floated through her head as she drew little dancing patterns across Beth's delicate skin. It was so easy. She didn't have to perform or be something she wasn't. Beth loved her, the real her. She didn't have to second-guess where she was supposed to be or what she was supposed to do. She was at ease with herself for the first time in over a decade. Love. She'd never experienced anything so beautiful or sexy. She wanted to laugh, or cry. Instead she hugged Beth, soaking up her scent, her feel, her taste.

Slowly her serenity gave way to a stirring just below the surface. Her body demanded attention. The way Beth was lightly kissing her chest was the cause, but once she started, would she be able to stop? Her need surged through her so quickly she worried that her desire would scare Beth. Her pulse quickened as Beth's kisses became more insistent, and she clutched the sheets for fear of hurting Beth.

"I want to make you feel good," Beth said, rolling Rory onto her back and straddling her waist. Rory wanted to say she already felt better, but the sight of Beth naked and rocking against her hips was too much. She only nodded and tried to swallow the dryness in her throat. Beth was even more striking than she'd dreamed. Tantalizing skin covered ample curves and full breasts that Rory had to fight not to grab. Her own need frightened her. She'd never let herself need anyone, and now she remembered why. It terrified her to feel this vulnerable, but it exhilarated her too.

Beth bent down so their bare chests met skin to skin. She kissed along Rory's throat and neck up to her ear before she whispered, "Tell me what you want."

"You." Rory choked on the word. "I want you so much I can hardly hold back."

Beth rolled onto her side, still pressed close as she ran her hand over Rory's breasts and down her stomach. "Don't hold back, Rory. Don't keep any part of you from me."

Rory exhaled shakily. She was right. It was time to let go. This was Beth, the woman who'd seen through all her charades. This was the woman she wanted to build a life with. If Rory's only sin was wanting Beth too much, then they'd both have to learn to live with it.

She kissed Beth again, this time allowing her passion to flow freely as she laced her fingers through dark silky curls. Beth worked her hand between their bodies and under the waistband of Rory's boxers, pushing them down over her hips. Rory didn't bother to kick the shorts all the way off. Instead she freed one leg and threw it over Beth, offering her total access as they lay on their sides facing each other.

Beth gently ran her fingers through Rory's wetness, slowly parting delicate folds. Rory groaned when Beth skimmed lightly across her clit with tantalizing strokes before she pulled back again. Beth never rushed into anything, and her lovemaking was no different. She leisurely acquainted herself with every inch of Rory's body. While one hand stayed between Rory's legs, Beth kissed her along her jaw, down her neck, and onto her chest. She caressed each breast with her lips and then her tongue. Rory arched into her, searching for release while simultaneously praying this exquisite torture would never end.

Slowly Beth's kisses stilled, and her touch grew more insistent. Rory lifted her eyes and met Beth's deep blue gaze. Her breath caught at the overwhelming rush of emotions there. Lust, desire, love, and devotion all mingled in Beth's eyes, or maybe they mirrored her own. Rory was captivated. She was still drowning in those azure oceans when Beth moved inside her, blurring the boundaries between their bodies. The physical collided with the emotional, heartbeats fell into time, and the barriers that had once stood between them crumbled to dust.

Rory never closed her eyes to the blinding light that exploded within her, crashing through her chest and echoing through her limbs. She held Beth's stare as Beth held her shaking body until the tremors subsided completely.

"You're amazing," Beth finally said when they were breathing normally again.

"Me?" Rory laughed. "That was all you. I've never felt anything like that before."

"How can you say that? I'm sure you've been with plenty of women who are thinner, or prettier, or more practiced."

Rory sat up quickly. How could Beth doubt her right now? Why couldn't she see herself the way Rory saw her? "No one has ever loved me like you just did. I've never opened myself up to anyone that way. I've always been performing. Even in bed I played a role. The great Raine St. James had a reputation to protect or sometimes hide behind, but you didn't want that. You didn't want her. You wanted Rory, and Rory has never made love to anyone before."

Beth's eye's filled with tears, but the smile that accompanied them eased Rory's tension. "I'm honored to be your first."

Rory gave her a goofy grin as she dropped back on the bed and hugged Beth once more. "My first. I like the sound of that, but I want you to be more than that. I want you to be the first, last, and only woman Rory St. James ever sleeps with."

Beth kissed her fully on the mouth before she leaned back long enough to ask, "How do you always know the right thing to say?"

"You inspire me to greatness."

Beth gave her a playful shove but quickly closed the distance between them with another searing kiss. This time they didn't pull away but allowed their hands to roam over each other's bare skin. They were lost in an eternity of exploration when a loud knock on Rory's apartment door interrupted their reverie.

"Go away," Rory groaned.

Beth sighed. "What if it's important?"

"I don't care if it's the pope," Rory grumbled, and stepped into her boxers. "You stay here while I go kill whoever's at the door, and we'll go back to where we left off."

Beth laughed as the door knocker struck again. "I'll be here as long as you want."

The words were almost as beautiful as the woman who'd said them. Rory thought about diving back in bed, but another loud knock made her growl and head toward the door, pulling on a T-shirt as she went.

Rory unlatched the deadbolt and swung open the door. "This better be good."

"That's not the way the dean of the college usually gets greeted," Flores said with a grin. "It's kind of refreshing, actually. You never cease to surprise me, like your speech today."

"Oh?" Why would the dean come to her personal apartment without warning, Rory wondered, but her body was still screaming at her to go back to bed.

"You surprised the board of trustees too," Flores continued quickly. "They'd been worried about you pushing a gay agenda, whatever that means, but now they're all convinced you're the kind of person they've been dreaming of."

"How's that?"

"Cultured enough to be credible, level-headed enough not to be threatening. One of them said, and I quote, 'Big-city ideas with a small-town sensibility.'"

Rory smiled and remembered her conversation with Miles about having to choose between small towns and diversity. "I guess we can have it all."

"Right now, you can have just about anything you want at this college, because I've been authorized to offer you a full-time job heading up our new Gender and Sexuality certificate program. It'll fall under Women's Studies, but you'll have a lot of say in the courses you design."

"Wow." Now Flores had Rory's full attention. This was her chance to secure her future in Darlington, her future with Beth. A week ago she would've felt nauseated at the thought of a life in her hometown. Even now it worried her that she didn't feel more unease at the prospect, but all she could think about was Beth. She wanted to drive to work with her in the morning, meet her on the quad for lunch, have dinner with Beth and her family, and make love to her every night. And she had the added bonus of continuing to work with the students she adored. "You've got a deal."

Flores seemed skeptical. "Don't you want to talk to your agent?"

"No, I want the job." The words were barely out of her mouth before someone slapped the back of her head.

Beth appeared beside her, wearing the green, button-down shirt Rory had discarded during their lovemaking. It came halfway down her thighs, covering enough to be decent but not enough to keep Rory's libido in check. "Hi, Flores. She'll accept on the condition that she teaches on a Tuesday/Thursday schedule and gets time for travel. She shouldn't give up the public speaking altogether."

Flores gave them a bemused smile. "And the surprises just keep on coming. I don't imagine there'll be any problem with those conditions. Whom should I send the contract to?"

Rory shrugged. She didn't know what was happening. All she could think about was how good Beth looked in her shirt and how much better she'd look out of it.

"Send it to Edmond. I'll read it before she signs."

"Great, then. I'll let you ladies get back to your evening," Flores said with a chuckle. "I won't expect to see you at any of the Homecoming festivities tonight."

Beth closed the door and pushed Rory up against it, kissing her forcefully on the mouth. Then she pulled back and punched her lightly on the arm.

"What was that for?"

"The kiss was for taking the job. The hit was for not talking to me about it first."

"I'm sorry. I thought you'd like having me around all the time." Rory found Beth genuinely perplexing, but somehow that only enhanced her charm.

"I'll love having you around all the time, but I don't want you to stop being you. You can't stay cooped up here forever. You're too good onstage to give that up, and I don't want to be the one who keeps Rory St. James from her adoring public."

"What if they don't like Rory? She's not as exciting as Raine was."

"She's more exciting." Beth slipped her hands under Rory's T-shirt, dragging her fingernails across the bare skin of her ribcage. "Audiences will love you almost as much as I do."

Rory shuddered at Beth's touch and allowed herself to be led back to bed. She couldn't imagine being apart from Beth even for one night. "If you love me so much, then how will you stand me being away on these speaking dates?"

Beth pushed her down on the bed. "Who said I wasn't going with you? I've still got a lot of ballparks to see."

Rory pulled Beth down on top of her, wrapping her in her arms and holding her tight. "I'll go anywhere you want to go or we'll stay right here forever. Whatever we do, I want to do it together."

About the Author

Rachel Spangler never set out to be an award winning author. She was just so poor and so easily bored during her college years that she had to come up with creative ways to entertain herself, and her first novel, *Learning Curve,* was born out of one such attempt. She was sincerely surprised when it was accepted for publication and even more shocked when it won the Golden Crown Literary Award for Debut Author. Since writing was turning out to be a real blast, Rachel decided to combine it with another passion and set her next romance on the ski slopes, and was absolutely stunned when her second novel, *Trails Merge,* won a Goldie in the category of Contemporary Romance. However, no amount of book signing or award winning can really change a Midwestern boi, and her third novel, *The Long Way Home,* is just that, a return to the themes and settings that mean the most in Rachel's life and writing.

Rachel and her partner, Susan, are raising their young son in small-town western New York, where during the winter they all make the most of the lake-effect snow on local ski slopes, and in summer they love to travel and watch their beloved St. Louis Cardinals. Regardless of the season, Rachel always makes time for a good romance, whether she's reading it, writing it, or living it.

Rachel can be found online at www.rachelspangler.com as well as on Facebook.

Books Available From Bold Strokes Books

The Long Way Home by Rachel Spangler. They say you can't go home again, but Raine St. James doesn't know why anyone would want to. When she is forced to accept a job in the town she's been publicly bashing for the last decade, she has to face down old hurts and the woman she left behind. (978-1-60282-178-1)

Water Mark by J.M. Redmann. PI Micky Knight's professional and personal lives are torn asunder by Katrina and its aftermath. She needs to solve a murder and recapture the woman she lost while struggling to simply survive in a world gone mad. (978-1-60282-179-8)

Picture Imperfect by Lea Santos. Young love doesn't always stand the test of time, but Deanne is determined to get her marriage to childhood sweetheart Paloma back on the road to happily ever after, by way of Memory Lane-and Lover's Lane. (978-1-60282-180-4)

The Perfect Family by Kathryn Shay. A mother and her gay son stand hand in hand as the storms of change engulf their perfect family and the life they knew. (978-1-60282-181-1)

Raven Mask by Winter Pennington. Preternatural Private Investigator (and closeted werewolf) Kassandra Lyall needs to solve a murder and protect her Vampire lover Lenorre, Countess Vampire of Oklahoma all while fending off the advances of the local werewolf alpha female. (978-1-60282-182-8)

The Devil be Damned by Ali Vali. The fourth book in the best-selling Cain Casey Devil series. (978-1-60282-159-0)

Descent by Julie Cannon. Shannon Roberts and Caroline Davis compete in the world of world-class bike racing and pretend that the fire between them is just professional rivalry, not desire. (978-1-60282-160-6)

Kiss of Noir by Clara Nipper. Nora Delany is a hard-living, sweet-talking woman who can't say no to a beautiful babe or a friend in danger a darkly humorous homage to a bygone era of tough broads and murder in steamy New Orleans. (978-1-60282-161-3)

Under Her Skin by Lea Santos. Supermodel Lilly Lujan hasn't a care in the world, except life is lonely in the spotlight until Mexican gardener Torien Pacias sees through Lilly's façade and offers gentle understanding and friendship when Lilly most needs it. (978-1-60282-162-0)

Fierce Overture by Gun Brooke. Helena Forsythe is a hard-hitting CEO who gets what she wants by taking no prisoners when negotiating until she meets a woman who convinces her that charm may be the way to win a battle, and a heart. (978-1-60282-156-9)

Trauma Alert by Radclyffe. Dr. Ali Torveau has no trouble saying no to romance until the day firefighter Beau Cross shows up in her ER and sets her carefully ordered world aflame. (978-1-60282-157-6)

Wolfsbane Winter by Jane Fletcher. Iron Wolf mercenary Deryn faces down demon magic and otherworldly foes with a smile, but she's defenseless when healer Alana wages war on her heart. (978-1-60282-158-3)

Little White Lie by Lea Santos. Emie Jaramillo knows relationships are for other people, and beautiful women like Gia Mendez don't belong anywhere near her boring world of academia until Gia sets out to convince Emie she has not only brains, but beauty, and that she's the only woman Gia wants in her life. (978-1-60282-163-7)

Witch Wolf by Winter Pennington. In a world where vampires have charmed their way into modern society, where werewolves walk the streets with their beasts disguised by human skin, Investigator Kassandra Lyall has a secret of her own to protect. She's one of them. (978-1-60282-177-4)

Do Not Disturb by Carsen Taite. Ainsley Faraday, a high-powered executive, and rock music celebrity Greer Davis couldn't be less well suited for one another, and yet they soon discover passion has a way of designing its own future. (978-1-60282-153-8)

From This Moment On by PJ Trebelhorn. Devon Conway and Katherine Hunter both lost love and neither believes they will ever find it again until the moment they meet and everything changes. (978-1-60282-154-5)

Vapor by Larkin Rose. When erotic romance writer Ashley Vaughn decides to take her research into the bedroom for a night of passion with Victoria Hadley, she discovers that fact is hotter than fiction. (978-1-60282-155-2)

Wind and Bones by Kristin Marra. Jill O'Hara, award-winning journalist, just wants to settle her deceased father's affairs and leave Prairie View, Montana, far, far behind but an old girlfriend, a sexy sheriff, and a dangerous secret keep her down on the ranch. (978-1-60282-150-7)

Nightshade by Shea Godfrey. The story of a princess, betrothed as a political pawn, who falls for her intended husband's soldier sister, is a modern-day fairy tale to capture the heart. (978-1-60282-151-4)

Vieux Carré Voodoo by Greg Herren. Popular New Orleans detective Scotty Bradley just can't stay out of trouble especially when an old flame turns up asking for help. (978-1-60282-152-1)

The Pleasure Set by Lisa Girolami. Laney DeGraff, a successful president of a family-owned bank on Rodeo Drive, finds her comfortable life taking a turn toward danger when Theresa Aguilar, a sleek, sexy lawyer, invites her to join an exclusive, secret group of powerful, alluring women. (978-1-60282-144-6)

A Perfect Match by Erin Dutton. The exciting world of pro golf forms the backdrop for a fast-paced, sexy romance. (978-1-60282-145-3)

Father Knows Best by Lynda Sandoval. High school juniors and best friends Lila Moreno, Meryl Morganstern, and Caressa Thibodoux plan to make the most of the summer before senior year. What they discover that amazing summer about girl power, growing up, and trusting friends and family more than prepares them to tackle that all-important senior year! (978-1-60282-147-7)

The Midnight Hunt by L.L. Raand. Medic Drake McKennan takes a chance and loses, and her life will never be the same because when she wakes up after surviving a life-threatening illness, she is no longer human. (978-1-60282-140-8)

Long Shot by D. Jackson Leigh. Love isn't safe, which is exactly why equine veterinarian Tory Greyson wants no part of it until Leah Montgomery and a horse that won't give up convince her otherwise. (978-1-60282-141-5)

In Medias Res by Yolanda Wallace. Sydney has forgotten her entire life, and the one woman who holds the key to her memory, and her heart, doesn't want to be found. (978-1-60282-142-2)

Awakening to Sunlight by Lindsey Stone. Neither Judith or Lizzy is looking for companionship, and certainly not love but when their lives become entangled, they discover both. (978-1-60282-143-9)

Fever by VK Powell. Hired gun Zakaria Chambers is hired to provide a simple escort service to philanthropist Sara Ambrosini, but nothing is as simple as it seems, especially love. (978-1-60282-135-4)

Truths by Rebecca S. Buck. Two women separated by two hundred years are connected by fate and love. (978-1-60282-146-0)

High Risk by JLee Meyer. Can actress Kate Hoffman really risk all she's worked for to take a chance on love? Or is it already too late? (978-1-60282-136-1)

Spanking New by Clifford Henderson. A poignant, hilarious, unforgettable look at life, love, gender, and the essence of what makes us who we are. (978-1-60282-138-5)

Missing Lynx by Kim Baldwin and Xenia Alexiou. On the trail of a notorious serial killer, Elite Operative Lynx's growing attraction to a mysterious mercenary could be her path to love or to death. (978-1-60282-137-8)

Magic of the Heart by C.J. Harte. CEO Susan Hettinger and wild, impulsive rock star M.J. Carson couldn't be more different if they tried but opposites attract in ways neither woman can resist. (978-1-60282-131-6)

Ambereye by Gill McKnight. Jolie Garoul is falling in love with her assistant. The big problem is, Jolie is a werewolf. (978-1-60282-132-3)

Collision Course by C.P. Rowlands. Tragedy leaves Brie O'Malley and Jordan Carter fearful and alone. Can they find the courage to take a second chance on love? (978-1-60282-133-0)

Mephisto Aria by Justine Saracen. Opera singer Katherina Marov's destiny may be to repeat the mistakes of her father when she becomes involved in a dangerous love affair. (978-1-60282-134-7)